praise for get cozy, josey

I love this series. I now have it in hard copy and on my kindle! I reread it every year. Josie is a great character and if she were real, I would want to be her friend. There is humor and romance along with spiritual lessons. I love it!!!

— Susan, Amazon

Warren once again blends in real life frustrations, honesty, and plenty of spiritual insights to delight the reader. I stayed up way too late last night desiring to finish this one and see how Warren would work things all out. You won't be disappointed!

— Kindle Customer, Amazon

As usual, Susan May Warren delivers a book that is both funny and thought provoking. One of the things I like best about the Josey books, is the relationship between Josey and Chase. They've known each other since kindergarten and although they have their rough spots like any other married couple, the affection and deep love between them is well portrayed.

— Loralee, Goodreads

I actually slowed down towards the end because I didn't want the book to be over. I felt like Josey was a friend. Loved this series!

— Tricia, Goodreads

Susan May Warren surprises me over and over again! I love her writing style, her in depth view of the characters and her ability to NOT let me put the book down! I'm loving ALL her books!

— Terra, Amazon

get cozy, josey

The Josey Series || Book Three

susan may warren

Get Cozy, Josey
The Josey Series, Book 3

(Originally published 2008 by Steeple Hill)
Ebook ISBN: 978-1-962036-14-6
Print ISBN: 978-1-962036-16-0 (hc.)
Print ISBN: 978-1-962036-15-3 (pb.)

For more information about Susan May Warren, please access the author's website at the following address: www.susanmaywarren.com.

Published in the United States of America.

Cover design by Courtney Walsh

my evil plot

. . .

It's on account of the jellyfish that I ended up in Siberia. That, and a can of Pringles, a volleyball, and two very sloppy *plombir* vanilla ice cream cones that ended up down the front of my Tasmanian devil pajamas.

But I should probably tell the entire story, not only of how Chase talked me into moving to the backside of the world, where the snow crests off the tundra like whirling dervishes, where a person can literally freeze her nose off her face, and where people eat pig fat for snacks, but also of how it made me reach deep inside myself to find more of myself than I'd ever dreamed.

Definitely more than Chase ever dreamed. But we'll get there.

I need to state, for the record, that I, Josey Berglund Anderson, never liked camping. At least, not my husband Chase's definition of camping, which I've discovered is vastly different from my own. But that, in part, is what marriage is all about—discovering the definitions of our personal vocabulary.

Case in point—to me, camping is s'mores over a crackling fire after a day of hiking some well-sculpted trail along a northern river while the sun sets above a perfect rose-gilded lake, fireflies twinkling in the indigo twilight. It's watching the moon rise and heating up coffee in a Sierra cup as the night settles in around us. That much, I believe Chase and I can agree on. However, it is here that our definitions diverge and trek off into opposite accommodations. I retire to a cabin, with indoor plumbing, screens, and although I'm willing not to have a real bed, I do want to be on something padded and at least away from the creepy-crawlies that live in the dirt. In short, when I camp, I want to just add water. This, however, is not Chase's definition. Chase likes to camp from scratch.

I should have known that Chase's interpretation of camping might be different. After all, as an anthropologist—or former anthropologist—his greatest dreams are along the lines of living among the Nepalis, trekking up the sides of mountains clad in only felt moccasins, sleeping in clay-covered huts, and eating boiled *dal bhat* while playing the *sarangi*. I know because he has a fifty-pound textbook on the subject. My Chase likes doing things like bathing in a glacial river and wearing the same natty attire for two weeks.

And you ask, I know, how we ended up together. Alas, the camping differences didn't surface until long after our wedding day, even after the birth of our twins, Chloe and Justin. Perhaps Chase snowed me with his black motorcycle and the way he filled out a football letter jacket. Perhaps it was the way he chased me across the planet to get my attention and win my heart.

Or maybe, as usual, it was the way he backed me into a corner, one hand propped over my shoulder as he leaned into my neck to plant a kiss and whisper, "C'mon, G.I., it'll be fun."

Fun, yeah. As I've discovered, that word, too, has vastly different definitions. For example, I do not think it is *fun* to pack everything we own—including buckets for hauling water (aka, the kitchen sink), swim gear, sleeping bags, clothes, pots and pans, plates, cups, silverware, tents, blankets, a shovel, and enough food for ten days—into backpacks, spend two days on a train from Moscow to Simferopol, Ukraine, then four hours on a bus, hike across the treeless rolling steppe to a cliff that drops one hundred meters or so of sure death to the sea, where we have to erect our own shelter like nomads, all the while carrying two munchkins (who have their own backpacks, I might add).

I should have realized, as we stood on the high cliffs overlooking the Black Sea and the waves crashing against the boulders below, across a pebbled, not-so-sandy beach, that setting up camp in a still-rustic yet sturdy cabin hadn't even been a blip on Chase's list of expectations.

Which led to panic and a softly breathed question. "Where are the bathrooms?"

"Outhouses." Chase pointed to the shovel attached to his pack. "Do it yourself."

Of course.

I stood there a moment, breathing in the view, trying to make it all better by focusing on the aqua-green bay under a cloudless sky; the way the beach curved as if cupping the water, rimmed by rugged, orange, lichen-covered cliffs and lush green brush. A road wound down to this Chasonian paradise from the cliff, and with a grin, Chase headed for it.

Justin and Chloe ran after him, as if he were the Pied Piper of Hamlin.

I sacrificed three things the day I gave birth to my twins.

1. My waistline. I must have offended it with one too many peanut butter cookies, because it hasn't come back, something my maternity clothes are all too happy to embrace. Chase says two children are enough, especially living in a high-rise two-bedroom flat in the center of Russia, but I've been holding on to my painfully acquired pregnancy

wardrobe (yoga pants and all of Chase's extra-large shirts) just in case. (At least, that's the story I'm sticking to.)

2. My sense of adventure. No longer do I run down the beach, Ray Conniff and the Singers' "Love Story" in my head, listening to the waves of the sea lapping the shore and the seagulls crying as they soar above.

Instead, as we descended the cliff to the Black Sea beach, my mother's eye saw broken glass, jagged beer cans, and old cigarette butts hidden in the sand like land mines. Three-year-old Justin rushed into the water up to his knees, laughing, splashing. I stepped close to grab him in case he went under.

I'll probably never enjoy water again.

3. My bladder. Which has decided that when it wants attention, it gets it.

Chase dropped our gear in an empty lot of dirty sand and dug out the shovel. I looked at it, looked at Chase, and tried not to cry.

I've come to expect a few inconveniences while living in Russia over the past four-plus years. For example, I don't really expect the electricity to stay on the entire time I'm cooking the Thanksgiving turkey. I know that the hot water will shut off from May until November, and that if I want a bath, I need to prepare at least twelve hours in advance. I have every public bathroom in Moscow plotted out and have rated them on a scale of *good idea* to *desperate*. And I know that when Chase latches on to a new idea, it's much like body surfing. Catch the idea at the right time, and you're on top of the wave, enjoying the view. Spring too late and the wave crests over your head, saltwater up your nose. You land choking and gasping and even a little roughed up by the sand and shells.

I've been wondering—at what point does a girl get to stand in the surf, let the wave crash against her knees, and say *Nyet!*

Clearly, I'm not there yet. Which is why, now, I find myself one outpost in a sea of tents facing Russia and Ukraine's idea of paradise, smack in the middle of Chase's idea of a vacation. He's been planning said vacation since we arrived in Russia, and I figure it's his well-earned bonus for three years of dedication to WorldMar, his NGO (non-government-organization) in Moscow. Over the past four years, he's launched and managed an entrepreneurial peanut butter company that's created a new love for creamy spreads all the way down the Yalta.

Here's where I admit to my evil master plan, the real reason why I agreed to set up camp at the edge of the world. The project has ended, and we've got two choices on the horizon.

Choice One: Head back to Gull Lake, Minnesota, buy a house, and enroll the kids in soccer and ballet lessons. Chase will work for my dad until a position at the school opens up, and we'll finally get to live somewhere where the backyard isn't a hazardous waste zone. (This is obviously my vote.)

Choice Two: Another NGO project, this time working with private local chicken farmers.

Can you believe Chase is actually considering it? Not that I have anything against chickens. Rather, I'm thinking that maybe I've done my time and it's my turn.

So, my thinking is, give the man a camping trip, he'll give me Gull Lake. Because, well, four years into marriage, I'm learning fast how to bargain. All that time in the market haggling over potatoes has made me a master.

Hence, this last adventure to the south of Ukraine. As far as the eye can see, tents—blue, orange, brown—dot the coast. All of Russia, Ukraine, and Eastern Europe takes a vacation in August, most cities emptying out to the sea where, although some make, uh, *reservations* and stay at a *resort* (which, by the way, has been my family's livelihood back home in Minnesota for nearly forty years), others find a space of land and set up a homestead. With kitchens (portable stoves and campfires) and laundry facilities (buckets and clotheslines) and living rooms (tarps staked over cars and paddles and other makeshift walls). Kids run naked or half naked to the sea and back—my preschoolers are overdressed in their pull-ups, T-shirts, and sunhats. The smell of fish and smoke taints the fresh air. Someone has decided to run the battery down on their boom box and picked up a radio station. I recognize a Machina Vreminya song.

Behind all this chaos, about fifty paces, is another village—of outhouses. Most are made of driftwood or scrap lumber shoved into the ground and covered on three sides, some of them poorly, with an old sheet. (The backside is open to face . . . uh, nature.) Not ours. The American outhouse is made from four rebars, a dark sheet secured on three sides, and a hanging door for privacy. It's plumb and sturdy, and I have a feeling it could survive a typhoon.

The fact that my backside is protected from flashing the world, even in the direst of weather, is my one consolation for having to spend every waking moment sweeping out the tent, making sure our children don't kick off their beach shoes or disappear forever into the sea, cooking another pot of potatoes, or lathering on another layer of sunblock.

Yeah, I'm having fun. I love camping.

Gull Lake, think Gull Lake. Three-bedroom home. Swing set.

Dog. A black lab, or maybe a collie—

"Josey, look what Sveta and Vadeem gave us." Chase comes tromping across the sand, all grins. Of course Chase is on a first-name basis with the "neighbors." Another day, and they'll adopt him.

Okay, yes, I have some attitude issues. Although I came to

Russia *first*, five years ago, learned to speak Russian *first*, learned how to negotiate the Moscow subway *first*, Chase was born to live in Russia. He even looks Russian, and he speaks it so well after three years that someone even asked him how he, as a Russian, managed to nab an American wife. That particular day, I didn't have an answer for that.

Today I might. Because he's looking tanned and toned, his dark-blond needing-a-cut hair curly on his neck and shiny in the sun. He smiles at me, his blue eyes lit with mischief. Wearing a red handkerchief he's tied in four corners on his head like a candy wrapper, a T-shirt with the arms cut off, and a pair of swim trunks (the American kind, not Speedo-style), he crouches where I'm sitting, accidentally kicking sand and pebbles onto my towel. I have an eye on Chloe, who is standing just at the edge of the water with a plastic shovel, perhaps contemplating how long it might take to fill the hole she's just dug with water. Her blonde hair is nearly white, curling out under her hat, like Chase's. Justin is napping in the tent behind me, his lips askew, a fine bead of sweat along his blond brow line. He's going to be a charmer, just like his dad. Someday his wife will wonder just how she agreed to live three billion miles away from her family and home in a country whose word for "hello" sounds like someone is clearing their throat of phlegm. *Zdravstvuyte?* Please.

I'll just smile. Because I know the answer. "What?" I ask Chase.

Chase plunks down a blue bucket—*my* blue bucket, formerly used to wash preschooler underwear in—"Flounder!"

I stare at the bucket, and my stomach responds before I do. Because the shiny, smelly *thing* is staring at me with both glassy eyes, his fins still twitching. "Both eyes are on the same side of his head," I say, not sure what Chase wants me to do with it.

"That's because he lies on the bottom of the sea, hiding in the sand, waiting to surprise his prey."

Creepy. "Is he a pet?"

Chase laughs. "We're invited to Vadeem and Sveta's place for dinner. We just have to clean it."

Not I, said the little red hen.

But before I can refuse, I'm distracted by a cry from Chloe. She's wandered into the water and has picked up a bag, dripping, see-through—

"That's a jellyfish!" I am on my feet, running toward Chloe, who's laughing and flinging the fish around like she might her teddy bear.

Jellyfish abound in the Black Sea, so much so that the first time I waded out into the water, it felt as if I might be swimming through Jell-O. "They won't sting," Chase the jellyfish expert had assured as I made a face and cleared a path back to shore.

Sure. Because they like me and want to be my friend?

Now, I grab the jellyfish and fling it out of Chloe's hand. She's startled and starts to cry. I sweep her up. Glare at Chase.

"I'll clean the fish," he says.

Ya think?

I dig into my mommy supply bag and hand Chloe a cookie. She takes it in her grubby little hands, grinning up at me through her tears. Yeah, I have her number. But I take one too.

The Black Sea at dusk is nearly magical, with the colors of autumn streaked like watercolors across the western sky, slowly absorbed into a perfect, diamond-studded canvas that seems so close I could probably reach out and wrap my fingers around a star. The wind off the sea is cool and smells of bigness, of the places it's traveled. Sitting before the fire as Sveta fries fish on her portable stove, listening to Chase converse with Vadeem, I'm reminded so much of Gull Lake and magical moments back home that melancholy finds me, wets my eyes. I love Gull Lake, the small town where I can walk down the street and know the names, even the secrets of everyone I meet. Where the Fourth of July parade circles the town twice and still only takes ten minutes. Where the most exciting article in the paper is the annual walleye fishing contest results. I miss fresh-brewed coffee and *kringle*, and my sister Jasmine, who just had baby number two. And H, my punk, now married, lead-singer friend, who just cut her second album.

I am on the other side of the planet, eating creepy fish, drowning it down with watery orange *sok*, praying my children don't pick up tuberculosis.

"Hey there," a voice says, in English.

I look up, startled. Above me stands a dark-haired man, brown eyes, nice smile, wearing dark shorts and a white "Vote for Pedro" T-shirt, holding a tube of Pringles. (Who is Pedro, and what is he running for?) My gaze latches on to the Pringles.

Pringles Man sits next to me. "Want one?"

I am a Minnesotan. I long for a Pringle with everything inside me, but you'll have to offer three times. That's only once.

"No, thanks."

He shrugs. "You look hungry."

I glance around for Justin. Chloe is sitting tucked into Chase's lap, playing with his hat tassels. Justin is crouched by the water, a tiny dark outline against the indigo prairie.

"Justin, honey, come to Mommy." I see him stand, look back, start to toddle toward me.

"I met your husband earlier today," Mysterious Pringle Man says. He crunches another Pringle. "He's an interesting guy."

I glance at Chase. He's in animated conversation. "He keeps me on my toes."

"You're a good wife to let him drag you out here."

Now he has my attention. I smile. Yeah, I am, I know. Mrs. Proverbs 31. "Thanks. We're headed stateside after this. He needed one last adventure."

Mr. Pringles crunches another one. "My name's Marc." He wipes his hand off on his T-shirt. "I'm with Voices International.

We represent the Fourth World, researching their cultures. Are you sure you don't want a Pringle?"

That's two. My mouth is salivating. "No, thanks," I say. "What is the Fourth World? I'm only aware of one." I laugh at my joke. He doesn't. Uh-oh, the Pringles might be in jeopardy.

"The Fourth World refers to the LDC, or least developed countries, usually within First or Third World nations. Namely, the indigenous groups who have been largely obliterated by the country in power. Currently, we're working with the Russian Ministry of Indigenous People out of Moscow to study their various people groups. Like the Nanai of Siberia. There are over thirty different indigenous groups in Russia, and the government is starting to realize they need to figure out ways to help preserve them rather than assimilate them."

"You make the Russians sound like the Borg."

He takes another chip. "It's not unlike what we did to our First Nations people in Canada, making them speak English, sending their children to boarding schools, obliterating their culture."

"I think we did that in America too."

Marc nods. He digs a little well into the pebbly beach, sets the Pringles can inside. "Where're you from?"

"Minnesota—a little town right in the middle."

"My backyard, eh? I'm from Winnipeg." He smiles at me, and the firelight reveals a twinkle in those brown eyes. For a second, the look in his eyes swoops my breath away. Not only is it aimed at still-pregnant-weight me, but I'm married, and I don't see too many of those zingers these days.

I don't know quite what to do. Is he . . . flirting with me? Gulp.

No, he can't be. I glance again toward Chase, who looks at me and grins. I grin back. See, happily married, Mr. Pringles.

He seems to have followed my gaze, because he waves to Chase. Grins.

Maybe I imagined all that. For sure I imagined it.

"I can't finish these. Are you sure you won't have one?"

That's three. Phew, I was starting to worry. I take the can, smile. If you insist. "Thanks."

Heaven, in one perfectly formed oval chip. I crunch it with my tongue, letting the salt fill my mouth.

Marc's eyes are on me, and he's smiling with one side of his mouth. "Methinks someone is missing America."

"Where did you find these?"

He lifts a shoulder. I see that it is muscled, well-defined. He must spend some of his research time in hands-on dogsled mushing through the frozen wasteland. "Spotted them in a kiosk in Simferopol. Bought all eight cans."

My eyes widen, and he laughs. "Yes, I have more."

"Oh, no, that's not—"

"I'll bring you a can tomorrow."

"No, I couldn't." But I could, I could!

I shouldn't.

I shouldn't.

But it tastes so good, so salty, so home. And I want more.

"Are you on vacation?" I ask, taking another chip.

He nods. "I'm with a group of other researchers. Taking a few days off before we head to an international conference in Kazakhstan." He stands up, dusting off his hands. "I came over to invite Chase to join us in a game of volleyball at our camp tomorrow. We have at least two Americans, and . . . "—he winks—"lots of Pringles. Come with him."

I shake out the crumbs into my hand. Look up at him. He smiles again, all white teeth and dark, friendly eyes.

I find myself saying "What time?"

just like camping

. . .

My hometown of Gull Lake, central Minnesota, population 2,500, thrives on sports. Our small high-school gym is hotter than a Finnish sauna during a January basketball game, and our cheerleaders can dance in hockey skates. We are a multisport town, and our trophy case has been reinforced three times to hold the weight of the embossed plastic accolades. I mention this only to say that I, Josey Berglund Anderson, have my name on a trophy in said case.

Girls Volleyball, 1996, State Champs, A Division. We were the Christmas parade mascots that year, and I made the front page of the *Gull Lake Gazette*—displaying "the Josey" spike—three times that season.

I lived and breathed volleyball. Pringle Marc has no idea what he's in for. More than that, Chase, being a football jock, rarely saw me play. I'm feeling seventeen all over again as I pull on my Tasmanian devil pajamas, tear off the already ratty arms, and tie the hem into a knot just below my waist.

"What are you doing?" Chase traps Justin under one arm, tickling him as Chloe climbs up his back, fire in her three-year-old blue eyes. She's such a chip off the old block (meaning me).

It's WWE hour in our tent, although I feel as if Jesse "The Bod" Ventura (aka the former governor of Minnesota) and I already did a few rounds due to Justin and Chloe's propensity to sleep with their feet in my face. Who, again, thought it was a good idea to go camping with two preschoolers who are barely potty trained?

"I got invited to play beach volleyball with you today," I say, pulling on a pair of shorts. Okay, yoga-pant cutoffs, but with my baggy Taz top, they look more like biking shorts, without the firm sheen (and you know what I mean). I'm wearing my swimsuit underneath, and I grab Chase's crazy hat, untying it for a headband.

"*You're* playing volleyball?" Chase asks, pulling Chloe frontward over his shoulder and then tickling her belly. She shrieks in delight.

I one-eye glare at him. Just because I've spent the past three years wiping snotty noses and cutting food into tiny pieces doesn't mean that the Josey inside, the one who came to Russia when hotdogs were still a delicacy, who gave birth in a Russian hospital, who helped her high-school sweetheart become a peanut-butter mogul, has lost her stride. I can still bump and spike. In fact, them sound like fightin' words.

"Did you think I forgot how?"

Chase gets that deer-in-the-headlight panic look on his face. Yeah, you're in trouble, pal. He deflects with a smile while Justin shoves his hand into his dad's mouth. "No," he says between little fingers. "I jush thouth—"

"I wanna play. I haven't played beach volleyball for years."

Chase pulls Justin's fingers away. "Of course."

"Can you help keep an eye on the twins?" Of course, in principle, I shouldn't have to ask the *father of our children* to watch the twins, but reality is, my man stepped outta line when the "equal responsibility" gene got handed out. Not that Chase is a bad father. For all his angst before the twins were born, he has plowed through midnight feedings, diaper changes, and pre-potty-training in stellar form. But—and I say this in love as he now holds down both kids and tickles their feet—he's sort of like a giant interactive toy.

I married a twelve-year-old. With great shoulders.

He flips Chloe over his shoulder as she slaps his back. "Sure. In fact, I'll sit it out and get them some ice cream. I saw a guy peddling some cones yesterday up the shore. It's almost lunchtime anyway."

Ice cream for lunch. See, I told you, twelve. But I lean over and give him a kiss because, well, he does have those shoulders.

The sun is hot, and the beach is warm through my rubber swim shoes as we walk to Pringle Marc's camp. No one with all their faculties intact would walk barefoot on the beach in Russia—not unless their tetanus shot is up-to-date. The sea is deep turquoise and so translucent that I spot the darkened underwater shoals where Chase went snorkeling yesterday. He brought us back a bag of clams and mussels. And then proceeded to clean them. And cook them.

I've lost about ten pounds on this trip.

Our neighbor Vadeem lifts his hand to wave—he's playing a card game of *Durak* (literal translation: "Fool") with his wife and mother-in-law and two naked daughters, ages six months and eighteen months. (One year apart. That must be nearly as fun as twins.) They've been here for a month now, all five of them sleeping in a tent made for four. I count my blessings as we weave our way through other camps, some constructed of brown Russian-army tents, one group sleeping under a giant nylon tarp. Russians on vacation are a friendly lot, and most of them smile at us. A few toast us with half-full glasses of warm vodka.

I spy the volleyball court and my team warming up.

Oh boy. Clearly, I'm the only woman in the group. Which, when surrounded by ten or so shirtless, tanned, just-sweaty-enough male volleyball players, isn't the worst situation in the world. I glance at Chase, smile.

He's wearing a frown. "I don't see the ice-cream man."

I'll just bet that's what he was thinking. But he hides it as he meets Marc's greeting with a handshake. "I brought you my secret weapon." He glances at me, winks. "Killer."

Oh, Chase. See, even though I'm surrounded by Baywatch, the man has nothing, not a thing, nada, *nichego*, to worry about.

"Then she's on my team," Marc says, pulling me into the game. He introduces me around—five Canadians, two Germans, an Italian, and two Americans. I don't catch all their names, because, you know, I'm focused on the *volleyball*, but I think there is a Joe, a Duncan, a Kurt, and a Paul on my team.

Their camp, adjacent to the court, is a beautiful array of orange and blue family-size tents, evidence that this group lives in luxury. And apparently they've taken the time to police the beach for glass, cigarettes, and other menaces, because most of the guys are barefoot. But I don't want anything to interfere with my game, so I'm keeping my shoes on as I line up in the back row for the serve.

"Let's play!" I say, clapping. Marc shoots me a look.

Where's the team spirit? The ball shoots across the net, and I go down for a perfect, beautiful bump. It sets up high for Duncan, who chooses to smash it into the net instead of setting it up for our spike-man, Kurt.

Apparently, my team needs to get their heads in the game. The next serve comes faster, and although I call it, Marc dives for the return, and we crash heads.

"Sorry," he says. I force a smile.

"No problem, it's just a game." It's just a game, *it's just a game.*

The third shot is out, and Marc takes the serve.

It's a net ball, and I shoot a look at Chase. He thumbs-ups

me. Justin is digging in the sand and dirt behind him. Chloe is fighting with the sunhat I double-tied under her chin.

I almost miss the serve but go to my knees to bump it. This time, Paul sets it for Duncan, who spikes it into the opposing team's court.

Now that's what I'm talkin' 'bout.

"Paul, that was an awesome set. Let's see if we can do that again."

Marc glances at me, and I nod at him, all smiles. All this team needs is a little leadership.

Paul steps up to serve for our team. He's got a wicked overhand serve, and pretty soon I'm covered in sand, we're five points up, and Marc is wagering his Pringles against the win.

"I think I see the ice-cream guy," says Chase somewhere in my peripheral vision. Yeah, yeah. Marc bumps the service up to me, I set up a beauty of a spike, and Kurt arrows it over. We're a well-oiled machine, we are, and even attracting an audience as we rack up three more points. I see fire in the other team's eyes, in the way they have their hands at the ready, in a crouch, poised to volley.

Paul finally nets the ball. But that's okay, because we win back the serve in a second, and Kurt's up. Beautiful service over, but German Guy bumps it back. Kurt bumps it up, Marc sets it, and I go airborne, feeling my wings, that old juice in my veins as I slam the ball over, hard, fast, just skimming the net and landing at German Guy's feet.

"She's hot now!" Marc says. And I go warm to my toes. But he just means it in a very volleyball kind of way.

I glance at Chase, who has Chloe in his arms. He's wearing a strange look, one I haven't seen in years. The same one he gave me from across the room at Lew Sulzbach's graduation party, right before I went joyriding with two of his football buddies. I remember returning to find him sitting in the front yard, arms dangling over his knees, waiting. He corralled me for a ride on his motorcycle—a long ride that lasted until sunrise.

It wasn't long after that that he told me he was attending college far, far away from Gull Lake.

The look rattles me for a moment, and then he breaks it, smiling. "I'm going for ice cream!"

Maybe I misread all that.

I wave at him and turn back to the game.

We're up by eight, and although the other team makes a valiant effort, they can't overcome the mighty power of, um, Josey and the Guys.

"Okay, Josey, I'll give you your own can of Pringles if you can bring it home!" Marc tosses me the ball to serve for game point, and I turn it in my hands, getting my rhythm as I step back to toss the ball in the air.

I send it over the net with a satisfying thwack.

The other team volleys well, spikes it hard, but Paul dives deep and rescues with a bump. Kurt sets it, and I realize it's all mine. A spike from the back row. I wind up, jump, connect—

A scream, right behind me, tears my attention. My mother instinct kicks in before I land.

I'm already turning, the word *rebenok* registering in my adrenaline-laced brain without needing translation.

Baby.

My baby. In the water, jellyfish wrapped around his little body, Justin is screaming. He's up to his chest, and if he falls—

Please, God.

I am in the water before anyone even moves, thrashing my way to Justin. "It's okay, honey, Mommy's coming." Jellyfish swarm me, wrapping like cellophane around my legs and arms as I scoop Justin up, pulling the fishy Jell-O from his body. But they cling to me and, apparently agitated, begin to sting.

A thousand needles into my legs, my arms, across my back. I'm shaking them off even as I run to shore, ignoring the fire that consumes me. Marc is there with a towel for Justin, but I don't hand him off. Just wrap his little preschool body in terrycloth and hold him close. He's crying.

I'm breathing hard. Great gasps of forced air. I . . . can't . . . breathe.

I drop to my knees. Let go of Justin. He stands there as I put a hand into the sand, another to my throat. I . . . can't . . .

"Josey, are you okay?"

"What's wrong with her?"

I look up, blinking, but the world is starting to fade, shadows and . . .

"She's—"

"Josey? Josey?"

I come to in a rush, and Chase is right there, above me. His hand is around my neck, and a coldness presses into my chest. I'm lying in the sand, a bed of grit. I feel heavy, groggy. My lips are thick.

"Whaf happen—"

"You had an allergic reaction to the jellyfish." Chase touches his forehead to mine, and I can feel him tremble. "You really scared us." As he pulls away, I see a crowd standing around me, Russians wearing their Speedos. That's a sight that will wake anyone from a sound coma. Thankfully, I see others, in swim trunks. A man is holding a ball in his hands.

A volleyball.

The game.

Justin!

I start to sit up, but Chase pushes me back. "Justin!"

"He's fine." He gestures to a place above my head, and I

crane my neck to see Chloe and Justin playing in the sand, aided by Sveta, our Russian neighbor. "He was a little shook up, but he wasn't stung. They don't usually sting—"

I raise my eyebrow.

"Unless provoked."

That's me, the Jellyfish Provoker. I close my eyes, aching from head to toe, feeling the stings. I shiver. "What happened?" My voice sounds tight, raspy, as if choked. My throat hurts.

"Your throat closed up. Good thing Duncan is allergic to bees. He carries an EpiPen with him." Chase's eyes begin to glisten.

I shiver again, cold spreading down my chest. No, *running* down my chest, into my armpits. I reach up to touch the sensation. It's sticky. Gooey. "What—"

Chase is making a face. "Yeah, well, I got sorta carried away. I saw you collapse and forgot I was carrying ice cream, and . . . "

"You smeared ice cream on me?" I lick my finger. "*Plombir.*"

"Your favorite kind."

Uh, *no*. Chase's favorite kind. Shortly after we moved to Russia, we spent a month deciding what flavor and brand of ice cream Chase liked, which involved testing every ice-cream vendor and flavor in the city. Not that I'm complaining about his methods.

I pull the sodden shirt away from my body. "Yuck."

"I'm so sorry, G.I. I thought you knew Justin was still here. You waved at me when I told you I was just taking Chloe."

I stare at him. I don't remember that. Do you remember that?

All I remember is, is . . . I sit up, looking past Chase, and zero in on Marc, standing right above him. "Did we get the point?"

Slowly, a smile breaks out across Marc's face.

Then he turns to Chase and utters the words that will change my life. And I know then that Chase is a flounder, two eyes on one side of his head, hiding in the sand on the bottom, awaiting his prey.

“See, I told you she’d do fine in Siberia,” says Marc. “She’s a trooper. Besides, it’s just like camping.”

Wait! Did someone say *camping*?

Or—worse yet—Siberia?

no pressure or anything

. . .

"He did what?"

I'm so relieved at my friend Maggie Calhoun's tone of voice, that slight shrill that says I'm not nuts to be on a full-out strike against Chase's methods of mind control, that I'm willing to forgive her for the fact she's lost all her pregnancy weight and is back down to a size six and wearing the cutest pair of Ann Taylor jeans and a cable-knit sweater. I feel like the hometown bum in my fat jeans and Chase's old Gull Lake sweatshirt.

"He planned it. The entire camping trip, the meeting with Marc. The volleyball game. If I hadn't nearly perished, I would have thought he'd planned the jellyfish too." I'm at Gorky Park, standing in line for popcorn, watching some lovebirds paddle through the lake in the center of the park in a paddleboat. Chase and I used to paddle this lake.

The thing about paddleboats is that the paddlers have to have rhythm and a commitment to work together. Today, Chase and I would probably swamp the boat.

"He wanted me to meet Marc, knowing I'd be swayed by the whole 'underprivileged and ignored people groups' line."

"You were, weren't you?" This from Daphne, my very pregnant friend, wife of my pal Caleb, and fellow orphanage fundraiser. She has a cute butterball tummy even at seven months, which she hides under a large long-sleeve Gap shirt and a pair of Caleb's baggy pants. I keep pressing her to travel stateside for the birth. To which she replies, "If you can do it, I can do it."

Yeah, well, if I'd had a choice, I would have had soft lights, soothing music, and the E-word. Epidural.

But I don't want to scare the girl.

Daphne, better than anyone, knows how my heartstrings are strummed by the weak and helpless, how Chase played me.

I purse my lips. "Yeah, okay, Marc did wage a convincing argument. Small community on the edge of nowhere, going under economically, trying desperately to hold on to their culture, their way of life. And apparently the research he wants Chase to do might help them figure out ways to thrive."

The cause calls to the hidden Mother Teresa inside me—the one who keeps trying to find a foothold in this country. But what about Gull Lake? Our dog, Shep?

"The way Marc put it, it felt like Chase was practically daring me to go to Siberia."

"And we all know how you do with dares."

Okay, yes, I do respond to the whole "wimp" taunt. Once, when Chase and I were eight, he double-dog dared me to touch my tongue to the icy playground slide.

That's a memory I don't want to dredge up.

The short of it is, I'm not good at backing down from a dare. And Chase knows it all too well.

I can't help but be proud of the fact that Chase married me for my ability to keep up, even forge ahead of his challenges. But it bugs me more than a little that he used it against me, the sneak.

"Mommy—me, corn!" Chloe is jumping up and down beside me, clapping her hands. Maggie's little boy, Steven, about four months younger than my twins, is pulling on his mother's arm, his eyes wide at the blowup trampoline with balls. Justin is driving the Hot Wheels car he got for his birthday along the metal railings that edge the pathways of the park. When we're out in public, my eyes are ever riveted on the twins. Russia is riddled with safety hazards—from open manholes to wild drivers. And when I say *wild*, I mean the kind that drive on sidewalks. Lest you think I jest, let me just say that winter is Chase's favorite season because there are no lines in the road, no sidewalk curbs. Hence, he drives anywhere his black Moskvich decides to go. No Rules Chase. All I can say is that the government didn't ask *me* before they gave him his driver's license, or I would have told them he had an aversion to driving—or living, for that matter—inside the lines.

A guy who lived by the rules would see how out of the question it is to ask his wife to move a billion miles to the east into snow and ice.

Sure, Minnesota has plenty of snow and ice. But we also have SUVs and lots of goose down. And snowmobiles. Betcha there aren't any snowmobiles in Siberia.

"Does that mean he's not going to take over the chicken project?" Maggie asks, giving in to Steven. Maggie's husband, Dalton, is the chief of party of Chase's NGO. And his soon-to-be-former boss.

I give Maggie a wry smile. "I was really hoping we'd be heading back to Gull Lake. I wanted to live in a real house and give my children the life I had growing up."

I hand Chloe the bag of popcorn, steering her to a bench, while Maggie pays the trampoline vendor and Steven pries off his shoes. He's got the cutest head of black curls and dark eyes, just like his father.

Justin spies him and comes running to me. “Me too! Me too!”

“Stay here,” I command Chloe. She grins at me, the devil in her eyes. Clearly she’s inherited that dare-me mentality. Where is the duct tape when I need it? I glance at Daphne. “Can you watch her?”

Daphne reaches for Chloe’s hand. Chloe yanks it away and glares at her. That’s my girl—don’t let anyone hold you back.

I take Justin’s hand (which he surrenders easily), and we join the line for the trampoline.

“Tired of living overseas?” Maggie asks. Technically, she’s lived in Moscow longer than I have, although I’ve accumulated an impressive five total years of Russia time. (Which should equal about twelve years in any other European country.) Before marrying Dalton, Maggie worked for the state department.

I pay the vendor and help Justin off with his shoes. “It’s not so much overseas as Moscow. The novelty of subway surfing has worn off, and I’d give my left foot for a backyard for the kids.” I help Justin into the trampoline door. Turn back.

Chloe is just disappearing down the path, Daphne waddling after her.

I take off at a run. “Chloe! Stop!”

She looks back at me. And, like the rascal she is, pumps it up to a full-out run.

Oh, I love motherhood.

A girl would think, with all this running, I might rid myself of those extra pregnancy pounds. I pass Daph, who’s stopped and bent over, gripping her knees (which she can still see), breathing hard. For Pete’s sake, I hiked all over Moscow while roughly twice the size of Daphne.

But it’s not her fault I gave birth to the Great Houdini, Master of the Vanishing Act. Already, Chloe’s been lost twice in

Gorky Park. One time involved the local police and forty very long, stomach-churning minutes.

I catch up with her and scoop her up. "Chloe, you have to listen to Mommy! It's not safe."

That's an understatement. It's not just the hidden hazards . . . it's the fact that with her pigtails and blonde hair and her clearly American attire (that is, no snowsuit in the middle of summer), Chloe practically wears a "kidnap me" sign.

I rejoin Maggie, who's watching the boys.

"Speedy Gonzales get away again?"

I plop Chloe onto the bench. "More than anything, I long for safety, and perhaps quiet."

"Siberia sounds quiet. All that snow sort of muffles everything."

Oh, hardy har har. "What's wrong with doing it my way, just for once? Can't we just go home, live a calm, predictable life?"

But even as I say it, I know that answer. Living a normal life would require living with a calm, predictable *man*. And much of what I love about Chase is his wild, adventurous side.

Maggie lifts a shoulder. "Here's my question—is your way the best way? What's best for you and Chase?"

Daphne rejoins us, easing herself onto the bench. A sweat has broken out over her forehead where she's pulled back her brown hair into two pigtails. She looks about sixteen, not at all like the twenty-six-year-old nurse. "Maybe it's just a matter of submitting to your husband."

Maggie's head swivels Daph's direction. Everything inside me goes still.

"Did you say 'submit'?"

I raise an eyebrow. It's not a secret that Maggie and Daphne hold vastly different viewpoints on the role of women, but I'm usually able to divert us around any philosophical land mines.

"Yes, *submit*. Wives submit to their hus—"

"Daph—"

But I'm too late. Maggie has fire in her eyes.

"I can't believe that in this day and age, you still think that. There goes sixty years of progress."

"Don't you believe in submission?" Daphne asks, ignoring me waving her off. What, do I need semaphores? It doesn't take a PhD to figure out that a woman who ran her own department in Moscow, who speaks four languages, isn't about to "submit" to anyone. And on the other side, it doesn't take a Strong's Concordance to figure out that a newly married missionary who loves Russia is sure she has this "submission" thing down pat.

"I believe in respect," Maggie says, and the air turns icy despite the warm September breeze. I know that Maggie, if she had ever been on Chase's side, would now go to the mattresses for my right to return to Gull Lake.

Daphne shoots me a *help me* look, but I'm useless. Because even though she and I are Christians, I'm not sure I'm *not* on Maggie's side.

After all, a girl should be able to have *some* say where she lives, right? And how?

"Someone has to give in," Daphne says, finally. "Obviously Chase and Josey are on different pages here. And if they want a happy ending to their fairy tale, someone has to make the sacrifice."

I'm narrowing my eyes at her. Hello, if it's a contest, I know who's been making all the sacrifices. Ever try grocery shopping in Russia? Ever try grocery shopping in Russia, where you have to hit eight different stores because no one store has everything? Ever try grocery shopping in Russia, where you have to hit eight different stores because no one store has everything, and then have to lug twenty bags home on the subway and up nine flights of stairs because the elevator is out?

Now try it *with two three-year-olds*. Then come talk to me about sacrifice.

But it's more than that. It's that I deserve to go home. I've been a noncomplaining trooper of a wife. I've lived in a two-bedroom high-rise, shopped with infants strapped to my front and back. Eaten caviar and carp.

I even went camping.

"Listen, Chase has a perfectly good job waiting for him back in Gull Lake."

"Teaching?" Daphne is squirming, trying to get comfortable on the bench.

"Uh, no. Helping my dad at Berglund Acres. He's getting old and needs the help."

"So Chase is going to run the resort?" Maggie asks.

"Um, well, I mean Jasmine and Milton are there, and they run the restaurant and the books . . . "

"So Chase would . . . ?" Daphne finally stands up. Folds her hands over her curves.

"Uh . . . " What would Chase do? Mow lawns? Plunge toilets? "I'm not moving to Siberia. That's just too much to ask of any woman."

Maggie nods. Daphne raises an eyebrow.

"Siberia, ladies! Where the snow comes sweeping down the plain. They subsist on stewed caribou and live in igloos . . . "

"I don't think they live in igloo—" Daph starts.

"I'm going home to Gull Lake. Period. End of sentence, end of paragraph, end of book."

"Mommy, I'm all done!" Justin is leaning against the edge of the net. Steven is already climbing out on his own.

Maggie gets up to retrieve her son. "You stick to your guns, honey."

Daphne rubs her hand over her stomach. "I'll make you a scarf."

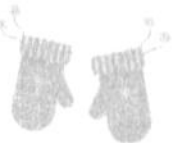

Wildflower: Siberia? Did you say Siberia? Isn't that where they sent people to gulag?

GI:Yes! See, I'm not overreacting. And worse, Chase is all, "Whatever you want to do, Josey, we'll do. No pressure." Yeah, right, like he won't blame me for his horrible life when he's plunging toilets and cleaning litter off the beach in Gull Lake.

Wildflower: Yeah, but Siberia. I mean, if you want to stay in Russia, why don't you stick around Moscow? At least you're assured a supply of bagels.

GI: I DON'T WANT TO STAY IN RUSSIA!

Wildflower: Calm down. I'm just saying, if you're worried about Chase, maybe there are other options that won't give you frostbite.

GI: He got a packet of literature from Voices International. Spent the night reading it. Got out his Nepali book. You know the one.

Wildflower: Listen. Just tell him that you're ready for a real life. For fast food. TiVo. Running hot water all year round.

GI: I'm just ready to be safe.

Wildflower: Then don't come back to Gull Lake. Because just last week, Bruce Minson busted a meth operation just outside town. And someone ran their truck into the Holiday station and took out the front window and the entire DVD rental section.

GI:Yeah, but no one is going to kidnap Justin off Main Street. And Chloe's not going to end up at the bottom of the sewer system.

Wildflower: No, but she could wade into Gull Lake.

GI: What's your problem? I thought you were on my side.

Wildflower: I'm just saying, if you're looking for safety, I think you'll have to invest in a bubble home. Or a couple of leashes.

GI: Where are you right now?

Wildflower: In Hutchison. We have a gig tonight.

GI: How is your album selling?

Wildflower: I just took on an extra shift at the Wolf. And Rex is working full-time at the paper. We're rolling in cash. Oh, and don't worry—Mildred still says no one can write the police report like you.

GI: My calling in life. *Sigh* I'll never write again.

Wildflower: What are you doing right now? I'm confused, because wasn't that you who wrote the fundraising newsletter for your orphanage program the past three years?

GI: I just thought by now I'd be back in my groove, maybe be editor of the Gazette.

Wildflower: So your fear of Siberia is because you want Mildred's orange chair and view of the Harbor Hotel?

GI: My fear of Siberia has to do with a thirty-below windchill. My depression has to do with the view. Which, from here, looks like moon boots, snowdrifts, and dogsleds. It just seems like I've pushed pause on my life, and everyone is passing me by.

Wildflower: Who, me? Because Letterman hasn't exactly been burning up my line leaving me voice messages.

GI: He will.

Wildflower: What happened to the woman who wanted to change the world?

GI: She expired due to lack of sleep. I just want to come home.

Wildflower: So come home.

GI: I don't think it's all up to me.

Wildflower: Just say no.

GI:Thanks, Nancy.

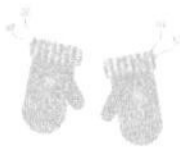

Living in Russia hasn't been a total nightmare. I have a cleaning lady. And for a while, I had a chauffeur. Sveta and Thug, aka Igor, who got married (thanks, I'd like to think, to me) right before the twins were born. Now, Sveta cleans my house once a week, while Igor drives for Dalton and Maggie. I am glad to surf the Moscow subway. In fact, I carry my subway pass with pride.

See, that "dare me" mentality can come back to bite me.

Especially now, as I'm hiking back from the metro. My backpack is bulging with meat, milk, cheese, bread, potatoes, and *podushki* (translation: pillows, which are really puffs of cereal filled with chocolate, my reward for stopping at four different stores and chasing Chloe through the fish aisle at the market), and I've got an iron grip on Justin and Chloe. Chloe is fighting me with every step, occasionally doing her I-am-rubber act. Justin, my *good* child, is only concerned about missing *Nu, Pogodi!*, his favorite Russian cartoon.

The sky is purple, as if bruised from the day, and I totally agree. Two weeks have passed since our camping trip, since I was shanghaied by Marc and Chase, since my grip on Gull Lake began to slide out of my hands, and I feel as if I've been through a sausage press.

And shoot, if Chase isn't being cooperative and romantic and *submissive* with his "Whatever you want to do, honey."

Yeah, sure. Whatever I want to do.

We live in a gated community, but it's not impressive, because that only means we have a guard at the front gate who protects all the mafia-connected tenants in our nine-story high-rise. It's a sad commentary about life in Russia when Mafia Central is the safest place in town. We live right above the mayor and his wife. Which should raise serious questions about his political connections.

Then again, the president of the country is former KGB.

I enter my code into the door, and it squeals open. Chloe wrenches herself free and runs for the lift, which is just opening. She's too short to smash the ninth-floor button, so she hits One. Justin runs in, jumping up and down. "*Nu, Pogodi! Nu, Pogodi!*"

I suppose I should be happy my child is learning Russian. Except *Nu, pogodi!* means, "I'll get you!" His other words are *Ruki vverkh!* Which, sadly, means, "Hands up!" I guess he fits into the neighborhood.

We all tumble out of the lift, and I open the three-ton metal door that barricades our flat. Sometimes I feel like I live in Folsom Prison, what with the metal door and the bars on the windows. I long for a vista without vertical lines.

Sveta's obviously been here, because the flat smells like lemon, the rug by the door is freshly shaken, the shoes are lined up in little rows. Justin wrestles off his shoes, and he and Chloe run for the television in our family room. I am just closing the door when I feel hands on my waist.

I jump, barely stifling a scream.

"Sorry. I didn't mean to startle you." Chase is behind me. I turn and barely stifle a scream.

"What are you wearing?" And I'm not talking about his jeans or his black WorldMar T-shirt, but the rather large, um, *animal* on his head, and the fuzzy sheepskin boots on his feet.

"I'm a Cossack."

"You're a crazy person." I touch the hat, which makes him look like an eighties rock star, a fuzzy brownish-blond mullet that extends down over his ears like a basset hound.

"I got you one too." And without warning, he pulls a matching hat out from behind his back and plunks it onto my head. It engulfs me, and I can't see. "It's red fox. Cool, huh?"

No, actually. Not cool. Sweltering.

"This is your idea of no pressure?" I push the hat up with one finger. But he's grinning at me with his devastating powers of persuasion.

He lifts a shoulder. "If we don't go, we'll wear them in Gull Lake."

"Where?" At the annual ice-fishing festival? A three-day dogsled race?

"Maybe when I shovel the driveway." He picks up the tassel attached to one of my basset ears and tickles my chin with the fuzzy ball at the end.

And right then, I know. I can't doom my man to a life of fixing water heaters or putting in the dock. It might be fine for my father, but Chase was born for adventure. For challenges.

For Siberia.

I close my eyes. Sigh. "Promise you'll find me a house, with a backyard?"

He wraps those muscled arms around me and pulls me tight, prods my head against his chest. He smells good, of shampoo and shaving cream. "That's my girl," he says softly.

Yeah, I'm his girl. Chase's girl. And his girl isn't going to hold him back.

Which, by the way, isn't the same as submission. Just so we have that straight.

He leans back, lifts my chin with his hand, runs his thumb along my cheek. His gaze runs over my face, one side of his beautiful mouth lifting up a second before he kisses me.

And let me tell you, Chase knows how to kiss.

This is the right decision. I can feel it in my stomach, all the way down to my bones. Peace.

I wrap my arms around those strong shoulders and deepen our kiss.

When Chase finally pulls away, I've forgotten that we have kids, forgotten that he's practically tricked me into moving to a snowy nowhere, forgotten that I'm still wearing a dead fox on my head. I'm just ready to pull him into the grown-up room and pretend we're still newlyweds.

Until he nuzzles into my neck and whispers, "We're going to have so much fun."

There's that word again.

I sigh. And inside, I'm quoting my favorite movie. "*I do not think that word means what you think it means.*"

a very small town

. . .

"I'M SO PROUD OF YOU, JOSEY!"

Daphne is sitting on her sofa, bouncing Chloe on her what's-left-of-it lap as I set the fold-out table for dinner. I hear Chase in the kitchen talking to Daphne's husband, Caleb, his voice bubbling with excitement as they do the dishes, good domestic men that they are. I am still in shock at my impulsive yes, and something akin to buyer's remorse has haunted me for a week.

Especially when Chase brought home my own pair of fuzzy sheepskin-covered Cossack boots. Ah . . . never in this lifetime, bub. But he was so thrilled, his eyes dancing as he pulled out mini boots for Justin and Chloe. What's a girl to do?

I swear, the boots will never leave my house with my feet in them.

Daphne's enthusiasm for our sentence to Siberia has me smiling, though. She looks at life through rose-colored glasses, and it's catchy. It helps that summer is giving way to fall in Moscow, and the slightest breeze filled with the scent of decaying leaves filters in through her open windows. Outside, the sun is still high and the sky a turquoise blue over the Volga, the kind of sunny Sunday that would have found me, in a previous life, playing touch football outside after dinner with Chase and my younger brother, Buddy.

"It's just for a year, Daph—not even that, really. Just until summer. Voices International only has nine months left in their gig with the Ministry of Native Affairs." I'm folding up the golden tablecloth to catch the crumbs. "I can do anything for a year."

Daphne lets a wiggling Chloe down, who runs off to tackle her brother playing sweetly and quietly in the next room. "Still, it's not every woman who would let her husband drag her thousands of miles into the endless tundra just so he can watch people."

Oh, thanks for putting it like that. I wad the tablecloth into a ball, stand up to take down the table. In Russia, the kitchens are so small that a group larger than three requires the use of the fold-out table in the family room.

Daphne runs her hand down her stomach. "Especially when you want to go home, when you've been looking forward to this for four years."

Only making it worse here, Daph.

"I have to tell you something."

The look on her face has me drawing out a chair, sitting. She doesn't meet my eyes. "Caleb and I are moving stateside."

I wait for more, something like "to have the baby." Or "for a year." But nothing. I raise my eyebrows, and my voice betrays my surprise. Caleb has lived in Russia longer than anyone I know. I thought for sure they were lifers. "Permanently?"

She looks up, and her eyes are red-rimmed. "I guess submission is harder than I thought."

Uh-oh, the bubble has popped. I wisely (see, I'm learning!) say nothing.

"Caleb wants our baby to live in America, be around family." She sighs, and for the first time I realize that we are living each other's lives. I want to be in America, living around family.

She desperately wants to stay in Russia.

Ah, says the blind girl. I finally get why she's proud of me. I put my hand over hers. "I'm proud of you too."

She sighs and looks up. I'm thinking that she's running our last conversation over in her mind, the one about someone having to compromise to make marriage work. The expression on her face tells me that words are easier than actions.

Her voice drops. "What if he's wrong?"

I frown at her. My voice also drops. "Wrong about what?"

"What if we're not supposed to go home? What if we're supposed to stay in Russia? What if we're missing the opportunity of a lifetime, to change hearts and minds, to help people see Jesus loves them?"

Okay, see, this is why I should never be Daphne's mentor. Because she is deeper than me. More committed to the eternal.

My primary worry has been about what I'm going to do about my bagel and coffee supply.

I stand up, fold in the legs of the table, lower down one side, then the other.

"Caleb will move it back to the wall," Daphne says, but I shrug her off and pick up the table, moving it back into place.

Then I sit beside her.

"I don't know, Daph. But I have learned that when I leap off the edge of my own understanding into the great unknown of faith, God has a way of catching me."

I'm not sure where that came from, but I believe it.

Please, God, make me believe it.

"You're going to be amazing in Siberia," Daphne says, reaching over to hug me.

I just hope to be warm.

Russia is a very large place. According to Chase, Russia is two and a half times the size of the continental United States. Two and one half. I know—it was hard for me to grasp, too, until Chase bought a map at the *rynok* (read: market) and spread it out on our living room floor. It barely fits between the black leather couches, even with the duct-taped glass coffee table pushed into the hallway.

I can lie down on this map, spread-eagle, and still not reach from one end to the other.

"Where are we going to live?"

"This is Moscow," Chase says, pointing to a dot on the far left of the map. At the moment, I don't care so much about where we're going, just who I'm going with, because Chase is looking devastating with his dark blond curls and two-day beard. He's stretched out on his side, one hand propped under his head. He's wearing a pair of faded jeans, his brown T-shirt bearing the wreckage from supper. That Chloe doesn't love oatmeal.

Hey, oatmeal is a perfectly decent food choice any time of the day.

Chloe and Justin are in bed for the night—or at least, we put them in bed. I can still hear Chloe singing to anyone who will listen.

"And we're going here." Chase has to sit up to move his hand over to the other end of the map. He peers closely at it, finds a speck the size of a mustard seed, points to it, and smiles. "Bursk."

I look back at the Moscow dot. "There's a size difference."

"That's because Bursk is really just a village."

Now, when I hear the word *village*, I think of quaint German towns, houses with thatched roofs, outside bistros, artists painting on the sidewalk while happy pigeons coo at their feet. I hear the jingle bell of bicyclists pedaling two-wheelers, their handlebar baskets filled with crusty wheat bread and a spray of daisies. I can even smell the bread baking from a nearby bakery.

Village means quiet. It means provincial. It means . . . vacation.

I've been on a Russian vacation. I'm no longer that ignorant girl.

But I am hopeful.

"Where's the nearest town?"

"Two hours by boat."

I narrow my eyes. Did he say . . . boat? I sit up, move his hand away from the speck. Read the name of the narrow strip of blue next to it. It's in Russian, and I sound it out. "Amore."

"Amur, yes. It connects the village—"

"Stop saying *village*. It raises too many expectations. Let's call it a . . . small town."

"A very small town . . . "

"How small are we talking?"

"Less than five hundred?"

I lie back on the floor, staring at the ceiling. I grew up in a small town, and more than anything, I long for my children to know the charm of living in a small town. But not an on-the-backside-of-the-world small town.

"Less than five hundred, Chase?"

"The people were formerly nomadic. Only since the Soviet Union took over have they settled down in one location. They're still largely hunters and make their living hunting and trapping animals for their fur. That's why Voices International wants us to study them. They want to figure out ways for them to survive in today's capitalist Russia without having to compromise their society or culture. Too many of their children are abandoning their heritage and moving to cities like Khabarovsk or Vladivostok or even Irkutsk and forgetting the family and life they left behind. It's destroying their culture and possibly their future."

I get it. And I agree with Voices International's mission. I do. And I believe he can help.

I believe *we* can help. That old feeling, the one that churned in me right before I took off for a year, so long ago, to teach English in Russia, burns inside me. We can make a difference, change the landscape from despair to hope for these people.

See, inside me still simmers the idea that I can change my world . . . their world. Our world.

There's the eternal perspective I've been waiting for.

However, "Is it really in Siberia?" Even the word makes me shiver. Yes, I'm a Minnesota girl and can handle a few snowdrifts, but I also remember, in my college days, reading something about Stalin sending people east to gulag, to Siberia . . . and we're going there by choice?

"Everything east of the Urals is Siberia." Chase draws an invisible north-south line down the mountains on the map. The line is a lot closer to Moscow than the little blip in the east.

"How cold do you think it gets?"

"You do remember the fur part, right?" Chase leans over, kisses me quickly. "I'll keep you warm."

Yeah, sure you will. I give him a playful push away. "No, seriously."

"Siberia is actually hotter than people think. They have summer, and the snow does melt, and Bursk isn't any farther north than Moscow."

I'm not appeased. "How far is it from here?"

"By plane or train?"

Oh no. "Plane, please."

"Nine hours."

Okay, nine hours. That's nearly as far as it is from here to

Boston. However, my stomach has clenched. I do *not* want to ask this question. Most wives wouldn't even have to think about it. However, most wives aren't married to Adventure Boy. "And by train?"

"Seven days."

"Please don't tell me—"

"We're taking the train." He scoots over on the map, right down the Volga River, to where I'm perched on the border of Ukraine. He's got a twinkle in his eyes, probably cornering me so I can't flee. "Seven days in our own train compartment on the Trans-Siberian Railway, watching Russia drift by."

He tucks his arm around my waist, leans over me, a gleam in his blue eyes.

Oh, Chase. I trace my finger in the well of his neck, trying not to smile. "Why can't we fly?"

"Voices International is on a tight allotment. We either fly with just four suitcases, or we ship our belongings, with us, on the train."

Four suitcases or a train for a week. Shoes, think of your shoes, Josey. I know that my style standards have plummeted to an all-time low from those days when I wore my leather pants without shame, but here's a fact: feet stay roughly the same size regardless of waist size.

My saving grace. Still, right behind the realization that Chase has opted for *more* suitcases (catching on, are we, Chase?) is the sinking feeling at his word *tight*. I generally hate this word, but even more so when it comes to money.

"Just how 'tight' is this allotment, Chase?"

His face does the math for me. Oh.

"It's just for a year. We can tap into our savings."

What savings? Oh, that $5,467.42 we saved up over the past four years? Sure, that'll get us real far.

"C'mon, G.I., the train. We've always wanted to take the train."

That sounds a lot like a he-we to me. You know, the *we* that doesn't really mean *we*, but rather the *we* that he'd like it to mean.

But nestled here in Chase's strong embrace . . . "It does sound romantic."

"We can go to the dining car. Read a book. Sleep late—"

"Mommy!" Justin shoots out of the bedroom, his jammies off, of course. He's just in his cloth pull-up and plastic pants. "Chloe is kicking me!"

Of course she is.

Chase rolls over to his side and scoops up Justin. "C'mon, buddy. We'll go have a talk with Chloe."

Good luck with that.

I watch him throw Justin over his shoulder and tickle him as they disappear into our bedroom. We've been living in a one-bedroom flat for four years now, pulling out the sofa bed every night in the living room just like the Russians do. Chloe and Justin share a giant double bed in the room where we keep our clothing. It's cramped with their toys shoved up against every wall, and shoes and coats overflow by the door. Our flat isn't much bigger than one of the cabins back at Berglund Acres in Minnesota.

Please, Lord, I want a house.

They have to have houses in a village, right?

When we first got married, Chase and I (okay, just I) wanted to buy a cute little Cape Cod I'd found in the middle of Gull Lake. This was, however, before Chase lost his job—or rather, before he told me how he lost his job—and found another in Moscow. I never dreamed I'd spend four years surfing the subway and shopping in the open market in Moscow. But the Josey that still lives under this long blonde hair that needs a cut, who wears faded yoga pants, loves the city life, the hustle of Moscow.

A village. It might be quaint.

Please, let it be quaint.

I hear Chloe now, laughing. I give it five minutes before I have to go in there and calm everyone down.

But listening to the ruckus makes me smile. Chase can make anyone laugh with his disarming grin, the twinkle in his blue eyes. His charm snuck up on me when we met in kindergarten, and by the time we were in third grade, he and I spent every waking moment racing bicycles, building woodland forts, and swimming in Gull Lake. I don't remember life before Chase . . .

Frankly, I don't want to.

I love the fact that Chase doesn't doubt that I'll move to the end of the earth with him, that I can keep up with him. Especially, that I believe in him.

I believe in us.

We can do this. We can change the future for this little town, this people group. We can help them survive, keep their traditions, entice their young people to stay. And a good Minnesota girl knows how to stretch her pennies.

Maybe I'll grow a garden. Learn how to put up beans.

I roll over and trace the length of the map with a finger. Its smooth, shiny surface flows under my skin as I travel over the Urals, across steppe, tundra, river, forest, and finally to tiny Bursk, the little village on the Amur River.

Bursk. Sounds an awful lot like Burrrrrr, doesn't it?

It's just a year.

I can do anything for a year.

"you're going to be fine"

. . .

Dear Jasmine,

Thank you for the anniversary card. No, I can't believe that Chase and I have been married for four years, and I have to agree that it's convenient that Amelia's birthday falls on the same day as our wedding anniversary. Although, you'd think, then, that I'd remember to send her a birthday card. Her party sounds great—love the fact that little Clay stuck both of his grimy hands in the cake—that's a one-year-old for you! Good idea making two cakes. I can just imagine Dad and Mom and Uncle Bert and Aunt Myrtle standing around the grill, watching your two little ones splashing in Gull Lake. I remember those days of summer, running barefoot, lying out on the beach . . . did I mention that Chase and I went to the Black Sea just a few weeks ago?

Which brings me to some news. I'm actually writing to you from . . . well, a Trans-Siberian train compartment. We've decided—well, that's not entirely accurate. Chase wants to, and I'm a reluctant but willing participant—to take a new job in . . . the truth is, it's in Siberia. Before you jump up and start accusing me of betrayal (I know you had us all signed up for the Gull Lake Community Church book club), let me say that this is going to be good.

Remember that time Chase got injured during his junior year playing football? He got hit in the ribs, right under his pads, and had a bruise along his side that took up half his body? He had to sit out two long games—I know, because I was there, in the stands, watching him pout on the bench. (I also remember the team losing those two weeks, due to the loss of their starting wide receiver.) Not only that, do you recall the night during that time that he snuck over to our house, climbed up on the roof, and knocked on our window? Halloween—I'd dressed up as the Queen of Hearts, complete with tiara and gown. I remember it well because he made me sneak out while I was still in my costume . . . oh, wait, you had stayed home, sick with the flu. I should probably tell you now that the reason I never answered your moaning in the middle of the night was because that lump you were whining at was actually a wad of pillows. Sorry. Anyway, Chase and I went out on his motorcycle, and we drove down to the football field, and he made me throw him spirals for two hours, just so he could feel the pigskin in his hands. He had this look in his eyes, too—a sort of desperation, like he might forget how to catch it, and his life would then unravel before his eyes. You know how much football meant to him, especially after his mom died. He acted like it was the only thing worth living for. Although, if I had a dad like Chase's, I might have hid out on the football field and kept my motorcycle tuned too.

So, the point is, I got to thinking about that and decided that going home for Chase would be like being benched from playing football. And I know when Mom finds out we're staying for another year (and that's all, really. I promise), she'll probably cry and box up one of her famous lasagnas and Fed Ex it to Moscow, or rather, Siberia. So you need to be there, explain it to her.

Cookies, by the way, make it through the mail just fine.

Lest you think that I'm losing my mind—and yes, I'm aware that brain cells diminish with pregnancy, but out-thinking Chloe has me at the top of my game—I did extract some promises from Chase.

1. We will live in a house. Seriously. Do you know how often the elevator dies on us? Just last week, we made it to floor eight and one half, waited for a half hour before help arrived. I long for a yard—something free of needles, cigarette butts, broken beer bottles, and open manholes.

I am going to miss, however, the sunset over the skyline of Moscow. The way the sun bleeds out through the tops of buildings, bruising the twilight above Gorky Park and turning the walls of the Kremlin to bright crimson. I'll miss the way the winter snow hides the despair of Moscow under a blanket of grace and how, as I stare down on it from nine flights, it resembles icing.

Which suddenly makes me miss your *kringle*. I think that could also ship well . . .

How are things at the restaurant going? So nice of you to take over Mom's job as head baker. Sounds like Mom and Dad's new place in Arizona is nice also. I hope we're not leaving you and Milton in too much of a bind running Berglund Acres.

But I digress.

2. We are going to homeschool. I've already started teaching Chloe and Justin their ABCs. I was reading up on homeschooling material, and it's not too soon to teach them to read. Justin is exceptionally smart. (After all, he knows how to dodge Chloe's teeth better than I do!) How hard can it be, really? I love to read, and Chase has a couple very large books here, one chronicling the history of the world. My kids have to be brilliant.

3. I am buying a car. Seriously. I am tired of lugging

groceries home on my back, dragging two toddlers (well, only one, really, since Justin actually uses his legs for more than just dead weight) on the subway. I want wheels. Especially since we'll be living in a village. Yes, I said village. I'm not even sure what a village is. I'm seeing thatched roofs and busy bakers' daughters, but knowing Russia like I do, I know it can't be accurate. After four years, I know I have to be ready for anything.

I know you think these might be large requests. But a girl has to put her foot down sometimes.

WorldMar took Chase's decision to turn down the chicken coop project pretty well. Maggie and Dalton were sad to see us move, but they promised to visit. As for Sveta and Igor . . . they're expecting! Finally, little Ryslan will have a brother or a sister.

Meanwhile, I've spent the past two weeks packing. Thanks to Aeroflot, which won't allow us to take more than one suitcase weighing twenty kilos (that's roughly forty pounds), and Chase's fear that anything we put in a container to send east will disappear forever, we decided to take the train.

Yes, I said train. For seven days. Across Russia.

Chase was so enamored by the idea that I actually bought into the romance. I packed a few read-alouds for Justin and Chloe, along with a bag of toys, and even slipped in two (okay, five, but what if I run out of reading material?) books to read.

Nostalgia meets reality. It isn't pretty.

Everyone in Russia takes the train. This fact should, I would think, guarantee some amount of standardized comfort. It's true that we took the train from Moscow to Ukraine for our vacation. But I thought we'd just gotten a very old one that didn't represent all Russian trains. Silly me.

Have I mentioned that all of Russia is caught in the 1940s? Think World War II movies, with long green train cars, smoke puffing out from under the giant metal wheels, and officers dressed in uniform, standing on either end of the platform, holding what look to be AK-47s. It made it worse when Daphne and Caleb came to say goodbye, and there we were crying, as if we were being sent off to gulag. (I can't get this out of my mind!)

Thankfully, Chase reserved us a private compartment. I had whittled our belongings down to fit into eight suitcases, but they still filled the upper bunks of our compartment to the brim. Chloe and Justin have had to share our lower bunks the past two nights. Remember: cloth diapers.

Our bunks are made of cracked brown vinyl, and someone turned the heat up to broil (probably in anticipation of never having heat again once we get to Siberia). Justin and Chloe are stripped to the waist and spend their days leaping from bunk to bunk. Between the bunks is a small table on which we picnic each day.

Lest you think that Russia is without comforts, they do serve complimentary tea every morning. And although we did venture down to the dining car the first day, the pileup of grease hanging from the ceiling above the stove made me turn back to my stash of bagels. Our saving grace is the food vendors lined up outside on the train platform at every little town we roll through. The train stops for twenty or so minutes, during which Chase darts out and buys items such as roasted potatoes in a bag, cooked *pelmeni*, winter salad (think potato salad with cooked carrots, pickles, and beets), and fresh bread.

The conductors (who aren't nice, stately English gentlemen, but plump, angry near-babushkas who would just as soon throw us from the train as bring us our tea) close the bathrooms during these stops. This annoyed me until I took the time to, um, explore this inconvenience. One look through the escape hatch of the toilet directly onto the tracks, and I understood why. Travel note: never walk on a railroad track in Russia.

Chase, of course, has made friends with our entire car of fellow passengers. Last night, the fellows next door knocked on our door and invited Chase over for smoked fish and vodka.

Now, don't get excited—Chase isn't a vodka drinker. But the man loves his fish, and three hours later, I could hear him leading singing next door.

This just might be the longest week of my life.

Once we get there, we're going to be just fine. I know it's Siberia, but really, how cold can it get?

Don't worry about me. It's only a year. I can do anything for a year.

My love to Milton, and kisses to Amelia and baby Clay.

Josey

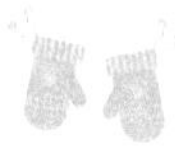

"Chloe!"

They say that all your sins come back to haunt you when you have children. I'm here to tell you that they're right. I gave birth to a child who is constantly reminding me of every dark night that I slipped out of the house to hang out with Chase and disappear on the back of his motorcycle. "Chloe!"

She's dressed in just her underwear and T-shirt since we're travelling in a moving sauna. I get up, duck my head out the door, and peer down the hallway. The compartment doors are open—to circulate the heat, apparently—and the little scamp looks back at me, gives me a grin, and bolts.

Oh, good, it's a game. "Chloe!" I step out into the hall, on the chase.

Outside, the terrain is chapped and brown, evidence of the upcoming winter. Occasionally, we pass through villages, and I see the same tired, scarf-outlined faces staring up at the train—old faces that wear travail and exhaustion in their lines, that look at me with eyes that wonder where I'm going, what I'm doing.

I'm mesmerized by these faces, the same question in my mind, numbed by the never-ending landscape of identically forlorn villages, the wisps of black coal smoke from broken chimneys, the blue and green houses, poorly hidden behind lopsided fences.

I'm starting to dread what I'll find in Bursk.

"Chloe!" She weaves in and out of legs, fellow sojourners who have their elbows propped up on the railing that runs along the window, most dressed in nylon sports pants and sleeveless army T-shirts. They all wear the monotony of our trans-Russian trip on their faces. No one makes a move toward the runaway.

"Chloe, stop!"

I've nearly caught up to her when I see a man turn from the window and crouch, right in her path. "Hey there, tyke," he says, and I just about fall over. English!

He's slowed her enough for me to catch up, and I scoop her into my arms, throw her wiggling and laughing body over my shoulder. "Thanks."

"I see I'm not the only crazy non-Russian taking the train across the Motherland," he says, standing. "Nathan Blume."

"Thanks, Nathan," I say. "Josey Anderson."

"Oh, a Scandinavian," he says, smiling. He's got dark eyes and dark hair and is wearing a T-shirt, sweatpants, and flip-flops. His version of Russian casual.

"From Minnesota," I say, filling in the blanks, holding out my hand.

"South Dakota," Nathan says, taking it. He's got a firm grip.

"And who is the escapee?" He nods to my daughter, who I now spin around and prop on my hip. She claps at this acrobatic move.

"This is Chloe."

He takes her hand and gives it a little pump.

"I have a matching one, male version, back in the compartment."

"Twins. Wow. Bet that's fun in Russia." His eyes are twinkling, and from his comment, I realize he's been in Russia long enough to understand that twins in this culture are an oddity . . . and a collective joy. I can't walk down the street without having babushki stop and make comments about my bookends—from attire and footwear to parenting advice. Russians have no problem asking personal questions, and the most common is, Where is their babushka? Apparently, someone my age isn't equipped to raise twins.

I sort of agree with that one. But I smile at Nathan. "Oh, yes, it's been so much fun. And now we're moving to Siberia."

"You and the kids?"

"And my husband, Chase. He's working with Voices International to help create industries in a Nanai village."

"Oh? Where?"

"A little town called Bursk. It's north of Kha . . . Kha . . . "

"Khabarovsk. And by the way, technically, it's called Far East Russia. But it feels like Siberia. Can get pretty cold there, even if it is on the Amur River. I hope you brought your *dublenka*."

"My what?"

"It's a thick fur coat. You'll need that and a *shapka*—it's a fur hat."

"I know. I do speak Russian, although lately my vocabulary is limited to childcare and household products." I laugh, but there's a sad irony in the fact that I came to Russia four years ago knowing the language, and now my husband can chat circles around me.

Nathan smiles, and it's warm, his eyes finding mine. "A few grunts and sign language will get you a long way. The people in Bursk are very nice. They're used to having tourists come by in the summertime, on excursions up the Amur River. They take them mushroom picking. And of course, it's on my route."

"Route? Are you a postman?" I'm jesting, of course, and he laughs. I think I like Nathan.

"I'm a missionary. I visit all the northern villages a couple times a month."

"Josey?" Chase comes up behind me, puts his hand on my shoulder. Chloe squirms in my arms and reaches out to him.

"This is Nathan," I say, handing off the renegade. She doubles over in shrieks as Chase runs his fingers against her tummy. "He's a missionary from South Dakota. Apparently, he knows where Bursk is. He travels there on his missionary route."

Chase shakes his hand, warmth in his eyes. "Come by our house when you're in town. We'd be glad to feed you."

Chase means *he'd* be glad to feed him, because our visitor would perish before he found something edible, besides chocolate chip cookies, made by my hands. The Berglund *Iron Chef* talents I did not inherit.

Besides, I'm caught on the word *house*. House! And I have a witness!

I beam up at Chase. "Yes, stop by the house when you're in town."

Nathan chuckles, shaking his head. "A house, huh? Okay."

It's his tone that lingers on in my head like the dying, dismal sound of a gong as I stare out at the shadowed steppe, the train chugging toward my future.

Chase's ability to navigate through a country he's never set foot in before astonishes me. He was born to be on the Travel Channel. Or maybe a reality show—*The Amazing Race*. Because we pull up to the train station in Khabarovsk (from where we'll take our two-hour boat ride to Bursk), and he has a fleet of men helping us out of our compartment. (The fish and vodka breath is my first hint as to where he dredged them up). Nathan is there, holding Chloe, keeping her from making another escape. Justin is a man after his father's heart, lugging out a duffel bag about twice his size, aided surreptitiously by, again, Nathan.

I really like Nathan. He's probably nondescript by today's standards—very short brown hair, dark brown eyes, a now six-day beard on his chin. He carries himself like Chase—confidently—and Russian rolls off his tongue like he might be half Slavic, although he indeed proves he's from South Dakota by expertly handling the Minnesota three-hour goodbye. Thus, he finds himself standing beside us and all our gear while Chase hails a cab.

"Chase says that you taught ESL?" Nathan says, letting Justin take a running dive at him from the edge of a bone-dry water fountain while I attempt to keep Chloe away from the feral kitties that roam the sidewalk.

"Kitty! Kitty!" Chloe reaches for one as it hisses at her and scampers away. I spot Chase standing on the curb, his hand in the air in Russian "catch a cab" language. In Russia, anyone can be a cabbie—yes, there are official cabbies, but even Chase has been known to pull over, name his price, and give the occasional fare a ride across town.

"I taught English once upon a time at Moscow Bible Church," I say, shooing away another kitty from Chloe.

"I had friends there," Nathan says. "Matt and Becky Winneman. But they went stateside quite a few years ago. Probably before you got there."

I smile at him. Because I know more about the Winnemans

than is acceptable to discuss in polite conversation. Like how Matthew nearly cheated on his wife with a slinky Russian translator, and how Rebecca turned her insecurities toward me and tried to teach me to cross-stitch. I glance at Chase, at the way he's now negotiating a possible ride. I'm fairly sure Chase would never cheat on me—at least, now I'm sure. But I know how easily it can happen.

Not to me, of course. But others.

"So, what is it that you do, exactly, in Bursk?" I hook my foot around one of my bags as I see a woman, dressed in acrylic layers of headscarves and flanked by dirty children, edge toward us. The first time I saw Romani beggars was in Moscow, at the train station. My heart cries out for their poverty, but I've also been told that they are essentially an organized crime syndicate. I'm not sure what to believe.

I pull Chloe up to my hip.

"I'm trying to plant a church there, but so far, I can't get the men to come, and the women don't trust me. So"—he gives a shrug—"I'm trying to talk the local *detskiy sad* into letting me teach Bible stories."

Justin launches himself again, and Nathan catches him, throwing him over his shoulder. The move reminds me so much of Chase that I'm wondering if these two have been separated at birth. No wonder they hit it off so well. He looks at me. "The kindergarten is going to love having Justin and Chloe."

Uh, no. "I'm going to homeschool."

Nathan gives me a look I can't interpret, just as Chase returns. "I found us a cab."

I'm eyeing the tiny Lada with concern. It's roughly the size of a Volkswagen Jetta, and I wonder if Chase has counted how many bags we have, or if perhaps he's trying to pull one of those collegiate how-many-people-can-we-fit-into-a-phonebooth challenges.

My face apparently betrays me.

"I'll go with the bags if you can take another cab," he says.

I'm speechless for a moment, because, hello, I have no idea where I'm going. Or, for that matter, where I am.

I know I must be in Siberia, because we've been on a train for way too many days, rumbling across steppe and prairie, through forests and even mountains. But Khabarovsk resembles Moscow, minus the subway and towering Baroque architecture. Crimson maples and yellow poplars line the center boulevards, and Ladas and Zhigulis—cars from the Cold War era—clog the streets. The requisite statue of Lenin sits in the center of a circle outside the train station, pointing east, as if a reminder of where we've come from. I smell fried meat sandwiches and exhaust, and the four-story yellow-and-faded-blue apartment buildings with the tiny curved metal balconies and ornate moldings look like they've been plucked from Moscow's Pushkin Square. But we're not in Moscow. We're in Siberia. Which reminds me . . .

"Where are we going?"

"To the port," Chase says, already throwing our suitcases into the car. Nathan hands Justin over and picks up a bag. Chase turns to me. "I'm so sorry, Josey." He picks up another bag. "I can't find a bigger car, and if I come back to get you, there's no one to watch our bags."

Shoes. Think of your shoes. "Of course, Chase, I totally—"

"I'll ride with you," Nathan says, throwing in the last of our bags.

He glances at me, and for a second, his smile knocks me off guard, reaches in and touches my heart and gives it a good tug.

We Americans have to stick together.

"Thanks, Nate," Chase says, holding out his hand. "I'll meet you there." He lands a quick kiss on my cheek and jumps into the cab.

I watch him go as Nathan hails another cab.

We climb in, and Justin and Chloe momentarily fight for lap space—on Nathan. But I'm so tired, so grimy, I don't care. I'm wearing dirty yoga pants, a pair of Converse tennis shoes I found at the market (and have long since realized are knock-offs), and a sweatshirt that is stained with Chloe's chocolate handprint. I just want a warm bath and a change of clothes.

But Chase did look so cute in his excitement, didn't he?

Nathan tickles them both as I try not to think about the lack of seatbelts and the way we weave in and out of traffic.

Apparently, the drivers have been imported from Moscow also.

I lean my head back against the seat, close my eyes. I'm just now picking up an odor of something stronger than beer emanating from the front seat.

Please, God, let us get there.

"Tired?" Nathan asks.

He has no idea. I merely nod.

"Chase says you're staying with the town elders tonight. Probably Anton Vasillyech and his wife. They're nice folks. In fact, I think you'll like Bursk. It's one of my favorite villages. They have an annual winter carnival, complete with reindeer-pulled sleigh rides and ice sculptures. It's gorgeous."

Gorgeous. Hmm.

"And if you need anything, you can always send me an email, and I'll bring it up on my route."

I open an eye. "Email? They have Internet?"

He nods. "Dial-up, although only at the city government building."

Close enough. As long as I can write home.

Nathan reaches over and taps my forearm. "You're going to be fine."

I hate how much I need those words. But with Chase dashing off to port (he sounds like a sailor, doesn't he?), I'm wondering just what I'm getting myself into. We had problems our first year of marriage—the kind that made me wonder if Chase even remembered he had a wife. But we learned. We grew. We got cell phones.

Please, God, I don't want to return to that life.

We ride in silence until the taxi pulls up to the wharf. Sure enough, there's Chase, sitting atop our luggage like some explorer, grinning. Chloe jumps off Nathan and dives into his arms as if she hasn't seen him for a decade instead of just twenty minutes.

"Our boat leaves in a half hour," he says, grabbing a bag. I stand guard while he and Nathan shuffle our belongings down a gangplank to what looks like a rusty tugboat with portholes along the sides. Justin can't wait to climb aboard.

"See you in a few weeks," Nathan says after Chase stows the last bag. His eyes find mine, and he smiles, and I see encouragement in the dark depths. *You're going to be fine*, he mouths.

You're going to be fine!

I climb aboard and walk down the steps into the belly of the boat. Our gear is stashed in the back, and I find a seat on one of the molded vinyl chairs. The sea is at eye level, or nearly, and I can't help but calculate my escape route should we take on a leak. Or a tidal wave. I probably can't fit my body through a porthole, but I could shove Justin through and maybe Chloe if she cooperates and . . .

Okay, the contingency plan is starting to make me queasy. I lift my hand in a meager wave as we leave shore and head out to sea, as it were.

"Isn't this fun?" Chase says, pulling Chloe onto his lap. She stands up, puts her nose to the window.

"See water, Daddy. Fishes!"

Poor Justin has his arms around my neck, cutting off my air supply. At least *one* of my children remembers our vacation and the narrow miss with the jellyfish.

Chase grins at me. "We took the Trans-Siberian Railroad, babe. Across Russia."

Yay us. I can barely contain my joy.

But I give him a smile. Who can be a grump with all that enthusiasm?

Siberia is lush and beautiful. Who would have thunk it? Amethyst and ruby, amber and gold—a potpourri of jewels arrays the shoreline dotted here and again with stately buildings, probably former Communist leaders' beach—er, river—homes. Fishermen watch us motor by, and we pass an occasional barge.

As we travel north, my body settles into the rocking of the boat, the hum of the motor. We are the only travelers, which I'm not sure bodes well, but it does give us room to move about the cabin. Justin finally finds his sea legs and leaps from seat to seat. Chloe has decided that since she can't have a kitty, she'll become one, and is crawling along the molded seats, her hands in tiny paws, purring and pawing at our faces. Chase plays along and pets her. She snuggles into his lap as I give him a dirty look. Guess who's going to have to play Mommy Kitty all day now?

I focus on the sun hovering low over the horizon. I miss my skyline. *You'll like Bursk*. Nathan's words buoy my hopes. Because here, finally, I'll make us a home—one that we can stretch out in—maybe build a sandbox for the kids. And a dog. I'd love a dog—

"We're here!" Chase displaces his kitty and stares out the window. I'm not sure how he knows this, because I don't see any "Welcome to Bursk" signs. But sure enough, we've angled toward shore and a long pier that looks like it might be washed away with one good squall.

Here?

Chloe makes a run for the stairs, but I grab her. "Not yet, sweetie."

We walk up to the deck together as a family to glimpse our new hometown.

Or . . . muddy hovel. You pick, because I see only muddy, rutted streets, rickety fences that border tiny houses, a trickle of coal smoke darkening the sky. I spy a pack of mangy dogs, ribs corrugating their sides, staring at us from the weedy beach. Unfortunately, I pick up the faintest odor of manure.

I hold on to the edge of the boat as we glide in.

You're going to be fine!

the little lies

. . .

My brain can often fool me. Not that this is a surprise. We all know that my mouth often runs off on its own rampant course without a thought to the repercussions. However, my brain has decided that it also has no accountability, and on occasion, I've awakened in Moscow over the past few years confused at my whereabouts. The birds are singing and the fragrance from a spray of lilacs on the window fills my nose, and I'm suddenly back in Gull Lake, waking to a fresh summer morning. I hear the clatter of dishes—my mother cooking up breakfast at the restaurant next door—and I pull the cotton sheet close to my nose and smell the fresh-from-the-line crispness of the sun.

In that moment, life is good.

Simple.

And doesn't come accompanied by . . . oh, I'm wet! I open my eyes to reality, and I'm staring at a paint-peeling ceiling, dark walls covered in patterned brown Turkish-style rugs, and a very damp Chloe, sleeping on top of me.

Soaking me through as she snoozes through her early morning accident.

Where am I?

I ease Chloe off me and onto Chase's side of the bed—which is empty—pull the sodden sheet away from me, and memory rushes back.

I am in Mayor Anton and his wife Ulia's bedroom. In their three-room house. Located three muddy blocks from the boat dock in the tiny town of Bursk.

In Siberia.

Russia.

Oh boy.

Sun filters through a flimsy lace curtain and across the brown painted floor covered with a worn red throw rug. Standing now in the middle of the room, I start to shiver. Although it's September, the house, which must be made of cement, collects the chill like a meat freezer. We've left most of our bags in the family room, as I can recall, but I find the one containing my clothes and change quickly, wishing, oh, wishing for a shower.

But today we move into our house. Our *house*.

Chase promised.

I take care of Chloe, who sleeps through the changing, and I tuck her into a warm, dry portion of the bed. Then I venture out to find my husband.

Chase already has a fan club. Three men sit at the kitchen table, drinking tea with him while he bounces Justin on his knee. I spot Ulia at the sink. She's a strong Russian woman with a wide, tanned, weathered face and the hands of a lumberjack. The house has a coal furnace the size of a Hereford in the kitchen, and it's on this she has simmering a pot of what looks like kasha.

"Good morning, G.I.," Chase says, scooting over on the bowed bench. "Want some breakfast?"

I notice that his bowl is half empty and Justin's is clean. Or maybe Chase is on seconds.

"Pumpkin kasha. You gotta get the recipe."

Oh sure. Has the man learned nothing since the day I nearly set the kitchen on fire, a week after our marriage? Do the words *instant oatmeal* mean anything to him?

He picks up his cup of tea. "These are the town elders—Misha, Alex, and of course, Anton." They nod at me, without smiling.

I scoot in beside Chase, and Justin climbs on my lap. The kitchen bears the markings of age, with a saggy, formerly white cupboard hanging from the far wall, a bowed hutch with chipped china behind us. The room is about as big as my parents' walk-in closet, and with six people at the table, I'm wondering how Ulia manages to scurry about, let alone ladle me up a bowl of the pale-orange kasha.

"*Spasibo*," I say, and she gives me a tight smile. I can read "go away" clearly in almost any language.

I'm starting to wonder if Voices International neglected to preapprove our visit with the locals.

I dive into the kasha, eyeing the tea, wishing for coffee.

No. I am sacrificing for others. For Chase. I am learning submission.

Coffee is probably the last thing I need.

The kasha crunches in my mouth, and although I've only eaten pumpkin in pie, I have to admit the flavor wins me.

I listen to the men talk about people and life in the village. They're telling Chase their history and how they've made their living by hunting fox and trapping mink and beaver for the past fifty million decades. Anton's two children live in Khabarovsk, the city we left yesterday, and Misha has a son that moved to Moscow when he was seventeen. He hasn't seen him since. I eye Ulia and notice that she doesn't say a word.

I hope this is a personality quirk and not SOP.

Submission. Maybe she has the corner on it.

Chloe shuffles into the room in her full-length footie

jammies. Her hair sticks straight up, and her eyes are huge at the changes in her world. Yes, well, like mother, like daughter. I pull her up on my lap. "Would you like some nummy kasha for breakfast?" I scoop up some and aim for her mouth. She turns her head at the last minute, and it narrowly misses her hair.

"Chloe!"

"No like Kasha! No Kasha!" She pushes at the spoon, which goes flying out of my grasp. It hits Alex the elder, who makes a face that looks uncannily like Chloe's.

"Chloe!" I'm trying to figure out who to clean first when Ulia crouches before me and hands Chloe a piece of brown bread, buttered, covered in what an un-Moscowed person might think is red jam.

"She's not going to like caviar," I say quietly to Chase as Chloe reaches for it. "What do I do?"

Before Chase can answer, however, Chloe takes the bread and takes a bite. Oh no, here it comes—

"Mmm. Try, Mommy!" Chloe holds out the bread to me as Ulia stands up, a satisfied smile on her face.

Mommy tries some. Smiles. Oh boy. Gone are the days when I used to eat caviar for breakfast. Like, when I was pregnant, which I suppose fits perfectly with Chloe's instant love of the delicacy.

Satisfied, Chloe finishes off the bread, pounds the table for more.

Figures that I'd have a diva for a daughter.

"Anton told me that he harvests the roe from his own catch," Chase says, as he accepts the offer of a caviar-laden piece of black bread from Ulia.

"What kind of fish?"

Chase asks, and it takes a second for him to translate. (Apparently, I need to work on my fishing terms.) "Carp."

Oh, perfect.

I manage to dodge my way around another caviar sandwich

before I'm able to escape with the kids to dress them. Chase joins me in the room moments later, closing the door behind him.

"I have good news and bad news."

See, here's the thing. When a woman lives in Russia, she doesn't need to be told there is bad news accompanying the good news. That's a given. She just wants to know how bad it is. "Lay it on me."

"They found us a house."

A house! I throw myself at Chase, and he's momentarily taken aback, apparent by the startled look in his blue eyes. Hey, someone should remind him that we just spent a week locked in a compartment the size of a caravan with our two kids. I'm a little on the emotional edge here.

He offers me a flimsy hug, then puts me away from him.

Long before Chase and I married, I had the ability to read his mind. Not only was he my best childhood pal, but he broadcasts his thoughts like the whistle of a locomotive, right before the news steamrolls in.

Right now, my Chase radar is telling me this one is a super freighter.

"You're starting to scare me."

"There's no plumbing."

I am eyeing him because, well, I'm not sure I've heard him correctly. "No . . . plumbing? Could you elaborate on that?"

"Well . . . " He looks away from me, wraps his hand around his neck. "I guess the entire town doesn't have indoor plumbing."

I'm still struggling here. Does he mean . . . "Are you saying that I have to lug my water in from . . . what, the river?"

His face brightens. Phew! For a second there, I was seeing *Little House on the Prairie*. And we all know I'm not Ma.

"There's a pump. Right there, in the house. You just have to, uh . . . lug the water from the pump to the kitchen sink."

Or, no phew. "So, no running water in the house."

" . . . Right . . . "

I can see I'm still not getting it, because he's staring at me like he's waiting for something to click.

No running water. No running water to fill the kitchen sink. Or the bathtub, or the only-in-my-dreams washing machine.

Or take . . . a . . . shower . . .

"Where do we bathe?"

"Well, at home, with a pot of water." Chase lifts Justin down from where he's jumping on the bed. "Or at the local bathhouse."

Local bathhouse.

"No chance it's a family bathhouse?"

"Segregated." He smiles, his eyes running over me dramatically. "Unfortunately."

"Please. So . . . " And then it hits me. No running water for a shower also means no running water to . . . flush the toilet . . .

"Oh . . . my." I touch the wall, because I think my knees might buckle.

Chase wraps his hand around my arm, because he sees that I've finally got it.

"I promise, I'll build you the best outhouse in Siberia."

I have no doubt it will win awards. But . . . "Chase, no indoor toilet?"

"Babe, c'mon." He leans in and touches his forehead to mine. "It's just for a year."

That'll be just about enough of that.

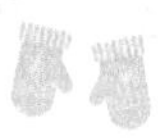

I'm still in a daze as we're given a tour of Bursk on our way to our new . . . what, shack? Hut?

I'm putting it out of my mind, however, trying to look for the shiny layers to this thundercloud. I'm especially not thinking about the word *outhouse*.

I blame my current fiasco on my waffling over our vacation accommodations. See, I let Chase, and apparently the cosmos at large, believe that I might be willing to live, permanently, without plumbing. Just for the record, that isn't the truth.

The one current benefit I'm spotting about our village is that there is no traffic under which Chloe or Justin might be killed. None. Not a car to be seen. Only carts, pulled by an occasional reindeer. And if that isn't enough to make one stop and stare, I don't know what is. Because I'm talking real reindeer here, with the soft moose-like noses, the big eyes, the tuft of white furry hair on their chests, and of course the antlers. I stand on the street corner (aka, the bump between two houses) and watch as a woman who looks like she might have been born at the dawn of time rides a reindeer down the street, her feet dangling in huge felt snow boots. She wears a worn-thin *shapka* and a wool jacket and gives me a look as if I'm naked in my jeans and sweatshirt, and how dare I bring those children out here with just a windbreaker? Where are their snowsuits?

Talk about Siberia.

Chase has Chloe up on his shoulders as he walks with the men. So far I've counted about eight light-blue or green houses—or rather, duplexes, because each house has two entrances and is a mirror of its twin. A fence encircles each yard on each side of the house. The yards contain chickens, cows, an occasional goat. And, once in a while, a reindeer.

I wonder if I'm going to get a reindeer. Instead of plumbing, of course.

"A long time ago, they used to herd reindeer, and these few animals are left over from those herds," Chase says when I ask him about Santa's pets.

How long ago, I'm wondering. Last week? The dawn of time?

"Anton says the market is only open on Saturdays, because that's when they get the shipment of food from Khabarovsk," Chase now says, over his shoulder. He's been passing on these incidentals the entire tour, like we're in the Smithsonian. He glances at me. "I suppose that'll leave you time to do other things."

Like what? Milk cows?

Attitude, attitude, Josey. *Please, Lord, help me see the good parts. Submission. Joy.*

I'm proud of you, Josey. Yeah, Daph, you'd better be.

Anton shows us the town hall—a long green building with saggy steps. "Anton says you can use his office to hook up to the Internet. There are no other phone lines in the village."

Of course there aren't.

Oops. Attitude.

Inside the town hall is a post office. Chase signs us up for a box and hands me a brass key.

At one point, years ago, my good friend H told me that I was a dreamer, looking for a happily-ever-after that didn't exist. Now I'm beginning to wonder if she might be right.

Finally, we arrive at our house.

Chase stands outside the gate.

I'm afraid to look.

"It's cute," Chase says, reaching over to wrap his arm around me. I take a breath. Crack open one of my tightly closed eyes.

It *is* cute, in a Siberian sort of way. See, I'm already seeing things with new eyes. It's blue, with giant, ornate, white-painted windows. A worn dirt path winds up to the front door. Beyond that, the path continues to the backyard, where I see trampled grass (read: weeds, but we're trying to have a good attitude, aren't we?). Along the back fence, which is painted green, I see a matching outbuilding.

I look away.

"C'mon," Chase says, letting Chloe down to run. She and Justin take off through the yard while Anton hands Chase the key to the house. I hear him say something about bringing our bags over.

I walk to the house, nearly holding my breath. Now, I have to admit, when I dreamed of a house, it had two stories and, of course, indoor plumbing, but most importantly, potential.

I hear the children's laughter as they chase each other.

Chase hands me the key, and I slowly unlock the door. Ease it open. It squeals on its loose hinges.

The door opens to a small foyer that is closed off from the house. Probably to keep the frost and chill from the warmth of the hearth. I can already smell the musty scent of damp, weathering boards, but at least the former owners were clean, because this room's brown linoleum floor has been swept. A row of homemade hooks by the door suggests the frequency of company, and a potato bin bulges with what looks like two sacks of potatoes. Chase gestures to it. "They had their potato delivery last week. Anton ordered us two fifty-pound bags. He told me we'd have to dry them."

Of course we will, whatever that means.

I nod, though, and push the next door open—the one that leads to the living quarters. Chase calls for Justin and Chloe, who scamper in past me, still laughing.

The house is cool, collecting the brisk Siberian air. A kitchen not much larger than Ulia's is on my right. I see a sink, with a bucket over the top.

"You fill the bucket and then lift the latch on the bottom, and it filters into the sink," Chase says, reading my thoughts. Oh, I get it—pretend plumbing. I give a shaky smile.

"I'll have to learn how to light the coal stove," Chase says, moving past me, opening the door to our own massive Hereford in the middle of the room. I note his choice of pronoun. Smart man.

"There's the pump," Chase says, gesturing to a . . . real pump. Now I am really feeling like Ma Ingalls, because it's the old-fashioned kind, with the long pump-by-hand handle and a bucket below the spigot. It's over a wood platform, of sorts, that covers a drain in the floor.

I stare at it as truth sinks its claws in.

"I'm not sure I can do this," I hear my mouth say. For once, it's actually cooperating with my brain.

Chase hooks his arm around my waist. "Misha and Anya moved out to live with his mother so we could have this place. Most of the other residents have to cart a watering can down to the village pump for their water."

Oh. Well. Lucky me.

But I still have no words.

"There are two bedrooms," he says, and I hear the note of panic in his voice. I am nearly numb as he moves me toward the first room, right behind the kitchen. Big enough for two beds, it's bright and has a throw rug that smells freshly washed. And of course, the requisite brown Turkish carpet on the wall—high Moscow fashion has found its way east. Chloe is jumping on what looks like a black-and-white striped prison mattress left behind on the floor. Justin is sitting, barking at her to stop jumping. Chloe responds with a No! No! No! No! No!

For once, I'm siding with my daughter.

The other bedroom is smaller, and is nearly engulfed by the double bed in the middle of the room. "Where do we put our clothes?"

"In the wardrobe in the family room," Chase answers softly. I can tell he's starting to get scared by the way he's still got a grip around my waist.

I suppose dressing in the family room is better than *sleeping* in the family room. I take a deep breath. Someone has left a glass filled with wilting orange, red, and yellow chrysanthemums on the windowsill.

"Well?" Chase says, swallowing hard.

I move past him, into the family room. Shadow seeps into the nooks and crannies of the room, so I open the curtains. The windows need a good cleaning, but the sunlight reveals pink wallpaper, a brown painted wood floor. Ornate crown molding along the ceiling.

And a crucifix over the door.

Chase takes my hand. "I know it's rough, G.I. Before you say anything"—he holds up his hand—"I want you to know that I agree we're in over our heads here. In fact, I wouldn't blame you a bit if you wanted to pack up and run. This isn't what you signed up for, isn't, in fact, what I signed up for either, although you and I know that I could sleep in a barn and probably be happy—and don't look at me like that. I'm not saying you're not as tough as I am by that statement. It's just that I don't really need things like running water or—stop looking at me like that! I know how important a bathroom is! But before you make a judgment, I have to tell you something—something that I should have probably mentioned to you before, but now I see as glaringly important."

He takes my other hand, and I'm so stymied, he assumes it's a "please go on."

"Anton and Ulia actually had three children."

I'm not sure why—

"Their oldest son committed suicide about a year ago. Right here in Bursk. Left behind a wife and two little kids."

I think of Justin and Chloe without Chase, and something inside me burns. But still, what does that have to do with—

"It was the third suicide in less than a month in this town. In fact, the suicide rate has skyrocketed over the past five years. That's one of the reasons Voices sent us here—because the alcoholism and despair has started an epidemic. Only one out of every four children stays in Bursk, and out of them, about a third have committed suicide. They're a culture without a future. You can see it in the eyes of the people, can't you?"

I remember Ulia, her almost reluctant smile at my two sweet babies. And severe Anton. Maybe not so severe. Maybe grieving.

"We need to find out why these men and women who have every bit of ability to make their lives better see suicide as a better alternative to their lives. We need to help them find a balance between embracing their culture and living in today's world. We need to give them hope." Chase runs his hands up to my forearms. "I know I'm not playing fair here, babe. But what if we can help? What if staying here and studying them and asking questions and maybe offering solutions actually changes—*saves* lives? What if we can make a difference?"

Oh no. He's singing my song. I swallow. Lean my head against his warm chest.

Spy the crucifix over the door.

Nobody is playing fair today.

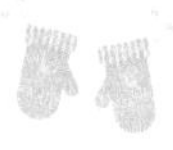

To do:

Rebuild the Outhouse

Learn how to pump water

I sit in the kitchen, in the windowsill that is large enough for my entire backside, since the walls are roughly a foot thick (I've solved the "where has all the heat gone?" question—it never got in!), and try to figure out where to start making this house a home. We need some furniture, a coat of paint on the walls, and food. But I haven't the faintest clue how to start the . . . stove? Furnace? What exactly do I call the behemoth in the middle of the room? Thankfully, I sent Chase in search of food. Nearly an hour ago.

"Mommy! Chloe is petting the big doggie!" Justin runs in, nearly in tears. Now how did she sneak past me? I thought I had her cornered in her new room, having shoved a couple duffels up to the door.

Then again, here's Justin too. Another escapee.

"What doggie?"

"Big one!" He's nearly hysterical now, and I scoop him up and shove him on my hip as I run out to the yard.

I spot Chloe standing stock-still next to the fence that separates us from our duplex neighbors as a rottweiler the size of a buffalo stares her down through a hole where a couple boards use to be. Only the horizontal beam holds him back. I wonder if he used his head to bust through. Oh, God, please, please.

He opens his mouth, and I'm about to scream when he slathers my daughter with a sloppy kiss. She giggles and then, to my horror, launches herself at the animal, both arms around its neck.

"Chloe!" I, in turn, launch myself toward her, scooping her up. "Shoo!" I say to the dog, while newspaper headlines run through my mind. "Rottweiler Mauls Child . . . "

"Lydia!" The voice comes from the other side of the fence. I'm holding Chloe football-style on my other hip, backing away from the fence. I see a woman in a housedress and slippers appear in the hole. She hooks a hand around the dog, pulling him back. "Lydia! *Nyet!*"

Lydia?

I come closer to the fence to get a better look. The woman is wearing a green floral headscarf knotted under her chin, yet I see wisps of black hair stealing around the edges. Down one side of her face, an ugly bruise evidences a fall. Or something.

"*Izvinite*," she says, puling Lydia the Killer Dog away from the fence. She's apologizing, but she's also eyeing me, as if I might be from another planet.

I am. It's called the Land of Plumbing.

"*Zdravstvuyte*," I say, smiling widely, because I can't hold out my hand, due to the bundles of children I'm holding. "*Menya zovut* Josey."

She isn't meeting my eyes. "Olya," she responds. My ear easily switches to Russian when she says, "Lydia loves children."

Lydia *does* look like she loves children, the way she's whining and trying to get at mine. I hope that love isn't based on their taste.

"I'm your new neighbor," I say, gesturing toward my house. "My husband and I are from America."

She blinks at me, and since I feel I'm on a roll here, I point to Chloe. "This is my daughter, Chloe." And then to Justin. "And this is my son, Justin."

Justin sticks his thumb in his mouth, and I don't want to know where that thumb has been. Even so, it's so cute, I can't help but give him a little kiss on his pudgy, soft cheek.

However, Olya's face hardens, just slightly, and she purses her lips. "Keep your children away from my dog," she says with a growl. Then, to my shock, she turns and yanks Lydia away, stalking out of view.

Oh. Welcome to the neighborhood, Josey.

Chloe is already wiggling out of my grip as I turn toward the house. "Doggie!"

"No doggie, Chloe. Stay away from the doggie, do you hear me?" She looks as if I've burned her or taken away her blankie. Her cute little lip starts to tremble, and tears fill her giant blue eyes.

This is why I'm a terrible mother. Because my little girl has my number. "Seriously, Chloe, the doggie will hurt you. Bite you." I make a yucky face, but she isn't buying it. The wailing begins. Justin is running toward our house. I pick up Chloe and, in a last-ditch attempt, add desperation to my voice. "Mommy loves you and doesn't want the doggie to eat you."

She stops crying and looks at me. I feel like a rotten mommy, but you know, it could happen, and a little healthy fear is good for a kid.

"Daddy!" Justin's voice saves the day, and Chase is back, bread in hand.

"Anyone for peanut butter sandwiches?" He also has some unnamed orange soda and something in a bag that, if I can decipher hieroglyphics, looks like crab-flavored potato chips.

"You guys having any fun?" he says as we make a picnic in our family room. Chloe is on his lap, Justin draped over my shoulders.

"Big dog!" Justin says.

Chase looks at me, raises an eyebrow.

"Nothing I can't handle," I say and reach for the chips.

I can see that it is the little lies I tell myself that will help me make it through the day.

a matter of perspective

• • •

DIRECTIONS ON PUMPING WATER:

Pick handle up so plunger goes down, pour a glass of water on top of the piston so the seals make good suction. As you push the handle down slowly, it creates pressure below the piston. Repeat, increasing speed, until water starts to flow.

I've been spoiled. I admit it. Here I thought that when you opened up a spigot, water should simply run out. It shouldn't take faith and a slick sheet of sweat across one's brow or a puddle of rusty orange water at one's feet to obtain clean drinking water.

But I've learned a lot of things in the week we've lived in Burrr, Siberia, like:

1. Coal dust doesn't come out of clothing, regardless how much you scrub it in generic washing powder in a tin bucket of freezing water.

2. The meaning of a chamber pot.

3. I can have my milk hand-delivered . . . as in my hand milking the skinny Jersey milk cow gifted to us yesterday by the village elders. She's currently eating the yard. Chloe calls it the Moo. I just want it to go away.

4. A person can take a fairly decent bath in a pot of water ankle deep. It just takes creativity. And washing one's hair takes teamwork. All these things are a thousand times better than getting naked in front of a group of women at the local bathhouse.

5. We are something of an oddity. Every day I get someone knocking at my door, delivering canned varieties of beans, tomatoes, pickles, eggplant, peppers, berries, and cabbage, otherwise known as sauerkraut. The visitor then proceeds to plop herself in my kitchen for roughly four hours, observing. Like Anton's wife, Ulia, who also brought prune-filled *piroshki*. At least I'm losing weight. Seriously. I dug out my largest pair of pre-children jeans yesterday. (There are some things worth dragging across the world.)

6. There are people on earth who don't like chocolate chip cookies. I know, it's a bafflement to me also. But case in point: Crabby Neighbor Olya. After finally unpacking our supplies, which included a Finnish mixer (as in, from Finland) I purchased in Moscow, I decided to make war reparations and visit the one person who hasn't visited me. So, armed with cookies and little Justin in tow, I surveyed the battlefield for guards (aka, Lydia the rottweiler) and, seeing an all-clear, crossed the line of demarcation (the little hole in the fence) and rapped on her back door.

As Olya cracked it open, I spied, through the crack, one swollen eye and the haunted look on her sallow face.

"Cookies?" I offered, and she opened the door just wide enough for me to hand her the plate.

She looked at the plate, frowned, and then shuffled to the table, where she dumped the lot into a basket filled with breadcrumbs. Then she reached over to a plate on her table and grabbed four slices of what looked like cheese on black bread. Since she hadn't invited us in, Justin and I stood watching her from outside the door.

I'm used to this system, by the way. My first year in Russia, my neighbor, Tetye Milla, gifted me into a corner until I had to date her grandson, Vovka of the fish lips. But despite the fact that Vovka and his designer muscles finally made Chase figure out what he might lose, I've always been wary of the gifting process. Who knows what I might get in return? Pickled herring? Fish heads?

But the cheese looked good. I took the plate with a smile and tried to make small talk. Justin reached for the cheese and bread.

She closed the door in my face.

Okay.

"Want a snack?" I asked Justin as we picked our way back through the fence. I held him off until we reached the house, where Chase and Chloe sat in the kitchen, polishing off the rest of the cookies.

I plunked the plate down before them, and Chloe's grubby little hand snaked out for a piece just as Justin went for the other.

"What's this?" Chase asked, eyeing the cheese and bread. He took one, and I grabbed the last.

"A cheese and bread snack from our neighbor."

I was just taking the first bite when I saw Chase frown and make a face not unlike panic, or rather, warning.

The truth sank in as the cheesy something that was not cheese coated my teeth. Something hard crunched.

Cheese shouldn't crunch, should it? And it lacked flavor. Any flavor, except . . . the overpowering bite of . . . garlic. With a rush of heat, it seeped into my pores, burning my mouth. "Ahhh," I said, opening my mouth, not sure what to do. Spit it out? In front of the kids?

"Wha is ith?" I managed, not wanting to close my mouth. Help, help!

"*Salo*. Garlic *salo*." Chase, my hero, grabbed a piece of paper and handed it to me.

Ew. "What's *salo?*" I asked after I cleared my mouth. I could still taste the putty on my teeth.

"Uncooked pig fat soaked in garlic." Chase said it softly, barely a whisper, not looking at me.

Uncooked . . . pig . . . fat.

"And that crunch?" I asked, also barely aloud.

He reached out for the kids' pieces. "Hair."

But that wasn't the worst of it. Here's the final item on the list of things I've learned this week:

7. Roaches live in wooden houses, too.

I thought I'd left the land of the roaches when we departed Moscow. The roach wars rage on in all Moscow apartments, which are built with hidden passageways for roaches to hide in while their homes (read: nests under wallpaper and behind cupboards) are regularly bombed.

Never, however, did I expect to bring them with me to Siberia.

Or perhaps they were already here, waiting for me. Like an ambush.

Here's a little-known fact about roaches—they hate the light. Which tells you something about their character, doesn't it? Thankfully, Siberian roaches are only, say, an inch long.

But what they lack in size, they make up for in quantity.

Every single brother, sister, second cousin once removed, great-great-aunt, and shirttail uncle lives in my kitchen. I know, because last night, as Chloe whined for a glass of water, I picked her up and shuffled out to the darkness where our icebox fridge—the kind with a freezer inside the size of an ice-cream box—hummed. I've noticed the opening getting smaller and smaller each day as ice builds up in the box. Not sure what to do about that.

I didn't bother turning on the light. Just opened up the fridge to retrieve the pitcher of water.

And across the top of the fridge, Uncle Spike peered over the edge to see who was up at this late hour.

I screamed. He dropped to the floor next to my bare feet, and Chloe started to cry.

"Chase, Chase!" I hit the light.

And everything inside me sort of slid away into a puddle of horror. Across my ceiling, thousands of roaches scurried to safety, some parachuting in from the light fixture, others running for the border along the floor, the rest skittering to cracks in the wallpaper and disappearing behind its surface. How I love wallpaper . . .

"Chase!"

I stood frozen, afraid to move lest I step on a carcass, wedge a bug between my toes.

"*Chase!*"

"What?" He appeared wearing panic on his face, as if I might be fending off an army of assailants.

"Roaches! They're everywhere!"

Chase looked around, as if confirming my words. What, did he think I might be lying? I watched them scurry across the coal stove, along the sink, into the cupboards, along the floor. Over my bare toe.

I screamed again. Why should Chloe have the monopoly on terror?

"Stop screaming!" Chase said, grabbing his shoe and beginning a systematic yet hopeless attempt at annihilation.

Oh, no, pal. The screaming has only begun.

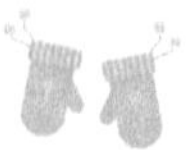

Wildflower: Have you completely lost your mind?

I'm sitting on a wooden stool in the cold Internet office of the Burrrrrrrr Town Hall. Chase has arranged our Internet use with Anton, and I've brought my laptop in, used the mayor's protocol, and hooked up. The building is long, built of cement, and echoes like a prison corridor. As in all pre-Soviet towns, it was set up by the government and contains the obligatory post office, police force, mayor's office, and most recently, communications center (aka the mayor's credenza, which he's moved into an empty office for us to use). There's nothing but me, the rickety wooden side table, a saggy bookshelf void of books, and a calendar for 1988 on the wall.

I consider it nothing short of a miracle they have Internet, even dial-up. And the fact that I have found H online (my time: 2:00 p.m., naptime; her time: 10:00 p.m., Sunday night) gives me hope that God still cares.

Although, currently, that belief is wavering. Yes, I've dug my Bible out since our move to Bursk, but I haven't opened it.

It's akin to Chloe putting her hands over her ears and humming in protest.

Probably, also, why I'm feeling as if I've been run over by a dogsled, pummeled and forgotten in the land of the sun-never-rises.

I ponder H's question a moment while the cursor blinks at me. Have I lost my mind?

No running water, a cow in my backyard that I must learn to milk, a neighbor who gives me pig fat as a gift, roaches as pets, and the best of all . . . my very own outhouse. I believe the answer would be yes.

GI: I don't know, maybe it's not that bad. In the last week, Chase and I have stripped all the wallpaper off the walls, repainted, cleaned the windows, built toddler beds, a sandbox, fixed the hole in the fence, and learned how to cook like pioneers. (Okay, Chase learned how to cook like a pioneer. I watched.) I'm feeling very Ma Ingalls here. And everyone loves Ma. It's only for a year.

Wildflower: If you say "It's only for a year" one more time, I'm coming over there. Let me be the bearer of truth—this is bad, Josey. Very, very bad. Even Chase should figure that out. I know that you'd like to change your world, and yes, you even taught the mayor of Moscow how to make peanut butter cookies, but this just might be over your head.

Oh, no, that almost sounds like a dare. Don't do it, H!

Wildflower: Yes, you showed all of Gull Lake that you were more than just the girl who pulled the fire alarm to get out of her calculus final.

GI: They never proved that.

Wildflower: Whatever. I get it—you're the Girl Who Doesn't Give Up. But seriously, enough. Come home. No plumbing? The smell alone should hit you upside the head and knock some sense into you. I'd be on the next plane.

GI: Boat.

Wildflower: See?

GI: But we're making progress. And you should see the outhouse Chase made me. He shored up the walls and added a little window on the side to let in light, and a shelf that holds, among other things, air freshening spray. He replaced the toilet seat cover with a brand new porcelain one and covered the "shelf" on either side of the seat with tile. There's a pull light that he rigged to flick on when the door is opened and turn off when it closes (almost like a motion detector!), and he painted the building a lovely light blue. He even put a bouquet of flowers in a vase he permanently attached to the door outside. It's a sight to behold.

Wildflower: I cannot believe you are finding this much joy in an outhouse.

GI: But isn't he impressive? He's even been invited to attend the council meeting tonight and is hoping to be invited on a hunt for . . . something. The mythical White Tiger, maybe.

Wildflower: We all know Chase is Captain Amazing.

GI: But it's more than that. I'm even seeing opportunities, like—my neighbor, who looks like she needs a friend.

Wildflower: I am the one who needs a friend. I am the one who needs a shoulder to cry on, a late-night drive out to Bloomquist Mountain where I unload my list of complaints to a willing ear and receive, in turn, timely and sage advice. I am the victim here.

GI: What do you mean?

Wildflower: Rex and I . . . need marriage advice.

GI: I'm probably the last person you should ask.

Wildflower: Rex wants to break up the Purple Monkeys.

Now, I've never understood why H named her band the Purple Monkeys. Yes, it's a punk band. Yes, I understand there's a deeper meaning to the name that I, as a non-songwriter, can't possibly understand. But it's never really made sense to me. However, I can grasp the concept of having an identity, a life that is stripped away due to no fault of your own. So I'm appropriate in my dismay.

GI: What? You've been together for over four years! You and Rex practically are the Purple Monkeys.

Wildflower: He wants to go to school for computer programming. And . . . have a family.

. . .

Wildflower: Are you there? Hello, Jose?

I have to admit, seeing H as a mom further pushes my imagination into never-never land. H is the last holdout, the woman most likely to cover her body with tattoos. But hey, if I can go from being a Gull Lake party girl to a missionary living in Siberia, then maybe . . .

GI: You should do it. It's time.

. . .

GI: H? Are you there?

Wildflower: I don't know if I can do this.

GI: Me neither. But I keep telling myself I can. Maybe that's what counts.

The cursor blinks and blinks as I wait for a reply, but I get nothing. It takes me about five minutes to realize I've been kicked off the Net.

In the other room, I hear voices—Russian voices—arguing. I rub my hands together, blow on them a bit, because although the temperatures have plummeted to just above freezing at night and a little lower than fifty in the daytime, the heat for the village has yet to be turned on. We may be on the backside of the planet, but this little town is heated exactly the same way as every other Russian town is—via a central heating source that runs pipes through the village like the tentacles of an octopus. I'm suddenly—and who would have thought it?—thankful for my little coal furnace that Chase keeps toasty warm.

Here's a thought. If they can get centralized heating, couldn't they also manage indoor plumbing? Isn't that just pipes running through the village? Maybe a little more something involved, but still . . . I'm just saying . . .

I'm already wearing a pair of leather boots—they're just over the ankles, and I picked them up for a song in the open market in Moscow. I purposely sized them big enough to fit my wool socks. I also dug out my peacoat—the one I rustled up last time we were in Gull Lake.

I am definitely thinner. Probably all those hiking trips to the outhouse.

I hear a knock at the door, and turn.

"*Vse?*" Anton says in his non-cheery voice. One would think that, as mayor, Anton would have to be at least moderately friendly.

"*Da,*" I say. Even if I wasn't done, I'd have to be because, apparently, I'm getting the boot. "*Spasibo,*" I add, thinking he'll disappear.

He stands there, watching me, his dark eyes holding a thousand private judgments as I pack up my laptop.

So he's not the warmest coat in the closet. His silent grief demands I give him grace. I smile at him.

"Be careful of your health," he says quietly, eyes not leaving mine. I frown at him. Then, abruptly, he turns away.

I was feeling fine until this moment.

Then again, the Nanai talk with a bit of an accent. He might have said "Be happy you have your health."

Which I am. Very. It just may be the only thing I have at the moment.

I close up the laptop, slide it into my bag.

I walk home. The leaves have already begun to turn to jewels in the scattered poplar and oak, and for a second, I am in Gull Lake.

The homey scent of bread baking drifts from a nearby house, the taste filling my memories, reminding me of Jasmine and Mom baking Saturday morning rolls.

Children, laughing from behind a fence, are Chase and me in the sandbox, fighting for Hot Wheels track space.

The crunch of leaves under my feet stirs the smell of decaying loam from the ground. I expect to see a football.

I lift my collar as the wind finds my ears, digging my chin into the wool.

As I near my house, I see a trickle of dark smoke etched into the gray pallor of the afternoon sky. The duplex next door, home of Lydia the Killer and Olya, is dark and quiet. Not a hint of life.

Not unlike Olya.

Shuffling toward me, up the muddy street, is a tall, gaunt man, weathered by environment rather than time. He's wearing a pair of Chase's Cossack boots, only covered in deer skin, a dirty and torn army jacket, and a misshapen fur hat worn so thin that the shiny surface of the hide glints through. He lifts his eyes to me, and even from ten feet away, I see emptiness in them, in the sallow face, in the grizzled brown beard.

His shoulders are hunched, and as he draws closer, the odor of alcohol hits me like a two-by-four. I stiffen, and he nods, curtly.

Then, as I pass, he stops. I can't help glancing over my shoulder, ready to swing my computer, or maybe just my boot. (After all, a laptop is a laptop.)

But he's not coming after me. He's opening the gate next to mine. Then, with another glance my direction, he enters, and the gate swings shut behind him.

The wind finds my neck, raises gooseflesh.

Unless I'm mistaken, I've just met my neighbor.

Olya's husband.

I remember our first year of marriage as a long, dark tunnel, during which I ballooned to twice my body size and eventually gave birth to two replicas of the childhood sweethearts I once knew and loved.

Chase remembers this time as the year life slid out from underneath him and he nearly lost me. (Not true.) We've since found our equilibrium, and the last three years have been as smooth as they can be with twins in a one-bedroom flat . . .

As I sit in our double bed, a cotton duvet tucked around my legs, listening to the Siberian wind howl amid Chloe's sweet voice singing herself to sleep, waiting for Chase to return home from his late-night council meeting, I have to wonder if we are again veering off course.

What are we doing here?

I understand all about the suicide issues, and the crevice of grace for my neighbor has grown into the Grand Canyon since I saw her husband. I also believe in the divine providence inherent in all life's roads less traveled. It's something I picked up my first year in Russia after I found myself teaching English in Moscow, having made what I thought might have been a rash life decision only to discover that God knew exactly what He was doing. In fact, He'd designed me and planned for me to be doing exactly what I was doing.

Then.

But I'm getting a little panicked now. I mean, after all, I am in *Siberia*.

I pull my Bible from my meager, well-read stack of books I've lugged from Moscow. I've been faithfully plowing through Ephesians, more or less. It's only taken me four years, but listen, I have twins. Cut me some slack.

"As a prisoner for the Lord, then, I urge you to live a life worthy of the calling you have received. Be completely humble and gentle; be patient, bearing with one another in love. Make every effort to keep the unity of the Spirit through the bond of peace."

I don't know about you, but anyone else see the word *prisoner*? Yeah, me too. In fact, I have to circle that. A few times.

Maybe I should focus on something else.

Worthy of the calling I've received. What calling? I'm familiar with this word, having grappled with the hidden meaning of it when I first came to Russia as a missionary. Calling isn't just something someone does on the telephone—it's deeper, that soul-deep passion that God puts inside someone. A faith that compels her to do what some might call stupid, like move to the backside of Russia with two preschoolers to change the world.

Apparently, by Paul's standards, a calling is supposed to be a privilege, something I need to be worthy of.

Maybe I'm looking at this thing entirely wrong.

I mean, how many women have the *opportunity* to learn how to kill roaches, milk a cow, and cook over a coal stove?

Okay, most of our nation's pioneers, and probably a third of the world, so don't answer that. But I'm seeing that it's all in perspective, and that perhaps God doesn't just send anyone to Siberia.

So, what does it mean to be worthy? The definition might be found in the next verse: humble, gentle, patient, peaceful.

When I was a missionary, I purchased a study Bible that came complete with a word study section.

It's helpful. Take, for example, the word *humble*, which also means lowly. It comes packaged with phrases like "compassion for the downtrodden."

Can anyone say Olya? I think of her now, in that dark house that is just on the other side of mine. Connected to me, in a way. Part of my world, whether I chose it or not.

Or how about *gentle*? My word study mentions meekness and stepping aside to let God fight your battles.

I can't even begin to list the battles. Maybe I should start with P for *plumbing*.

I think I can figure out *patient*, but when I look up the word I find *fortitude*. Makes me think of a fortress or a castle, like how our home is a castle. Inside is our home. Outside, the battle rages. Maybe if I can provide a fortress instead of a battlefront, then Chase will have a place to hide.

Maybe, even, God can use me to protect and nurture Chase as he hides inside our castle.

Yeah, see, I'm really good at this word study extrapolation. Too bad just understanding the words isn't the goal. Shoot!

Peace. I look this one up. Prosperity. Quietness. Rest.

It strikes me that these are the attributes of Christ. Humble. Gentle. Patient. Peace, as in Prince of Peace.

Is that what it means to be worthy? To be like Christ in this chilly world?

Maybe I *am* here for a reason. Of course, I knew that, but it helps to be reminded.

Especially when one is waging an ongoing (and often losing) battle against roaches.

I hear a thumping in the entryway and listen as Chase comes in, closes the door. In a moment he's climbing into bed, snuggling up next to me, his arm around my waist, his chin in my neck. "Hey, babe," he says, his voice husky and tired.

I reach up, rub my hand on his cheek. It's stubbly, and I hear him sigh.

"How was the meeting?"

He is silent for longer than necessary. "The council has a request."

I can't pinpoint exactly why, but that sentence tightens my jaw. I say nothing.

"They want you to send the twins to *detskiy sad*."

Kindergarten. I try—really, I do—to school my tone. "Since

when does the council get to decide what's best for my children?"

He tenses, and I know that he's trying to decide if he should run—metaphorically speaking, of course—or stay and fight. To be or not to be, that is the question.

"They're not trying to decide what's best for *our* children. It's just . . . they think that unless we're in the culture, we can't understand it. And all the kids attend school here by the time they're eighteen months old."

I think my bulging right arm muscle (why can't the pump be rotating? I'm going to have a huge right arm and a skinny left one) and hiking outside in the wind to use the biffy should help me understand this culture. I don't need to sacrifice my children, do I?

"I need to get them to trust me, Josey. To see that I value their values. The Nanai take their role as hunters very seriously. Their culture survived on fishing in the summer and hunting in the winter. They weren't unlike our Ojibwe in America. But when the Soviets took over, they made it illegal to hunt or fish, except for the collective, and they took away the men's ability to provide for their families. It dismantled centuries of tradition. More than that, they destroyed the symbiosis of their nomadic lifestyle. Before, the wives partnered with their husbands to find food, take care of the family. But once they built towns, their nomadic mindset began to vanish. Add to that the way the Communists sent all the kids to boarding school and you have a fractured, confused society. All they have left is their traditions, but even those seem to be unraveling."

I understand all about feeling confused. And life unraveling.

Chase's hand closes over mine. It's cold, and a little chapped. I weave my fingers through his, clasp the other over the top. It's warming under my touch.

"I need to get involved in their lives, to show them that I

understand. And the first step is letting my children become a part of their society. I even think it will be good for them. And you—maybe you could meet other mothers through the school. And you'd have more time to spend with our neighbor. She seems like she could use a friend."

Oh, what was your first clue? The big dog with the hungry bark?

Gentle, Josey, gentle.

"It's your call, G.I."

I pull the covers up to my chin. I've finally gotten the smell of mold out of the house after cleaning every last corner. I've picked the fresh chrysanthemums, the last of the wild batch in the backyard, and hung them upside down over the window to dry. And the smell from dinner—a pot of potatoes with clumps of onion and dried dill (I'm learning!)—lingers in the carpeted walls.

"I know it's a lot to ask."

Humble. Gentle.

"But maybe it'll make a difference."

As a prisoner for the Lord, then, I urge you to live a life worthy of the calling you have received.

What if . . . what if I had time to do something, like invite Olya over for tea? "Half days?"

"That might work." Chase is running his thumb over my hand, and I can already feel his breathing start to slow. Relax.

Patience. Peace.

"Give the cow away, and we have a deal."

He pulls me close, molds his body to mine. The wind rattles the windows, hinting at a coming storm, but I'm warm and dry.

We're going to make it.

I'm only here for a year. For the first time, I'm wondering if it's long enough.

catch me

. . .

I've always been enamored by people who homeschool. Science projects in cookie-making class (which seems right up my alley) and reading epic tales out loud, acting them out later in homemade costumes—I think I was born to be a homeschooler.

So it takes great submission (see that word? Yes, Daphne would be proud) to dress up my children and walk them to the preschool in the middle of town. It's the only building with playground equipment, although that is a questionable definition for the rusty, twisted metal in the yard. The merry-go-round is missing all the slats, and the slide has a puddle underneath that a two-year-old could drown in. The swings are metal, and all I can see is pinched fingers as I hear them squeal on rusty hinges. As for the monkey bars—why, exactly, do they have monkey bars for three-year-olds that I can walk under? Does anyone besides me see a broken neck?

However, the Bursk *detskiy-sad* has not only managed to keep children alive, but turned out the likes of Olya, Anton, Ulia and Vasilley. Except, did anyone get a good look at Vasilley?

Okay, that was judgmental. But I'm suddenly having all sorts of empathy for Olya.

I have to give the teachers credit for their creativity. Just like the orphanage I worked in outside Moscow, the *detskiy sad* is brightly painted, with yellow walls, big blue violets, and orange poppies. The room I pass, the one for three-year-olds, is large, with huge trundle bunks built into the wall and a giant table in the middle with adorable little chairs pushed up to it. A Cyrillic alphabet circles the wall, and an old carpet remnant parcels out the play area, where I see a few children holding dishes, a wooden truck, a naked doll.

A teacher—or should I say overstuffed babushka, which does much to hearten me—sits on a tiny chair with a group of children, reading aloud.

This might work.

I stroll down the halls until I find the office marked Director: Maya Kradenski. I knock on the door.

The woman who opens it scares me. She has short, nearly-shorn-to-the-scalp hair, and is wearing a high-necked blouse and a high-waisted wool skirt that makes her look like she might have come straight from the runways in France. Her footwear—a pair of thick-soled heels—makes me consider my hiking boots with some chagrin. (When did I sacrifice fashion for convenience? C'mon, Josey, don't fold!) No, it's not her attire that scares me (to be honest, I'm a little jealous). It's her eyes. Dark as night, they stare me down without compassion. "*Da?*" she says, and it's not a nice *da*, but a "why are you bothering me?" *da*.

"*Zdravstvuyte*. My name is Josey Anderson, and I, uh . . . want to enroll my children in your *detskiy sad*," I say, rethinking my words even as they come out of my mouth.

She raises one nicely sculptured eyebrow. "*Ladno*," she says after a moment, like, *Oh, well, I guess so*. "I'm Maya." But she doesn't hold out her hand. Instead, she returns to her desk and pulls out a form from her desk drawer.

Oh yeah, I'm feeling the love.

I take a deep breath, find a smile, and pull my beloved children into her office. We sit down on a plush black sofa that I know isn't leather, because I had one just like it in Moscow. I pull Chloe onto my lap as Maya starts asking questions.

It's a nice office. Typical Russian, with a bowed laminated wood desk and a file cabinet, the door of which opens from the top, along one wall. A fake plant stands in the corner, and tea accoutrements are laid out on a credenza behind her with a Korean hot water pot, a used cup, and a packet of tea.

Looks like she often drinks alone.

Chloe breaks away and starts to wander around the room. She has kitty paws and is meowing, eyeing me. I think that's a nervous meow. Justin climbs up on the sofa beside me, but before he can get his muddy feet beneath him, I pull him off.

"They're twins?" Maya asks.

I nod. "Three years old."

She writes that down. "And why do you want them here?"

Why, indeed. "My husband thinks it would be a good idea for them to get to know Russian culture." Okay, that was passing the buck a little, but accurate.

She puts her pen down. Folds her hands on top of her paper. Regards me without a smile. "And you?"

And me. Me? I'm submitting, but she doesn't have to know that. In fact, it lessens the impact of the submitting if I announce it to the world, doesn't it? But suddenly I want this woman to understand that these are my precious children, and I'm entrusting her and her staff with their little minds and, for that matter, lives.

I pet Chloe, who has climbed up to my leg, purring.

"I'm a mother," I say, and my smile vanishes. "Please take good care of them."

For a split second that might have only occurred in my imagination, her steely demeanor vanishes, and I glimpse the smallest hint of . . . curiosity. Even, tenderness.

Then it's gone. I'm left holding my breath and praying that my words of faith spoken so long ago to Daphne are true—that when we fling ourselves out there, God catches us.

Dear Josey,

By the time you get this, it will be nearly November, I guess. Or do you get mail in Siberia? I can't believe you moved to Siberia—you are so brave! And such a great inspiration to the rest of us. I was just getting used to you living in Moscow. And . . . the Internet!

Yes, your sister has finally figured out how to use the Internet—I know you thought I would never learn, but after reading your last letter about sending you *kringle*, Milton had this bright idea to put my *kringle* up on eBay, and we're an overnight success! Can you believe it? Go to www.kringlekompany.com. We ship overnight, and we're already talking about buying the old pizza joint in town to turn it into a commercial Kringle Kompany store!

You should see little Amelia and Clay in their *kringle* aprons! (I've enclosed two for the twins!) Mom has postponed moving permanently to Arizona so she can watch them every day—in fact, she's even teaching Amelia to read. I know, it seems early, but she's over four and is already keeping up with Sesame Street and the plethora of early learning shows. I know I shouldn't let her watch too much television, but today's programming is really quite educational.

Milton says that soon, we'll have enough to add on to the

house. I love the cute kitchen in our Cape Cod, but it's getting a little cramped. I'd love to add a granite island, and of course, upgrade to stainless appliances. We're also looking into a subzero fridge—after all, I can't neglect the family! But Milton has been so supportive—he's even sending me and Mom out to New York for the Kitchen Expo! I know you've been to NYC, but I've always wanted to see the Big Apple. We're even staying at the Waldorf!

Oh, I sent you a copy of the newspaper. Lew Sulzbach got the job at the high school after the entire town thought we'd be without a football coach this year (too bad Chase didn't want the job), but so far, the Gull Lake Gulls are undefeated! It's so fun to watch the games. Milton and I haven't missed a game—we love snuggling up together under a blanket in the bleachers. Makes a great date night!

We all miss you. Mom, of course, was saddened by the news you weren't coming home for another year. I think being near my kids helps a lot. I miss you!

Love,

Jasmine

I have heard stories from other mothers about their children who, after being so well nurtured in the home, suffer great anxiety when they are left at preschool for the first time. They throw themselves at their mother's legs, begging, *pleading* not to be left behind, wailing for hours after mom leaves, only to repeat the trauma the next day, for weeks.

This has not been my experience. Chloe has taken to *detskiy sad* like a second home. In her cute pigtails, tights, and dresses, she skips to class every day, yanking my arm from my socket in her excitement to get away from me.

Okay, maybe it's not away from me, but let's just say a little three-year-old angst would go a long way. Just one temper tantrum, one moment of agonizing goodbye? Justin isn't quite as excited, but when he saw that the children get treats—a lot of treats—and get to play games and draw and climb things, he was all-in.

I got a tour from Maya and discovered that the *detskiy sad* contains a music room, a nap room, and of course a potty room—a room with a long bench with little bowls attached to it underneath. I guess it's a group event. Three ages of children make up the three different classes, and Chloe and Justin's class has eight little adorable children who are already wearing their snowsuits.

My children are woefully underdressed in wool hats and coats, tights, and *valenki*—molded wool boots that Anton sent home with Chase. They resemble stiff brown stockings.

I pick the twins up every day at noon, right before naptime, which leaves me three empty hours every morning to do . . . I'm not sure what.

Maybe it's because my life has been replete with washing dishes and running after Chloe and doing laundry and running after Chloe and grocery shopping and running after Chloe and cleaning the house and, well, you get the picture, that the deafening silence in the house after the kids are gone paralyzes me.

Who thought I'd be the kind of mother who has made her children her entire life?

Then again, isn't that sort of the definition of *mother*? Don't ask me! I've never done this before!

I filled up the silences this week by reading a book.

Writing a letter home.

Actually purchasing everything on my grocery list.

Wow, I miss my kids.

I am seeing now that I gave birth so that I would have little people to keep me company.

I'm sitting outside in the *detskiy sad* yard, on the lead-painted railing, watching as the kids climb on the monkey bars and dig in the sand. Justin is chasing a little boy, playing tag. Chloe has joined a group of girls who have morphed into kitties. She probably taught them everything they know.

It's nippy out. The last of the leaves have fallen, a blanket of gold and yellow, browning nicely on the ground. The smell of decay is in the air, and the sun sinks lower earlier each day. I fold Jasmine's letter and shove it into my coat pocket, turn up the collar on my jacket. Football games. Thanksgiving.

I wonder where I can track down a turkey in this town.

And I don't need any wisecracks about looking in the mirror.

The novelty of moving to Siberia has worn off. I look down at my chapped hands and wonder if I can do one more load of laundry in that metal tub. With the cold bite of the fall wind, each item of laundry freezes into a stiff carcass before it dries. I especially love prizing myself into a pair of jeans every day.

Chase has interviewed nearly every man in town, chopped wood with them, hauled water, even fixed a few roofs, trying to unravel the layers of their lives. He keeps asking to go out to check the trap lines, and even visit a nearby mink farm (yes, I said mink), but so far, it's a right that he hasn't yet earned. He has earned, however, the right to attend every council meeting and stay long hours at Anton's house, eating fish.

Yeah, that's ever so fun.

I'm trying not to be negative, but as my hands become more chapped and cracked, as I trot out with a flashlight to use the biffy, as I fight my battle against the roaches, I'm feeling like a forgotten soldier.

But we're going to be fine. He's just busy.

However, to add to my feelings of defeat, I can't seem to muster the courage to face Olya. What happened to the fire of wanting to change lives? The compassion for my neighbor?

I suppose it died in the face of Vasilley, who just about glared at Chase when he offered him the cow. Although yes, he took it, I had to wonder if perhaps we'd offended him.

Then again, would I like to be given a cow? We all know how that turned out.

"Mommy!" Justin says, now spotting me. He runs toward me and dives into my arms. I hug him tight, smelling his curly blonde hair, and smooch him good on his pudgy cheeks.

"*Nel'zya!*" One of the teachers yells the Russian equivalent of "You must never do that again! Never, never, never!" (The Russians can get that conveniently all in one word.) I see that Justin's group is lining up to go inside. She's not smiling at me.

Apparently, my compromise to pick up my children every day at noon has angered the status quo. So much for being accepted.

"Go with your group, Justin. Mommy will be inside in a few minutes to collect you." I'm not sure why they make me come inside to get him, other than wanting to make a spectacle of his leaving.

Justin makes a face, then runs off to join his group.

"Josey?"

I turn, startled by the English, and a streak of warmth goes through me at the sight of . . . "Nathan?"

Our American missionary friend is exactly as I remember him—warm brown eyes, a matching smile, although now he's clean-shaven and wearing a black stocking cap and leather jacket that make him look more mafia than missionary. "I thought that was you." He climbs over the fence and sits beside me. "What are you doing here?"

"Waiting for my children to finish with *detskiy sad* for the day."

Nathan nods in what looks like approval. "How's that working out?"

I shrug. "Kids seem to like it." Do I like it? I'm trying not to need therapy.

"And Chase? How's he doing?"

"Busy. He's trying to get the council to let him go out with the fur trappers, but I guess there's some sort of rule against outsiders, so we're trying to become insiders . . . "

"When in Rome . . . sounds like something a missionary might do." Nathan picks up a dead leaf, begins to strip it. Inside are the pods of an oak tree. "So, I suppose you're keeping busy?"

"Uh, let's see. Hauling water. Doing laundry." I look at him. "I got out of milking the cow today . . . "

His eyes are huge, and I laugh. He has a nice smile, especially when he sees I'm joking. "Please tell me that you aren't milking cows."

"There is nothing wrong with milking a cow, Nathan."

"No, there's not. But you *can* buy milk at the market."

I nod, watching as he peels open the pod to the seeds. "Chase gave the cow to the neighbors."

Nathan blows the seeds into the wind. "I enjoyed getting to know Chase on the train. He told me you are both Christians."

I nod, although I feel that pinch of guilt in my spirit. Yes, Chase and I attended Moscow Bible Church for the past four years, and yes, we pray at mealtime, but no, we haven't really been on our knees together about our faith.

Which, perhaps, might be why we ended up in Siberia.

No, no. We're not being punished. Not being punished! I ball my chapped hands into fists.

"So, I saw Chase earlier today and asked him if you would be open to a project. He told me to run it by you."

I eye him, checking my watch. "What kind of project?"

He crumbles the rest of the dead leaf in his hand, drops it to the ground. "I'm starting a women's Bible study. I'm wondering if you would lead it."

My eyes widen. "I don't—"

"Listen, I know my limitations, the biggest being that I'm a, well"—he lifts a shoulder—"a man. But there are so many women in this town who need God's word in their lives. And Chase told me that you were once officially a missionary."

I nod and can't help the niggle of excitement inside me. Oh, I'm so pathetic.

But what if, you know, *this* is why I'm here?

What if God used Chase to get me here, even arranged for my beloved offspring to go to kindergarten so that I could lead hundreds—okay, maybe just a dozen women—to Christ? I now understand the sacrifices. The submission. And I can see the fruit. A group of women are packed into my living room, sitting on the fraying gold-and-brown sofas we inherited from some village elders, eating chocolate chip cookies, discussing the book of John, the peace of the gospel changing their lives one day at a time.

Maybe I can even find a way to reach my hurting neighbor.

I take a breath. The wind swirls the leaves piled at my feet. A tinge of smoke fragrances the air from the houses surrounding the kindergarten. I love the flow of seasons, the crisp anticipation of knowing things are about to change.

"I'm not sure, Nathan. I've never led a Bible study before." I stand to go inside to get Chloe and Justin.

"I'll help you," Nathan says, and the smile he gives me makes me believe him.

In fact, the thought grows as I retrieve Justin and Chloe, bundling them up like it might be minus thirty out, and rejoin Nathan on the street. He takes Chloe's hand as we head toward home. She looks at him with adoration in her eyes.

Unabashed loyalty, just because he plays to her kitty routine.

"I have errands to do, but Chase again mentioned letting me bunk with you guys. Will that work?"

I'm not sure. We only have a sofa . . .

"I'll make dinner," Nathan adds, smiling.

Oh, that rat, Chase. Someone told Nathan about my cooking abilities.

But a girl does get hungry . . .

Bursk has a main street, with four or five rickety side streets, hemmed in by tiny houses that look identical to mine—ornate windows, outhouses in the back, ringed by a wobbly fence. The roads then taper off to fields and finally black oak and spruce forests. As in every Russian town, there are two places to shop—the *gastronom* and the corner market, which in Bursk is a few rickety kiosks offering vegetables and frozen meats, flanked by a row of people sitting on wooden crates selling jars of *brusnika* (berries) or sunflower seeds or even cigarettes displayed on old towels. Occasionally, I spot someone trying to unload a pair of shoes or homemade mittens.

Today, as we stroll by, I take in the offerings—dried herring, squares of pumpkin, a spray of chrysanthemums, and . . . *salo*. With the skin on.

I slow, and sure enough, Olya is hunched over in a ragged wool coat with fraying sleeves and a holey knitted muffler. She glances up at me, and for a moment, our eyes meet.

And then I see it—a flicker, like a door opening to the inside, a peek into darkness.

Hope.

Just like that, it's gone. But I know I saw it. I know it's there.

Please, God, let that hope be because she sees You in me.

I point to the *salo*. "*Pa chom?*" I ask.

She doesn't look at me when she names an amount.

You know, Chase will eat almost anything for a good reason. I fork over the rubles. As she rolls up the piece of pig fat into a grease-dotted piece of paper and hands it over, she meets my eyes again.

And smiles.

the oddity

. . .

The first time I realized I loved Chase—or rather, wanted to let myself love him—we were making pizza in Moscow. Chase is an awesome cook—one of the primary reasons we are all still alive and not dead from scurvy. And during my first year in Moscow, he not only surprised me with a visit but made me dinner.

I love to watch a man make dinner.

I realize this as Nathan chops onions and browns some ground beef, using a portion of Olya's *salo*. I'm holding Justin, who has fallen asleep on my lap. Chloe is in her bed, curled up like a kitty. I expected Chase to be home, and I keep waiting for him to appear.

But he's probably somewhere mending a fence, building a bridge. Chase already has a fan club in this town, and I'm proud of him.

I do, however, feel a little strange sitting alone in the house with Nathan.

Especially with him singing, making himself at home in my kitchen. He's wearing an apron, and a towel hangs over his shoulder.

Darkness fills the windowpanes, and outside, it's started to rain.

"By the way, you're going to have to defrost your fridge soon if you hope to avoid salmonella poisoning," Nathan says over his shoulder.

Oh. "Uh . . . and having never defrosted a fridge before . . . ?" I smooth Justin's sweaty hair on his head.

Nathan glances at me and laughs. "How long have you lived in Russia, anyway?"

"Four years. But I had a . . . normal fridge."

He laughs again. "This is a normal fridge. And it's easy to defrost. I'll do it tomorrow before I leave."

He drains off grease into a tin can and adds carrots, potatoes, tomato sauce, beets, and dill to the pot, along with chicken broth.

My stomach is cheering wildly, but I manage to keep my voice steady. "What are you making?"

"Borscht. I learned it from my landlady in Khabarovsk. She's about eighty and nearly blind, but boy, can she cook." He takes a clove of garlic and grates it into the pot. Stirs.

"How long have you been here?"

"I've been here three years. I came over for just a year, but once I got involved with the Small Peoples groups, I couldn't go home."

"Small Peoples?"

He lifts a spoon from the cup where I keep them on the shelf. Someday I hope to have drawers in my kitchen. "It's the Russian name for the indigenous people groups." He takes a sip of soup.

"But they're not short."

He nearly chokes and covers his mouth, his shoulders shaking. "No . . . small in population, Josey."

He glances over at me, and my face heats.

"But that's cute."

Or stupid. Let's remember, shall we, that I had two kids. At once. There's been a drainage of the brain cells.

He turns back to the soup, and I turn my cheek into Justin's downy head. "Isn't it hard to be away from your family?"

"My family will be there when I get home. At least, my parents will. My siblings are spread out all over the world. My brother is a cop in Alaska, my sister is a diplomat of sorts in London, my other sister lives in Paris, working on some dissertation on water sources for third world countries." He adds salt, covers the soup. Wipes his hands as he turns to me. "I come from a long line of do-gooders."

"And chefs?"

He nods, and his smile is warm. "But I'm the only one who is doing it full-time, for the Lord."

My brain tells me that Nathan shouldn't be here when Chase is not, but it's nice to have someone to talk to.

Chloe wakes, and after a short, disgruntled cry, shuffles out to the kitchen. Her hair is standing on end, and her face is hot and red where she slept hard on her pillow. She is dragging her pink blankie my mother quilted for her. She stops just outside the kitchen, ponders me for a moment, and moves toward Nathan. Leans against his leg.

He rests his hand on her head. "Hungry, Kitty?"

She nods, makes paws.

I give Nathan a look. He grins at me. Troublemaker.

Justin wakes, and I take him to the outhouse before he makes a little accident on my lap. Every day, the lack of plumbing bothers me less. Or maybe I'm just like the proverbial poached frog—getting used to the heat.

I'm not sure what to think about that.

By the time we get back, Nathan has ladled out soup, cut bread, and put a jar of homemade *smetana* (or sour cream, in our language) on the table.

I sit down as Nathan joins me and bows his head. "Lord,

thank You for Josey and Chase and their willingness to be used by You. Please bless their home and family and work here."

Amen.

He raises his eyes to mine. "Amen."

I smile. "Thanks for the soup."

"How did you and Chase meet?" Nathan asks. I fill him in on our courtship, the one that began with a lunchbox fight at the bus stop and ended with Chase proposing to me at a bistro in Moscow.

"Did you always want to live in Siberia?"

Did I always—

"Oh," he says, reading my expression.

"This was Chase's brilliant idea."

"And you agreed because . . . " He raises an eyebrow.

Right now, sitting in the middle of Siberia, the coal furnace kicking out heat, eating borscht, my husband conspicuously absent, well, I'm not sure. I think it was something about a fur hat on my head, overheating my brain . . .

"Because Chase and I thought we could make a difference." I remember Chase's words about Anton and think of Olya. "I *know* we can make a difference."

"I believe you." Only, Nathan doesn't meet my eyes—his gaze stops at my angry, chapped hands. "Josey, those look bad."

I close them, tuck them into my lap.

"Are you washing clothes by hand?"

I lift a shoulder.

Nathan puts his spoon down. "I had no idea."

"It's okay. We didn't think about a washing machine until we arrived here."

"Chase needs to get you a machine—"

"He's been busy. We're only here for a year, you know."

But the way Nathan is looking at me, I'm thinking that doesn't matter.

"He and I need to have a chat," Nathan says.

I am not sure what to do with the swell of feelings inside me.

I grew up in the age of dinner parties. My mother, although busy with running the family resort, always threw the annual Christmas banquet in our resort dining room, an event open only to our little country church (and occasionally crashed by the other denominations). I have vivid memories of Mom planning out the appetizers (bacon-wrapped garlic bread with cheese spread), baking breads (ribbon bread), and marinating the cranberry pork roast. She pulled out the industrial-sized coffee maker for the buffet, ordered cheeses from Wisconsin, and once, even asked the organist from the Methodist church to play.

I am not my mother.

But I do know the elements of a great dinner. Food. Ambience. Entertainment.

Oh, and people. And while I'm not inviting the whole town of Bursk yet, I think having the mayor and his wife over merits a nod toward social decorum.

I'm very Martha when I want to be. I found a white sheet and had the kids color turkeys (out of their traced hands). I also cut little square napkins from the ends and hemmed them. Yes, that would be with a needle. And thread.

There might have been blood involved. But it's worth it, because Chase needs to buddy up to Anton, to know his life, his family, his traditions, his needs, if he hopes to find out how to help their village. And I am here to help.

Chase found a hunk of what might have been pork (but could be beef) at the market, and after lots of washing and seasoning and even some marinating in oil and wine and spices, it's baking in our oven, nestled inside a cradle of potatoes. The house smells like Sunday afternoon, and my stomach is alert and on the prowl.

I made, of course, cookies. Sugar cookies, and I even rolled them in what some highbrows might call "natural sugar" (known here in Siberia as unbleached, cheap sugar). They look sparkly and festive in the middle of the table.

Then there's the bread that I attempted to make. So I'm not Jasmine. Some people like flat bread. Maybe no one will notice.

I found two white, slightly bent candles for ambience and dressed Justin and Chloe up in their best brown and green harvest colors, teaching them "Jingle Bells" for a touch of cozy entertainment.

I think my mother would be proud.

The fact is, I miss having friends. I miss Dalton and Maggie Calhoun, Caleb and Daphne. I even miss Jasmine and Milton, although a gal can only be around her former-boyfriend-turned-brother-in-law so long without dropping to her knees to thank God for his goodness. So, I'm hoping that tonight will bode well for future game nights. Besides, I need a girl to talk to other than Chloe, who thinks active listening involves paws and purring.

I hear Chase come into the entryway, and in a moment, he's in the kitchen, brushing snow off his hair. He looks adorable tonight in a red sweater and black dress pants, his curly blond hair slightly wet. He hands me a bag. "I could only get orange-flavored soda."

It's better than vodka (which, of course, I wouldn't serve, and hope Anton doesn't expect).

I'm hauling the roast out of the oven when I hear them arrive, hear Chase greet them. I am pulling off the potholders from my hands when I see him give Ulia a little kiss on each cheek. When did he turn European? But even more shocking is

Ulia's hair. Where once it was long and black, it's now . . . what is that color? Marmalade? Auburn? Burnt pumpkin? I've seen that color before in Moscow but have never personally known anyone who has chosen it. Oddly enough, it's a good look for Ulia.

Anton double kisses me and then sits down at the table.

Ulia hands me a jar of pickles. "*Spasibo* for having us," she says. I like Ulia, despite her reserve. She's a little orange-haired Morticia Addams tonight, dressed in a black polyester wool skirt and V-neck sweater, her long hair down. She gives me a tight smile, and I think she's trying.

I've already served dinner to the kids, so I have them perform (okay, maybe I alone see their charm, but they are cute!), and settle them in their room to play while we eat.

I make a mean roast.

Okay, Chase makes a mean roast. But I carve and serve well. Dinner is delicious, and Anton nearly inhales it, cleaning his plate three times.

Ulia, on the other hand, picks at her food.

"How are the kids liking *detskiy sad?*" she asks, not looking at me.

Anton shoots her a dark look. She ignores him and lifts her eyes to mine. "How do they like it?"

My ego is wrapped up in the answer, so I nod, nicely. "They like their teacher. And Maya, the director, seems like she knows what she's doing."

Ulia's lips tighten. She looks back at her food. "Just don't let Chase pick up your kids."

Huh? I'm not sure I heard her right, but apparently Anton has, because he drops his fork. "That's all, Ulia."

But Ulia just looks at me and raises an eyebrow. I am suddenly remembering the time I was shopping with Chloe in the international food store in Moscow and she laid hold of a chocolate bear and refused to let go. The more I threatened, the louder she got.

She had me right where she wanted me. And apparently, so does Ulia with Anton.

"Maya lost her husband about two years ago in a fire. The drunk fell asleep smoking and burned his house down." She wipes her mouth. "So now she thinks she can have her pick of men in town."

I glance at Chase. He's giving Ulia a look that is reminiscent of his high-school days, when people would dish dirt on his poor mother.

Ulia, however, doesn't see it. I want to wave flags, warning her off.

"She seemed nice—" I offer.

"She's nice until she gets what she wants." Ulia takes a sip of her soda. Anton looks like he'd like to strangle her. "Which is Chase."

I glance at Chase, and he's shaking his head. "The kids sure like her." That's my Chase, taking up for the underdog.

"Don't trust her. She has a rock where her heart is."

"Ulia!"

She shrugs, picks up her fork again. "Then again, there's a few men she won't touch, like your neighbor, Vasilley." She gives me a smile. "Have you met him yet? The town drunk?"

Anton reaches out and grabs Ulia by the arm. She raises her chin, twists out of his grip. "Josey should know who she lives next to!"

I glance at Anton, remembering his cryptic words about my health. He meets my eyes. "Vasilley has a history of getting drunk and destroying property."

Oh. Like my fence?

"That's why Olya has that big dog, you know. It's not to protect her from the neighbors. It's to protect her from her husband," Ulia adds.

I have lost my appetite.

"Anyone want a cookie?" Chase asks.

It's a long evening, and I find out much, much more about Bursk than I ever needed to know. Like the fact that Misha and Anya, who lived in this house, were glad to move to get away from our loud neighbors.

Seeing as I've heard nary a sound from that side of the house, I have to wonder if their move might really have to do with the roaches.

I also hear about Ulia's daughter, Sasha, who lost her husband. She doesn't leave her house. Ulia and Anton have to bring her and her children food.

The fatigue on Anton's face as Ulia shares this tugs at my heart.

Still, I slouch down at the table as Chase finally bids them goodnight. The roast and potatoes are cold, the cookies are gone, and Justin and Chloe are asleep in their good clothes on the sofa.

Chase comes back in, closes the inner door behind him, folds his arms across his chest, and leans against the jamb. "So maybe they won't be our *best* friends."

I am the most popular person in town. In my family room, twenty women sit hip to hip on my sofa, every available chair, on the arms of the chairs, on the windowsill, and still others are standing. They're all wearing their *shapkas*—a necessity, thanks to the blanket of snow outside. Winter charged in like a herd of, well, reindeer two weeks ago on a surge of arctic wind that left the town blanketed in ice and sleet.

Now I live in Siberia.

The positive here is that the muddy road is frozen solid, which cuts my laundry pile in half. The negative, aside from the frost accumulating inside my windows, is that it takes us twice as long to dress the twins for the hike to *detskiy sad.*

Now add the outhouse into the mix, and you get a good picture of my current life.

But I'm popular!

And my house smells like brownies. I arrange the plates of chocolate on my kitchen table while Nathan talks to our guests. He and Chase have visited every family in town, inviting them to this event.

No pressure or anything.

I have to admit, however, that finally my life makes sense. Finally, I see why I'm here. See, my words to Daphne were true—you fling yourself out in faith, and God has a way of catching you.

I was born to be a missionary.

I even prepared a three-page Bible study on the opening verses of John. I figure that's the most popular book in the Bible to start an investigative Bible study, so we'll spend some time there, then maybe move to Ephesians. (Which would help me, perhaps, finish that book?)

Russian and American women are alike in many ways. We have kids, and hopes for them, and struggles, and dreams. But when we're together, I've discovered that American women like to talk.

Russian women observe.

Perhaps it's the collective wait-and-see-what-happens pose. But hardly a sound can be heard from the next room. I take a breath, shoot a prayer toward heaven, collect my Bible, and enter.

I see Ulia sitting in the corner, her hands folded on her lap. She's smiling at me, like this is her idea, although I have to wonder if she's hoping she can dish more dirt on poor Maya.

Still, I'm ashamed to admit that I've made a point of picking up the children alone since our conversation.

As I look around the room, I wonder how many women were commanded to attend my event.

No matter. God can use this anyway. His word never comes back void, right?

Nathan introduces me and then disappears into the kitchen, good man. He and I worked together on the Bible study—he helped me find the right references and create the probing study questions. He's stayed a couple nights a week at our house over the past three weeks, appearing randomly at my door, usually with the fixin's for dinner.

Like I'm going to turn him away. We Minnesotans don't do that.

He and Chase reunited like old war buddies, and most of the time they stay up late, talking, as I put the twins to bed.

I've learned a few things from their conversations. Like Nathan was once engaged. And when the river freezes, he'll take a snowmobile from Khabarovsk to get here. I even heard them talking about the apostle Paul and his singleness, and how he wished everyone could be like him.

Everyone? Even Chase?

I sit down on the floor. Open my Bible. "Thanks for coming," I say, smiling at the group. I've even practiced what I will say, so that it doesn't come out in garbled Russian.

"Today, I'd like to start studying in the book of John."

One of the women raises her hand. Like we're in class or something. But at least there's questions. I can hardly wait to get into a deep, penetrating spiritual discussion of life. I smile at her.

She looks briefly at the others, then ducks her head as she asks, "Are the women in America all like you?"

I'm not sure how to take that question. As I'm forming an answer, another woman pipes up. "And is it true that everyone in America has a swimming pool in their backyard?" She leans back, a smile on her lips. "They all have swimming pools on *Santa Barbara.*" She says it like Sonta Barrrrbarrra.

"*Santa Barbara*?" I ask.

As if I've lit a match under these women, they come alive. "I knew Cruz was B.J.'s father!"

"And I can't believe that Sawyer killed Frank."

"He deserved it after kidnapping B.J."

"Sawyer didn't do it—it was Reese!" The look on this woman's face has me afraid. I bounce to my feet.

"Ladies! I'm sorry, I have no idea what you're talking about."

Ulia looks up at me with a shake of her head.

"Okay, listen. No, we don't all have swimming pools, and don't believe everything you see on television." Wow, I sound like my mother.

The group falls quiet and looks chagrined. Way to make friends and influence people, Josey. So much for my ability to wow them with my scholarly Bible knowledge. As I look around the room, I see not even one Bible, and I'm realizing that none of them are here for a Bible study, probably.

They're here to view the oddity. At least they didn't bring sauerkraut. I close my Bible, sigh.

Another hand slips up. I feel like a schoolteacher. I quirk an eyebrow.

"Do you know how to make pizza?"

I glance toward the kitchen. "Uh . . . "

"What's that?" Another woman points to the plate of brownies on the kitchen table.

I'm not sure what to call it. "*Korichnevyy*," I say, which translates to . . . "brown." I make a face.

"She makes *pechen'ye*," says a voice, and I'm surprised to see, standing behind me, a woman I hardly recognize . . . my neighbor, Olya, who must have snuck in while I wasn't looking. She doesn't look at me, keeps her eyes to the ground. But her presence ignites a hope inside me that catches my breath. I don't glance at Ulia, and I'm wondering if our conversation is written all over my face. Oh! This is why I shouldn't listen to gossip!

I nod at Olya's words. I *do* make cookies. "Chocolate cookies," I add (because I don't know how to translate *chip*).

"Teach us," says a woman sitting on the arm of my sofa. "We want to learn to make American cookies."

Another woman points to the plate of brownies in the kitchen. Nods from around the room, and smiles. Cookies, huh?

Nathan peeks his head around the corner. "Say yes, say yes!"

Well, if cookies will make them listen. Show them that I care. Apparently Russian women and American women aren't that different after all.

"Please," I say, "come into my kitchen."

more than i expect

. . .

"So Olya actually came to your Bible study?"

Chase has brought home a hunk of venison and is pressing it through a grinder he borrowed from Anton. So this is how ground meat becomes . . . ground meat. He adds a little of Olya's *salo* to the mix (minus the hair and skin) to add fat. I know—adding fat? But deer meat is so lean it will dry out without it.

The things I learn in Siberia.

The kids are in bed, having eaten their fill of the three hundred thousand cookies I made in front of my willingly captivated audience today. The eagerness of the crowd prompted me to use my entire supply of chocolate chips and even crack open a jar of peanut butter for a batch of peanut butter delights.

I figure if Jesus can multiply a few loaves and fish, He can overflow my chocolate chip supply for the good of His kingdom.

Everyone went away with a doggie bag. A term, I've discovered, that doesn't translate well.

Nathan left also, catching a boat for his next stop north. I saw him talking to Chase in quiet tones in our entryway before he left. I hope he's not disappointed by my lack of spiritual accomplishment today.

I've never been so full. Yes, I know, I don't have to eat them . . . but what's the point of baking them if . . . oh, never mind.

"I can't believe Olya was here." I reach out for another cookie, then snatch my hand back. Just because they're there . . . "She acts like she hates me, but she'll smile when I buy *salo* from her, and she sort of . . . defended me today. Go figure."

"I think she does like you—she just doesn't know how to take you." Chase adds salt and pepper to the bowl of ground meat, begins to stir.

"I assume you mean that in the nicest of ways?"

Chase looks up at me, winks. "Of course."

"I just wish I knew what goes on over there." I nod toward the separating wall between our homes. "I never hear any fighting. But the first time we met, she definitely looked like she had a black eye."

Chase scoops out a hunk of meat, dumps it into a plastic bag. "Vasilley is a trapper. Although, I heard he was trained as a plumber, so who knows?"

Plumber? *Plumber?*

"According to Anton, they have a daughter, but she doesn't live with them." Chase twists the bag shut, opens the Nathan-defrosted freezer, and adds it to the already growing pile. "She lives in Moscow with Vasilley's mother."

Okay, I have to have another cookie. They'll just go bad.

"What is she doing there? Going to college?"

Chase is about to ladle another portion of meat into a bag but stops and gives me an odd look. "Olya's just a little older than we are. Her daughter is only five."

"Five? What's she doing in Moscow?"

Chase fixes another bag of meat. "I guess Vasilley's mother came out here for a visit and asked if Albena could visit her for the summer. That was three years ago, and evidently, no one has the money to fly Albena home."

He closes the bag and adds the meat to the freezer.

"She's been gone for three years?" I've lost my appetite. "Olya hasn't seen her daughter for three years? Because she can't afford a plane ticket?" I feel ill. I put the cookie back. "That's awful." I remember, suddenly, how she looked at Chloe and Justin.

Yes, definitely my stomach is turning. "We have to help her."

Chase is dismantling the grinder. "Vasilley already told the village council that he didn't want their help." He puts the pieces into the bowl I use for a sink. "Which is why they're somewhat ostracized from the community."

"Why won't they ask for help?" I let him pump water. He puts it on the stove to boil.

Chase wipes his hands on a towel. "Why doesn't anyone ask for help? Pride?"

"Oh, that's stupid."

He raises an eyebrow. "I know a few people who might suffer from the same ailment."

He comes over, kneels before me, takes my hands, rubs his thumbs over them. They've healed somewhat, but the tips of my fingers are still cracked. "How come you didn't tell me your hands were getting so chapped?"

He looks up, and his blue eyes hold pain. My throat tightens. "No, don't answer that. I should have noticed." He opens them and kisses the palms. "Forgive me?"

Oh, Chase.

I lean forward, wrap my arms around his neck. "Yes."

He cups his hand against my face, and I lean into realizing

how long it's been since we've had a quiet kitchen, sleeping children, no company.

Chase's arms can make me forget where I am, make me believe that everything is, and will be, right in the world.

It's a long time before we realize the water has begun to boil.

We do the dishes together—him washing, me drying. "Tell me something," he says, handing me a plate. "Did you come to Siberia because of me?"

I stare at him, not sure exactly what he means. "Do you mean because it was your idea?"

He is scrubbing the grinder, the hot water still sending up steam. I'd be crying in pain. "No. Because you thought . . . well, that you had to."

I eye him. "Isn't that what submission is all about?"

He looks up at me with something of a stricken look on his face. His eyes are wide and he's stopped scrubbing.

"What?" I ask. "Isn't that what it says in the Bible?"

He closes his eyes, hangs his head as he leans on the counter with sudsy hands. "I can't believe I got you into this mess."

Yeah, me too—No! Be humble. Gentle!

"I'm okay, Chase. We're okay." If he didn't figure that out a half hour ago, I'm going to have to try harder.

But he doesn't believe me. "No running water, the skin peeling off your hands. And now our house is covered in ice." He shakes his head. "I guess I was delusional to think that maybe you came here because you believed in the project."

I toss the towel over my shoulder, press my hand to his chest. "Chase. This is a great opportunity for you. That's why I came to Siberia." Because we all know it wasn't on account of my stellar evangelism skills or even my ability to make friends.

Chase closes his eyes in what looks like a little pain. "I

thought you'd find a way to help people—you always do. I would never have made it in Moscow without your brilliance."

Now you're singing my song, bub. Except he smiles on the last word, and I know he's trying to do a dodge around the deep fears lying just below the surface.

I'm having flashbacks of our high-school days, of him tapping on my bedroom window, begging me to take a motorcycle ride just so he could feel my arms around him. I did catch on to that, by the way. It just took a while for me to realize that sometimes a guy just wants to know that the girl will hang on, no matter where he takes her.

"I believe in you, Chase. That's why I'm in Siberia."

But Chase's smile dims, and he turns back to the dirty water. "I don't know, G.I. Maybe you should have said no."

I think back to the day he came home, plopped red fox fur on my head, and my brain had an allergic reaction and said yes. "You're pretty hard to say no to."

He doesn't look up.

"Besides, maybe I'm also here for a reason now."

He's wearing hope on his face as he rinses the grinder, hands it to me.

"Olya. Maybe I'm supposed to help her."

"How?" He's draining the water through a hole in the metal sink. Of course, it drains down into a bucket, which we then lug outside and toss into the outhouse, but still. It's a pretend sink that makes us all feel better.

"I don't know. Help get her child back from Moscow?"

He bends down, grabs the bucket. "How?"

"I don't know—you're the anthropologist. You figure it out." I snap the towel at him. At least he's smiling. He looks at the grimy water. Back to me.

"How about inviting her to Thanksgiving dinner this weekend?"

Thanksgiving dinner! My face must betray the fact that I've

completely forgotten Thanksgiving. C'mon, give me a break. It's not like any other person in Siberia is celebrating Thanksgiving. It's an American holiday. Chase just stares at me. "You forgot."

"I . . . ah . . . "

Now he's laughing.

"Don't laugh. We don't have a turkey or anything even remotely near it." I haven't seen chicken since Moscow. And even then, it didn't resemble the poultry I've come to know and love stateside.

"Let me take care of Thanksgiving," Chase says, turning toward the door. Then he stops and leans down, kisses me on the cheek. "The Lord knows I have plenty to be thankful for."

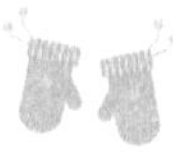

The fact that Russians don't celebrate Thanksgiving stymied me when the holiday rolled around during my first year in Moscow. While the rest of the city went to work, my fellow Americans and I stopped and gave thanks around a stuffed bird that cost roughly half a month's wages.

I fell for the turkey nostalgia during my first year of marriage also. It's more ingrained than one might think, but this year, as I stroll through the market, noticing the meager meat selection, I'm realizing something.

The rest of the world doesn't eat turkey. Lamb, cow, and reindeer, yes, but turkey, no. I can't even find a chicken leg.

It's not what you eat but that you eat it thankfully, right?

I've always enjoyed shopping at the market—even the tiny corner market staffed by eight to ten chilly vendors, most of them selling dirty potatoes and bags of ground venison, aka reindeer. They look cold, especially the woman with a fuzzy gray scarf tied under her chin. She's wearing mittens with the fingers cut off and is stamping her feet and blowing on her hands.

I know Chase said he'd take care of it, and we just ground venison, but I can't help it. My heart says to buy two kilos of venison. They probably had lots of venison at the first Thanksgiving, right?

Although the mercury is well into the zeros, it's a fresh and sunny day as I walk home. It snowed again last night, and a layer of sparkle bedazzles the ring of lush pine that encircles the village. It's a fairy-tale setting along the now frozen Amur, the sky a pale blue, the smell of woodsmoke curling in the breeze. I could be in the middle of a painting, and I find myself singing a Christmas carol.

"O little town of Burrrrr, how still we see thee lie . . . "

Lydia barks, shoving her nose through the slats of the fence as I pass by, enter my yard. I stomp off the snow from my boots, hang up my down parka, and enter my warm house to find Anton sitting at the table, enjoying a cup of tea with Chase.

I'm surprised to see them, given they left early this morning to do something manly.

"Hey," I say, still humming. I plop the venison on the table. "Thanksgiving dinner."

"Yum," Chase says, then glances at Anton and translates. I'm always amazed (and now admittedly jealous) of the way Russian rolls off Chase's tongue. I catch about half the words, but I can tell that Chase is explaining Thanksgiving to Anton. Anton is still wearing his dark fur *shapka*, and with those dark eyes and matching dark pants and sweater, he seems more imposing than he is. Or I'd like to think so.

"And about a month after Thanksgiving comes Christmas," I hear Chase say. He's on a roll now and talking about gifts and Christmas stockings and finally the trees we decorate. "Similar to your New Year's tree, but we go out and chop it down at a tree farm every year."

I'm not sure what year Chase is referring to, because never since we've been married have we chopped down a tree from a tree farm together. Perhaps he's remembering the year he tagged along when our family drove out to Uncle Bert's place and found our annual fir. It was the year after his mother died, his first Christmas alone with his father.

Probably, he needs all the happy memories he can get to fill in the dark crevasses.

I set a cup down, fill it with water, add a tea bag. If someone loves me, they'll send instant coffee from America for Christmas.

"It's a lucrative business," I say, stirring my tea. "My uncle Bert makes half his income for the year from his trees."

"A farm for trees?" Anton's eyes have begun to shine.

"Bert chops them down and runs a stand in town too." I sit down, reach for one of my cookies that Chase has pulled from the freezer. I keep a steady sanity supply. "Most people don't want to go hunt down their trees, so he makes a killing."

"I still like chopping down my own tree," Chase, my hunter-gatherer, says quietly, blowing into his cup.

Of course he does. "Maybe we can cut down a tree from around the village."

Chase shakes his head. "Those are owned by the government, we can't—"

"No. The town of Bursk owns those," Anton says. I can nearly hear his thoughts finish the sentence. *And I own the town of Bursk.*

"I can barely hear you, Maggie!"

I'm in the central phone station, in the room next to the Internet center, holding a phone that looks like it might have been installed under Alexander Graham Bell's direct supervision. I think these are the kind of phones they used in spy movies as lethal weapons.

Although, I'm thrilled that Maggie has tracked me down, ordering the call to our village the old-fashioned way—a day in advance, requiring the town operator to track me down and arrange a meeting.

She sounds like she might be calling from her space station on the moon.

"Daphne had a baby girl!" Maggie yells, and this time it comes through loud and clear.

"When?" I yell back.

"Two weeks ago. In Canton, Ohio. She and Caleb are doing great. They named the baby Isobel."

Oh. And for some strange reason I thought that maybe they'd name it after me. Okay, okay, I know, but for a long time I *was* her mentor.

"That's great! Tell her I'm thrilled for her!"

"How's Bursk?"

"Cold!" I say. But I don't hear the laughter on the other end. Why don't people get my jokes? "It's good. I have an outhouse!"

"A what?"

"An outdoor bathroom. A privy."

Silence.

"Hello?"

"Do you want me to come and get you?"

Was that a joke? "No! I'm fine." Better than fine, really. Because apparently my cookie party made a hit with the women. They've asked to come back.

They want to learn to make pizza, and Chase has agreed to guest star.

In fact, he's been doing a lot of guest starring around the house recently. Been nearly a regular.

Even started washing clothes.

"How's Chase's new venture? Is he making headway?"

"He still hasn't been asked to go on a hunt, but he attends all the council meetings and, well, you know Chase. The world loves Chase."

I don't hear her laughter. "Hello, hello?"

"How about you? Have you made any friends?"

"I've started a Bible study. But, well, I'm having a neighbor dilemma. Chase had this brilliant idea to invite her to Thanksgiving."

With our abundant supply of venison, his solution to turkey made me realize just why I love him. He formed a venison sculpture of a plump bird and cooked it in the oven, complete with stuffing and gravy. Even Nathan appreciated it, and the twins gobbled through the house all afternoon.

Not a kitty in sight.

My only disappointment was Olya's absence. I invited her, twice, when I purchased my daily *salo*.

We waited for her, the steam rising off the deer-turkey.

Finally, I fixed a plate and headed over to her house. I still have nightmares of how she opened the door, staring at the food as if it might be poisonous.

"It's a gift. American dinner," I added. I spied the panic on her face, something raw and desperate as she glanced back inside for something to give me.

"I don't want anything, Olya. Please, just take it."

She considered me a long moment. Then snaked her hand out and took the plate.

Closed the door on my nose.

"I think I offended her with my Thanksgiving dinner," I say now to Maggie.

Now she laughs?

"Maggie!"

"I'm sure your dinner was delicious, Josey. Maybe it's just . . . you know, sometimes it's hard to receive. I'm sure that's not easy for her. It's not easy for anyone."

I stare at my hands, which are healing. In my own defense, I didn't mention my hands to Chase because, well, I didn't want to complain.

Not because of my pride. Really.

But now that he's doing the laundry, I feel . . . indebted.

"Are you saying I shouldn't give her anything?"

The line begins to crackle, and I fear I'm losing her.

"I'm saying that it's going to be up to you to help her give back."

The line goes dead, and shoot, but I have no idea what she means.

I hang up the phone. The shadows are filling the hallways as I shuffle out into the snow. The wind is light, and the air is crisp. A full moon hangs against the dusky sky. I've always loved the metaphor of the moon, how it reflects the light of the sun.

Humble. Gentle. Patient. Worthy of the calling.

Help her give back. Really? Why can't she simply accept my gift without feeling like she has to repay?

Lord, help me give peace to Olya somehow. Help me find a way to reflect You.

In my experience with the Almighty, I've discovered that when I ask for something, He doesn't just give it to me. Instead, He gives me the opportunity to discover it. To grow into it.

Unfortunately, it's usually when my husband decides to leave town.

I'm a big girl, and I can take care of myself, but when Chase is away, things begin to unravel. I often wonder if it's God's way of reminding me I'm not invincible.

I get it! I get it!

I should have remembered my prayer when Chase left this morning in the darkness to take a snowmobile ride to Khabarovsk with Nathan. When I turned on the light to say goodbye, I heard a pop, and then a trickle of flame traveled along the ancient wires strung up outside of our house and exploded in a shower of brilliant sparks when it reached the transformer on the pole.

We stood there in silence in the predawn hour, the cold seeping up under my puffy jacket, through my flimsy jammies. Nathan looked at me. Chase looked at me.

"Do we have candles?"

I wasn't sure what to say to that, because apparently, he had no intention of staying home. I think I nodded. "I'll be home by dinnertime." Then he kissed me and was gone, slipping into the dawn.

I snuggled back in with the kids until early morning lit the room.

Here's a friendly motherhood tip: don't let your children get up before you. By the time I realized Chloe had risen, she'd got hold of the scissors and created a shimmering pool of featherlight blonde hair, in which she was the center attraction. I found her half bald and wet, eating a box of chocolate *podushki*.

At least she knows when to go for the chocolate.

I sat down beside her and joined her party. Justin dragged himself out of bed, stumbled out to us. He took one look at the *podushki* and crumpled into a ball, crying.

"No paddy!"

I simply don't understand a child who won't eat junk food

for breakfast. But I get up and try to fire up the stove to make oatmeal.

Nothing. Nada. Not even a whiff of gas. I came to expect occasional gas outages in Moscow, but I've been spoiled living in the village.

I'll have to cook the old-fashioned way. I fill the pot with water and set it on the furnace.

By the time we're finished with our morning constitutionals, the water is boiling. Justin gets his meal, and I attire the children in their layers. Chloe's head is lopsided, so I even her out and put on a hat.

Maybe no one at the school will notice the absence of her pigtails.

The sun is high, and it must be above freezing, because the ice is dripping from the icicles on the house. The snow is icy, and Justin's boot gets stuck in a drift. I have to pull him out, leaving behind his sock and boot. After much digging we retrieve them, but we're late to *detskiy sad*, and his foot is an ice cube.

On the way back, I stop by the market and buy a piece of *salo*, but today Olya doesn't look at me. Perfect. Now I've alienated her with my Thanksgiving offering.

I return home, pump a bucket of water, watch it heat over the stove, then wash the children's clothes. I wring them out, then hang them from the line that runs through my living room.

It's a lovely garland. Thomas the Tank Engine underwear and Strawberry Shortcake training pants, Chase's thermal underwear, my misshapen yoga pants. My hands burn, so I lather on lotion.

The sting makes my eyes water.

I've never seen a vacuum cleaner in Russia. Even when I lived in Moscow, my cleaning lady wet a towel and wrapped it around an empty mop head and scraped the carpets clean. I've modified her methods by wetting the ends of a bristle broom in a bucket and sweeping the carpet.

It's the hard-knock life, for me, it's the hard-knock life . . .

I shake the throw rugs and change the sheets and even debate whipping up a batch of cookies, then realize I have no gas. I probably shouldn't just eat the dough . . .

I finish off the *podushki* for lunch. I don't know what Justin's problem is.

I'm at *detskiy sad* early to pick up the kids. Maya is in the yard. I lift my hand in greeting. She seems to consider me for a moment, then turns away.

I don't know what Chase was thinking, but from my perspective, we're not exactly plowing highways into the culture.

We return home, and I lie down with everyone for a nap.

It's about three when I hear the barking. The door slams open, and I'm yanked out of a sound sleep—and you know the kind, where your body feels as if it's submerged in glue. As I waken, I'm pretty sure I'm back at home, at Berglund Acres, and Buddy has just returned from football practice.

"Mommy, doggie!"

Or maybe not. I pry open my eyes. Chloe is jumping on me, barely missing my gut. I wince and curl into a ball. Justin sits up, rubbing his eyes.

Lydia leaps onto the bed, barking. She looks like she dug her way to freedom under the fence (hello, could she not see the hole?), her body covered in mud and grime. She leans down and slathers my daughter with her sopping tongue. Justin screams. Chloe grabs the beast around the neck and nuzzles in. Perfect.

"Lydia!" I'm on my feet. "Lydia, get!"

She's plastered the bed with footprints and chunks of mud and now drops to the floor, presses her cheek to the carpet, and runs along my clean rug in a circle, cleaning herself.

"Shoo! Shoo!" I grab my multiuse broom. "Get!"

Lydia stops, looks at me, her bottom up, wriggling. She thinks it's a game. Leaping around me, she grabs Thomas the Tank Engine and pulls down the line.

Chloe cheers from the bed. Justin, the smart one, is crying.

"Get!"

"Lydia, *Idi syu-da!*" Olya appears at my door. She wears what I can only assume is an exact replica of my expression of horror. "Lydia!" She comes in and pounces on the dog, grabbing her by the collar. "*Izvinite,*" she says over and over as she drags the menace out.

The door shuts with a thud. The house shakes on its foundation.

I slide down to the floor. Justin launches himself into my arms. "I scared."

I wrap my arms around him, smell his hair, tuck his trembling body close.

The darkness is hovering, and the heat is waning from the furnace. Someone has to find the candles. And feed the children dinner.

I want my mother.

I'm still sitting in the silence when I hear the door creak open. From the shadows of the entryway, Olya emerges. She looks tired and wrecked. "*Izvinite,*" she says again.

"*Nu ladno,*" I say, pushing Justin off my lap. "It's okay."

It's hard to tell in the light, but I think relief washes over her face. We stand there a moment, in silence, neither of us knowing what to say.

But suddenly, it all bubbles out of me, and wouldn't you know it, I start to cry. I put my hand over my mouth, but I can't stifle the sound of my sobbing.

I'm just tired.

And cold.

And it's getting a little hard to see.

I think I scare Olya, because she abruptly turns and leaves. Probably running for dear life.

I give one last hiccup and sigh, not sure whether I should go after her. Instead, I decide to pick up my dirty laundry.

Moments later, she reappears, holding a pot in her arms. She sets the pot on the furnace and then opens the door and, taking the tongs, reloads the furnace, stirs the coal brick into the embers.

Then she takes a candle from her pocket.

I watch as she sticks the end into the furnace and emerges with it lit. She finds a teacup on the shelf and puts the candle inside, propping it up with a wadded napkin.

Then, turning, she gives me a small nod and again makes to exit.

But I grab her and, because I have to, because I can't think of anything else, I pull her into a hug.

She's a little bony, and even more surprised. But she lets me.

She lets me.

She leaves me with the smell of potato soup, the wan light, and the wild hope that maybe God can speak even through dumbfounded silence.

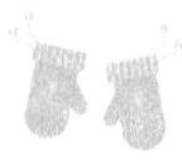

It's late and dark when the screaming starts. The soup was delicious—potatoes with chunks of cabbage and dill. And the candle burned long enough to read a story to Chloe and Justin.

I go to bed early, of course, which gives me plenty of time to ponder exactly what to do with Olya's behavior. Do I go over in the morning with the clean pot, perhaps filled with cookies, and say thank you? Or will that start the cycle of craziness all over? I feel that she might feel we're even, but I know (thanks to the way Justin and Chloe wolfed down the soup) that I'm woefully beholden.

I'm also worried. Where is Chase? He told me he'd be home by dinner.

The screaming starts sporadically, with a thump and then yelling. Everything inside me tightens. I've never heard them fight before, and everything inside me knots with the knowledge that I was right about Vasilley.

Please, Lord, tell me what to do.

I close my eyes, pull my covers up to my nose. I hear something crash. What is the number for 911? No, it's not 911, but I should know it.

Suddenly, everything goes quiet. I hear the door slam, and it shakes both our houses. I'm breathing hard, wondering. Should I go over there? I'm still talking myself into it, staring at the filmy darkness, when I hear another thump outside. Our door creaks open.

Please, let it be Chase. Please, let it be Chase.

"Shh." I hear a voice. "They're sleeping."

My breath trickles out. I didn't realize I'd been holding it.

"I'll grab the sofa." It's Nathan's voice.

A second later, Chase appears at the bedroom door. "Hey G.I.," he says, climbing into bed beside me. He's cold, his cheeks chapped. He pulls me close.

"What took you so long?" I try and keep the frantic out of my voice, but it's there. He nuzzles his cold chin into my neck.

"Halfway home, the snowmobile quit. We couldn't get it to turn over. Had to hitch a ride to the turnoff on the highway and then hike the rest of the way home."

"The highway is three miles from town."

"I know." His arm tightens around me. "But that's not the worst of it. While we were in Khabarovsk, I ran into Anton."

His beard rubs against my cheek as I turn. He props his head on his hand. "He was selling Christmas trees."

I search Chase's face to understand the significance of this.

Chase raises an eyebrow. "The Bursk trees. He cut them down."

"All of them?"

"I don't know. We'll find out in the morning. But we stopped by the town hall on the way home. Apparently the trappers in the village are furious. They say it'll upset their trap lines."

"Will it?"

Chase shakes his head, but even in the darkness, I see concern. "I dunno. I saw Olya's husband at the meeting. He was pretty angry."

I don't tell him about the fight. The door slamming.

Chase rolls back, throws his arm over his eyes. "I can't believe Anton did that. And worse, that it was all my idea."

"It was hardly your idea, Chase. You just told him about a childhood memory. He took it from there."

"They'll blame it on me."

"You're blaming it on you. Don't. It's not your fault."

He lowers his arm, and I see the faintest edge of despair shadow his eyes. He reaches out and takes my hand. "How are your hands today?"

I make to tug them away. He brings them to his mouth and kisses them. "First your hands, and now I've managed to wipe out the village economy. I'm really making an impact here."

"Shh." I put my finger over his mouth. "We're all going to be fine."

He sighs. "What is it they say about anthropologists . . . First do no harm?"

"I think that's for doctors," I whisper. He runs his hands around my neck and pulls me close, kissing me.

And for a sweet pocket of time, we do no harm.

"How was your day," he asks later, pulling me against him. He's warmer now.

"More than I expected," I say. Much, much more.

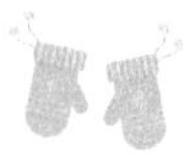

"Josey!"

Maya catches up to me in the hallway of the *detskiy sad* just as I'm leaving with Justin and Chloe. The preschool is decked out with paper chains and snowflakes on the windows. Again, I'm impressed with the use of the limited resources.

I'm not as impressed with the use of the town's resources by Anton and a small band of entrepreneurial accomplices who have, indeed, denuded the forest. He's swiped every tree under twelve feet, and the once-abundant embrace of pine is scraggly and sparse. Woodchips, pine needles, and stripped boughs now litter the once-pristine snow.

For this American Christmas event, Maya is her fashionable best in a tight black high-waisted skirt and black jacket, but I'm so, so sad to say that I can't shake Ulia's words from my head. They burn inside me.

This is what gossip does. Keeps you from thinking straight.

"*Privet, Maya*," I say.

She has her hair gelled today, and with her dark makeup, she looks exotically beautiful. I'm wondering, suddenly, if Ulia's words are born from jealousy.

Maya doesn't smile as she approaches me. I keep a firm grip on Chloe, just in case she does something. Like eat a decoration.

"I heard, in America, you do not have Father Frost." I appreciate the fact she's using her English, which comes out crisp and British.

"No," I say slowly. "We have . . . well, Christmas is supposed to be a religious holiday, so we have baby Jesus, angels and shepherds, and the three wise men."

We also have Santa, but I'm not sure what my stance is on

Santa yet. And I'm glad I'm not stateside, where I'd fold under the pressure. Jasmine and I grew up in a Santa-filled world, but she has recently taken a stand against Santa. I realize this sounds a lot like taking a stand against Bambi, but her argument is that she wants her children to grow up without the Big Lie.

My kids being only three, and in Russia, I've done an end run around Halloween, Santa, and the Easter Bunny. But I'm undecided.

"Tell that story, about baby Jesus, to our children. Please."

I eye Maya and speak very clearly. "It's from the Bible."

She stares at me.

"It's religious. And I happen to believe it's true. Are you sure you want me to tell it?"

She nods without a smile. "It's important to understand what other cultures believe."

You can believe too, honey, I think. Because Jesus isn't American, last time I checked. But you don't have to hit a former missionary over the head to wake her up to an opportunity.

"Where and when?"

Three days later, I'm sitting cross-legged in front of Justin and Chloe's class, a storybook my mother sent last year for Christmas open on my lap. They are cute, dressed up for the occasion with big bright bows on the girls and bow ties on the boys. I've made frosted Christmas cookies for the event and now have their rapt attention as I tell them about Mary being visited by an angel, and Joseph, the man who wants to marry her. I tell them about baby Jesus being born in a manger and field a few questions about what that might look like. I keep it G-rated, although I, too, have wondered what it might have really been like to give birth in a stable two thousand years before plumbing (although now I have the smallest of glimpses).

And then the wise men, with their gifts of gold, frankincense, and myrrh, on their camels (which takes some explaining also).

To my surprise, the teachers are listening, also with rapt attention.

And they, too, have a few questions after story time is over, after the cookies have been eaten, and after I get invited into Maya's office for a private "tea."

"Why did you come to Siberia?"

"Do your children like *detskiy sad*?"

"Why does your daughter think she's a cat?" (I love that one.)

"Do you plan on staying?"

Nothing easy there, but as I take my time answering, I notice Maya watching me from her perch behind her desk.

The room finally clears out, and I expect to leave too, but she motions for me to sit. She scares me a little, so I stay put.

"I don't believe your story."

I raise an eyebrow. Well, get in line with about half the world, I want to say, but I don't because I think, deep down, there's more to that statement.

"I don't believe that God would send His son to people who would kill Him."

Oh, so she's heard the rest of the story. I nod, listening.

"If He loved him, wanted the best for Him, and knew people were going to kill Him, why did he do it? A smart God—a loving God—wouldn't do that." She folds her hands over her chest. "I don't think I could trust that kind of God."

Oh, I see a gauntlet thrown down. I lean back on the sofa. "Why do you think I sent my kids to *detskiy sad*, Maya?"

She says nothing.

"I didn't know you. For all I knew, you could have hurt my children. But I believed that getting to know you and showing you that I cared about you was worth it. Now, I'm a human parent, and of course if I thought you were going to seriously hurt my children, I wouldn't have done it. But I felt the risk was worth the opportunity to know you. Which is also why Chase and I moved to Siberia."

Something again flickers in her eye. Hope? Curiosity?

Disgust?

I wonder at her stance, the way she has her arms folded across her chest, eyeing me, and I remember Maya's story. Not the sordid gossip but the part about her husband. Dying. In a fire.

And I wonder what, exactly, it might have been like to live with him.

Maybe we should all give the woman a little grace.

"God sent His son Jesus to earth because He loves you, Maya. And He wants to know you. That's the Christmas story."

The flicker is gone, and she gives me a tight smile, pushes her chair away from the desk, and stands up. "Thank you for your story, Josey."

open wide your mouth

. . .

Russians have a saying: everyone is an artist. This came about during the time of the Communists and communal labor. It was their way of remembering their true identities while being forced to work in suitcase and bread factories across Soviet-era Russia.

I have news for you. They sent all the real artists to Burrr, Russia. Did you know that Bursk has one of the most elaborate ice sculpture festivals on the planet? Didn't think so.

This just might be my favorite Christmas in Russia yet.

"Mommy, cream!"

Chloe is pulling on my hand—have you ever tried to hold on to a preschooler through two layers of wool?—and my only advantage is the fact that the ground is pure ice and she has no leverage. But her request has alerted Justin and Nathan to the ice-cream stand nearby. Here's a little-known fact about Siberians. They only eat ice cream in the winter. Because eating it in the summer will cause pneumonia of the throat. Really.

"Wait for Mommy, Justin!"

The sun is high and golden and shining down like a spotlight on the fifty or so ice carvings that decorate the central square. Every town has a central square, and Bursk's has come alive with twinkle lights and ice sculptures from every known Russian fairy tale: snow girls (*snegurochka*) and Father Frost (*Ded Moroz*), prancing horses (the *troika*) pulling a sledge, a Siberian bear with the white half moon on its chest, and a fierce White Tiger. There are also mermaids and dolphins, castles and ogres, a slide of ice, and a giant reindeer. At night, the village turns on red and blue lights, and the square becomes magical.

I love Burrrrrrrsk.

Nathan digs into his pocket to buy Justin an ice-cream cone. The vendor, only her eyes showing under a wool muffler, asks the flavor, and of course Nathan says, "*Plombir*." I should have guessed.

Chloe is clapping and meowing, and Nathan feeds the hysteria by handing her a cone also.

"Want one?" he asks. I'm scanning the square for Chase. It's Christmas Eve, and he left early this morning on an errand, telling me he'd be back before our celebration tonight.

"No, thanks," I say.

Nathan pays the vendor, and we help Chloe and Justin down the slide. They could live a week outside in subzero temperatures without even a shiver in the layers I've garbed them in. Tights, sweatpants, snowsuits, and *shuba*—fur coats that Anton and Ulia dug out of storage—all tied with big belts. They're wearing the requisite *valenki*, and fur *shapkas* that tie around their chins, further secured by scarves. The only way I know they're mine is by the way Chloe is constantly trying to escape. Oh, and the meowing helps.

Lest you think I concocted this system on my own, let me disappoint you. I was instructed by Ulia, who has appointed herself Keeper of the Americans. She brought over the clothes, gave me lessons, and kept me stocked in home remedy supplies. Like raspberry jam, which I guess cures all fevers.

And it's great on blini.

Which Nathan makes when he stays over.

It has not escaped me that God has provided, everywhere I've lived . . . food. There's a verse in the Psalms that says, "Open wide your mouth and I will fill it." I feel like a baby bird.

A happy, fat baby bird.

"Where is Chase?" Nathan asks as we stand at the end of the slide, watching Chloe slide down on her tummy.

"Feet first, Chloe!"

Justin follows her, on his back. Good boy.

"I don't know. He said he had to do something. But he promised he'd be back tonight. I made soup—"

Nathan is looking at me, a smile on his face. He's dressed light for the day—a green military coat with a wool layer, his fur boots, and his black wool hat. Looks like he should be in a movie as an undercover green beret.

"Stop. I can cook." Okay. Liar, liar. "I peeled the potatoes. Chase did the rest."

"What kind of soup?"

"Corn chowder."

Nathan claps his hands together, blows on them. "Can't believe it's already Christmas." He sighs, puts his hands in his pockets. "It sure is nice to be able to spend it with you."

I glance over at him. I know he means *us*. The family. But it warms me anyway. His friendship is starting to feel comfortable, like the one I have with my brother Buddy.

The kids finish sliding, and I run into Maya as we take another spin through the displays. She gives me a tight smile, but it breaks open a little when I introduce her to Nathan. Everyone smiles for Nathan.

We finally head for home. "I got you something," Nathan says as we near the house. I see the something leaning against our gate—a something that is dark and bushy.

A Christmas tree.

Since the Great Deforestation, Chase hasn't wanted to think about, let alone purchase, a tree. And frankly, there are none yet available in Bursk. Since Russians don't celebrate Christmas on December 25, they usually don't have trees for sale before New Year's Eve. Except, of course, this year, the trees are on sale early—in Khabarovsk, at least.

"Where did you get a tree?"

"I probably shouldn't tell you. I bought it from—"

"Nathan, you didn't—"

"Shh. Take it inside." He grabs it and follows Justin and Chloe into the yard. They're jumping up and down, screaming, laughing.

Nathan sets the tree up in the family room and produces lights from his coat pocket. We string them on the tree, relishing the smell of corn chowder.

"Let's make ornaments," Nathan says, and proceeds to cut out snowflakes from white scratch paper.

I never could figure out how to do that.

Darkness has blanketed the land, but inside we're warm, and the light is bright, giving off a magical glow as we sit and eat soup.

"Will Chase be back soon?" Nathan asks. Justin is bouncing on his knee.

I look at the clock. "I don't know."

Justin climbs down, races into his room.

"Is he gone a lot?"

Is Chase gone a lot?

"Our first year in Russia he was working on an NGO project and practically slept at his office. He's sort of a one-horse guy. When he gets something in his mind, it consumes him. So when he's here, he's here. But when someone else needs him . . ."

Nathan smiles. "What if you need him?"

"I don't want to burden Chase. He's busy." I get up and

retrieve the tea from the stove. Pour him a cup. "Chase loves God, and this is his way of making a difference, I think."

I sit down. "Once upon a time, he mentioned wanting to use his skills as a missionary. But that was years ago."

"Before wife and kids?"

I look at him, and just like that, it hits me, like a sledgehammer to the chest. Paul and his singleness. Have I been holding Chase back? Would he be doing great things for God if I weren't here? Am I slowing him down?

Wait. Wait. I sit down. I'm in Siberia. Hardly holding the guy back.

However, the thought has found a foothold.

Chase could do so much more if he didn't have the kids to worry about. I rub my raw hands together. He could be like Nathan, going from village to village, spreading hope. "Chase is exceptionally good at what he does," I say softly.

"I don't think he should leave you alone so much, though." I watch as Nathan pours a tablespoon of tea onto his saucer, then takes a sugar cube and dips it in the tea, sucking on it.

"Something my landlady taught me," he says. "Try it."

So I do. It's tangy and sweet. An unexpected delight.

"Good, huh? Some things just belong together," Nathan says, now picking up the plate and swilling the tea into his mouth. He puts the plate down. "Have you ever thought about being a pastor's wife?"

I laugh. "I don't think Chase will ever want to be a pastor. He loves helping people, but he's not real comfortable sharing his faith. Besides, I don't think I'd make a good pastor's wife at all." I take another taste of the sugar. "I can't even get my neighbor to talk to me."

Nathan is looking at me strangely, however, a sort of sadness in his eyes. "But you're willing to try, aren't you?"

I'm just picking up my saucer, not sure how to respond, when I hear a thump at the door.

I am out in the entryway, about to open the door, when Nathan stops me. He's got a grip on my arm. "Who is it?" he hollers.

"It's me! Chase! Open the door—my hands are full!"

"Chase!"

Nathan opens the door, and I see what looks like Chase, somewhere under the snowy, ice-crusted man stumbling inside. A trickle of red is frozen in a line down his nose, and his day-old whiskers are covered in frost. He's fashioned a backpack of sorts from twine that encircles a huge box, about half the size of my coal furnace. He leans back and lets the box thump to the ground.

"What are you—"

"Ho, ho, ho!" he says, and grabs my face in his snowy hands, gives me a quick kiss.

"What?"

"Merry Christmas, G.I." He starts to peel off his layers.

"You're bleeding!"

He frowns at me, and I point to his nose. He touches it, looks at his hand. "I didn't even feel it. Must have been the wind, cracking my skin. It was a long walk from Petrogorsk."

Nathan is helping him off with his giant, snow-encrusted jacket. "Petrogorsk is eight kilometers from here. And you walked it? What were you doing?"

"It's only six through the fields. I didn't know you were going to be here, or I would have borrowed your snow machine. I had to pick up something I ordered from Khabarovsk." Chase gestures to the package. "Open it, babe."

I stare at the package. Back at Santa. He's all grins.

Justin and Chloe have heard the commotion and barrel out from their bedroom. "Daddy!"

He gathers them in his arms as I attack the package, ripping it open at seams where the staples hold it together.

For a moment, a long moment, I can say nothing.

Everything drains out of me, and I reach out to grab Chase's arm. "You carried this home? For six miles?"

"Kilometers," Chase corrects.

"Same thing," I say as my eyes fill.

"What is it, Mommy?" Justin asks, wiggling out of Chase's grip. "Who brought it?"

"Santa, honey," I say, scooping him up, holding him close, smiling at my man through my watery eyes. "Santa brought me a washing machine."

Merry Christmas from the Kringle Kompany!
Enjoy your specially prepared
Almond Crème Kringle.
Now serving eight new flavors to make
every day a celebration!
www.kringlekompany.com

Dear Josey,

I'm not sure if this will reach you before Christmas, but I wanted you to have a taste of home for the holidays. I know you're probably making your own *kringle*, but I wasn't sure if you could get almond flavoring in Siberia, so . . .

Mom and Dad say hello, and by the way, I saw your friend H in town. She is working at the Red Rooster Grocery Store. Only six months until I see you again!

By then, maybe our new storefront in Minneapolis will be open! Milton just acquired a warehouse/commercial kitchen. I can't wait to move to the big city! Don't worry, Mom and Dad have agreed to stay on running Berglund Acres until you and Chase move home. I can't believe we'll be selling the Cape

Cod. But with prices skyrocketing over the past four years, we hope to find a place twice the size in the cities. I think Clay and Amelia need their own playroom, and Milton would love to have an office. I'll make sure we get one with at least four bedrooms so you and Chase can have a guest room when you visit us.

You're still planning on moving home, right? I know you're doing amazing work in Siberia and all, but maybe it's time, you know?

Sorry there's not more room on the card. I'll send you an email!

Merry Christmas!

Love, Jasmine

We're sitting at the table, Chase and I, eating *kringle*, drinking tea, enjoying the smell of pine as it fills our home, our New Year's Eve dinner simmering on the stove in the form of chicken soup. Chloe is playing with her new collection of stuffed animals (the only gifts we could find in Bursk). She loves her herd of kitties.

She's in the center, speaking in tongues.

Justin is watching *Nu, Pogodi!* Through fuzzy reception on the black-and-white television Anton gave us for Christmas. Evidently, he gave Ulia a new one—something to keep up her *Santa Barbara* habit.

"I can't believe Jasmine has an online business," I say to Chase, who looks amazing in the red flannel shirt I found in the market. He spent the day trying to hook up the washing machine while I chopped potatoes for soup.

"Why? It's easy. Set up an eBay account, sell the right merchandise. It's all about having a unique, quality product and decent advertising." He holds up the *kringle*. "Yum."

I narrow my eyes at him.

"Well, it is good." Chase takes a sip of tea. "But I'd take your cookies any day."

I'm glad he would, because my confidence took a header when I brought a batch of thank-you sugar cookies to Olya only to have her peek at me through the crack in the door. She stood there, silent, as I smiled and handed her the cookies.

She took them, again not meeting my eyes. And closed the door behind her.

I thought we were past this. I'm so confused.

I get up and put our cups into my sink-bowl. I stand there a moment, thinking about the cookies and the way the women from the Bible study packed my tiny kitchen. At least *they* seemed to like them.

"Nathan said I'd make a good pastor's wife."

Chase looks up at me. "A pastor's wife?"

See, even Chase is surprised. "I know. I told him how crazy—"

"I don't know, Jose. You care about people. Like wanting to figure out a way to get Olya's daughter back to her. I hear you talk in your sleep. You'd be a great pastor's wife. Only problem—you're already married. To me."

I stare at him to see if he's making some sort of joke. "I think he was suggesting *you* need to be a pastor."

Chase rolls his eyes. "Like God would ever use me like that." He takes another bite of *kringle*. "But I have to admit, I sometimes wish I was like Nathan—I'd love to get a glimpse at life in the other villages."

I knew it! I knew it. Paul. Single. I'm trying to get a fix on my reaction when I hear a knock at the door.

"Hello?"

"Nate!" Chase gets up, lets him in. Nathan has been acting strange ever since Christmas Eve, when he left early the next morning, even before Christmas dinner.

I hear him stomping off his feet, hitting his gloves together. He follows Chase in, wearing rosy cheeks, his eyes bright. "Happy New Year!" He pulls out from behind his back what looks like . . . a turkey!

"Where did you find it?"

"A little international foods store in Khabarovsk. It was frozen solid when I left this morning. I hope it's okay."

Since I know nearly nothing about turkey storage and thawing, I shrug and reach out for the bird. "I'll put it in the fridge and let it thaw." I think I remember my mother doing something like that.

"And there's something else." He holds out what looks like a plate. On top of it sits a pair of mittens and a small box.

"You stole one of my plates."

"No, I found it outside on your stoop. By your door." He hands it to me, and it occurs to me that this is the plate I gave Olya, with the cookies on it.

She's gifted me back a pair of mittens. Homemade mittens, it seems. They're soft, made of angora, maybe, with an intricate design along the top. "These are gorgeous."

"Take a look at this box." Chase hands it to me. It's made of birchbark and then overlaid with an intricate birchbark design.

"Do you think she made this?"

Nathan sits down at the table, takes it from me, and turns it over for scrutiny. "I'm sure of it. I've seen these at nearly every house in Bursk. It's one of the crafts the women make here."

"There's more of these?"

"I'll bet Olya has quite a few more. And if not, she can make them. It's one of the Nanai skills from long ago, along with making reindeer mittens and hats. I've even seen picture frames made of birchbark."

A unique and quality product . . .

Olya's house is dark when I cross through the hole in the fence, keeping my eyes peeled for Lydia. I hear someone or something come to life inside the house as I approach. I knock three times before the door opens, just a crack. Olya peers out.

I point to the box. "*Spasibo.*"

She nods.

"It's very pretty," I add, testing the water.

She says nothing but ducks her head.

"Do you have more of these, Olya? Just like this box? And maybe the mittens?"

She slowly looks up, frowning at me, and I see she needs further explanation into the labyrinth of my thoughts. "I think I've found a way to get your daughter back from Moscow."

She stands there a long moment, during which I feel the prick of cold on my toes, between the cracks of my hastily thrown-on jacket, nipping at my ears. The sun is low, the late-afternoon shadows already creeping into the yard.

As I watch, her eyes slowly start to glisten, to fill with tears. She puts a hand over her mouth. Then she starts to nod.

Keeps nodding, even as her other hand covers the first. She steps back, and the door creaks open.

"I have more," she says softly, in a voice that speaks of tentative hope. "Many more."

I glance at my house next door. The lights are bright, creating a glow of warmth and happiness. I suddenly want her to join us, to come next door.

But first, perhaps, I need to enter her world.

I stomp the snow off my feet, smile, and step into her dark home.

Open wide your mouth, and I will fill it.

do you trust me?

• • •

My mother always said that I was an entrepreneur at heart. Maybe it was the way I set up the petting zoo by the side of the road, filling it with the ducklings who had lost their mother, a bunny we'd rescued after dad mowed over the mother, my aunt Myrtle's deer lawn art, a cat from my uncle Bert's farm, and Sherlock the dog. I charged admission and, on one hot July day, made exactly three dollars and twenty-two cents.

The thing is, you have to believe in the idea to sell it. And not just believe it, but commit to it. Take, for example, the honey-coated peanuts the school forced me to sell in sixth grade so we could send our swim team to Minneapolis for the regionals. I'm all for honey-coated peanuts. But going door-to-door to convince my neighbors that a can was worth their hard-earned cash so we could hang out in a hotel room made me want to hide behind the shed.

And eat the peanuts.

I think my parents privately funded my trip after discovering my stash of empty peanut cans.

Except my problem wasn't salesmanship. It was vision (not to mention the tasty crunch of the peanuts).

I'm getting the impression that the ladies of Bursk lack vision, too, as I finish unveiling my Great Plan to market their handicrafts. The women huddle around the room, wearing their *shapkas* and knobby wool scarves around their shoulders. January's icy fist is slowly tightening around our village, darkening the days, isolating us from the world with the sleet and snow. The fear of windchill and frozen appendages shuts us up in our homes. I see it in their pale, lined faces, the tired eyes, and know that mine look the same. I smell it in the coal smoke on our clothes, feel it in my own grubby hair. (Here's a new dilemma—heating a second pot of water to bathe in before the previous batch cools to the point of uselessness. Sure, Chloe and Justin can take baths in two inches of water, but that ain't gonna cut it with me and my size fourteen—no, ten!—backside.)

Yep, winter has tightened its fists around Bursk, and even the women's spirits have been caught in its iron grip. Granted, it's a fledgling idea, still growing legs, but in my mind, I can see birchbark jewelry cases, picture frames, trivets, and even candleholders being bought by craft-hungry Americans. And I'm just getting started. A walk through Olya's dark house revealed sculptures and paintings, tapestries and table linens, painted *matryoshka* dolls, knitted scarves and mittens.

A supermarket of Russian goodies just waiting to be shipped to the Mall of America.

And with the new speedy postal rates (which I know about thanks to Jasmine's *kringle* experiment), it just might work.

If I can get the ladies to warm up to my idea. Sadly, their faces, like my house, stay rigid and cold.

Although Chase stocked the coal furnace today before heading out with Anton to ice-fish, the behemoth is fighting a losing battle against the below-freezing windchill battering the house and the creep of frost on the inside of the windows. Last night, both Justin and Chloe joined us in bed, and if someone doesn't get night-trained soon, I might move to the sofa. Our sheets hang outside, in the cold, and I'll have to thaw them inside before remaking the bed.

Siberia is just like Minnesota? Who said that? Chase? Uh, I don't remember my mother bringing home milk on a stick, frozen as if it were in a bucket. And my hair solidified into a knot this morning as I took Chloe to the outhouse.

No, I'm sorry, my fellow Minnesotans, but I win the cold weather war.

I am not going to let the creeping darkness—both in spirit and in climate—deter my entrepreneurial spirit. After all, I've spent the last few days learning new Russian vocabulary—words like *marketing* and *advertising*. I look around the room and put every ounce of "this is a fabulous idea" on my face.

"Okay, how many of you have items like this in your home?" I hold up the little birchbark box.

Nearly everyone raises their hand.

Now that's what I'm talkin' 'bout.

"What if I told you that I think we could make money by selling your crafts on eBay?"

The hands go down.

I must be talking Swahili.

"Have you ever thought of selling your products before?"

Ulia raises her hand. I again feel like a teacher. "Yes?"

"Sometimes in the summer, we have tourists. We've sold some crafts to them."

Bingo! "That's right. Only we'd do this year-round. We could use the money to . . . say . . . " I cast a look at Olya, who is sitting with her head down, her hands folded on her lap. "Buy something you might need. Like . . . a washing machine?"

Yes, I saw the small, intrigued crowd clustered around the newest member of my family. One would think that I've brought an alien spaceship into the house. Just to set the record straight, it's not a Maytag or anything. In fact, it's a little bigger than a dorm fridge. It has two compartments—the wash side, and the spin side—each roughly the equivalent of a three-gallon bucket. I add clothes and water to the wash side, and it spins the laundry in a circle.

After ten minutes or so, the agitator stops, and I drain the water. Then I lift the sopping laundry out of the wash bin and squeeze it into the spinning bucket. It then spins the laundry at warp speed, using the centrifugal force to wick out the water. The clothes are nearly dry by the time the spin cycle is finished.

Oh, don't worry—they're still wet enough to freeze on the line outside.

Each bucket only holds about five items of clothing—less if I'm washing Chase's or my jeans. So I get to repeat this process about five times a day.

All the same, gone are the hours of wringing the laundry out by hand, and the skin on my hands has actually begun to grow back.

I'm feeling like a queen, and apparently the village women agree, because after scrutinizing the machine, they all looked at me as if I had just told the peasants to fetch me my scepter.

Does anyone see a mink hat on *my* head? I'd just like to point out that I'm still wearing a puffy down jacket while the rest of the women in all of Russia wear fur, head to toe.

That's all I have to say about that.

"Listen, ladies. I think this will work." I hold up the birchbark box. "This is beautiful, and with the right marketing, I think we can really make some money here. Even buy food and medicines for your families." And plumbing. Maybe we can even put in plumbing!

Okay, Josey, settle down. But the idea has me buzzing. For the first time all day, I can feel my toes.

Ulia is looking at me hard with an expression I can't read.

Then, to my astonishment, she stands up. Digs into her bag and produces a key chain, braided with what might be deer hide. "Will this sell?"

I take it, look it over. The leather is soft, with a stamped design on the flat surface that holds the ring. "Yes. I think so."

She nods. "*Ladno*. I'll be back."

She glances at the others, and without smiling, gives a nod.

Olya, however, looks up, and briefly meets my eyes. Again, I get the smile.

Wildflower: I can't believe I caught you. Every time I go online, I hope you're there. How are you?

GI: I've been in Mayor Anton's office for six hours now, sitting on a broken stool, setting up an eBay site for our new business—Secrets of Siberia. It's a gift store for homemade products made by the locals.

Wildflower: Are you kidding me? See, that's the woman I know, the one who deserves to have a washing machine. I can't believe I am actually saying that. You know, I can't even think about the fact you were doing cloth diapers by hand. See, this is why people get scared of missions. Or motherhood. Or, for that matter, marriage.

GI: Marriage? Why?

Wildflower: Isn't it because of Chase that you're in this mess?

GI: Mess?

Wildflower: Predicament?

GI: I like it here.

Wildflower: You keep telling yourself that.

GI: Seriously. So I don't have hot water. So what?

Wildflower: You don't have running water. You have to put on your snow pants to go to the bathroom.

GI: I am here to help people. Change lives. But it is cold—still so cold that when I go outside, my tongue freezes to the roof of my mouth. But I'm hoping, at least, to earn enough to install a heater in the outhouse. Chloe sat on her little tin potty yesterday and it stuck to her bottom.

Wildflower: See, again, that's a visual I didn't need to have, thanks. Is there anything I can do to help?

GI: With Chloe's potty?

Wildflower: Uh . . . with the business?

GI: Really?

Wildflower: Sure.

GI: Could I send the boxes of gifts to you, all labeled with the addresses, and you could send them out from Gull Lake? I think it would be easier to track, and I could get them to you faster.

Wildflower: Of course. At least until you open your shipping center.

GI: You jest, but this is going to be big.

Wildflower: I'm not jesting—look at Jasmine. She and Milton are moving to Minneapolis. Can you believe it?

GI: How are you? Last time I talked to her, she said you were working at the grocery store?

Wildflower: I . . . ah . . . I was wondering . . . what would you think about me coming to visit you?

GI: In Siberia?

Wildflower: No, in Hawaii. Of course, Siberia.

GI: <><><><><><><> That's supposed to be clapping. Yes, Yes, YES! Seriously?

Wildflower: I don't know. It's just a thought. But I miss you. And I want to see the outhouse for myself.

GI: Okay, tell me why you really want to come here.

Wildflower: It can't be because I miss you?

GI: And?

Wildflower: Rex and I have separated. And, well, I'm hoping you can give me advice. I need you.

I hate to say it, but . . . I could give her great advice. Because I'm a wife who submits. Who flings herself into the arms of God with abandon, waiting to be caught. Who is the most popular woman in town, the entrepreneur of Bursk.

GI: I'll put clean sheets on the sofa.

We in America have birthday parties backwards. At least, according to Russians, we do. See, in Russia, the birthday girl throws her own party, cooks her own dinner, bakes her own cake, and invites her friends to celebrate with her. I see a number of positives to this. For one, you get to invite only the people you want to spend time with. Secondly, you get to eat only the foods you love.

In the Russian tradition, if one is invited to a birthday party, it's a big deal.

You attend.

Even if someone's scary husband is going to be there.

"How do I look?" I ask Chase as I emerge from our bedroom wearing a jean skirt and a sweater. Yes, it might be early millennium fashion, but anything other than my yoga pants makes me feel like a human again. And the fact that they're two sizes smaller, well, you know I'm doing a wild jig. I even wrestled myself into pantyhose. I'm not sure why—I'll never take off the wool leggings I'm wearing over them. Maybe it's simply the knowledge that I'm wearing pantyhose. That under the turtleneck, the jean jumper, and the wool long johns, I'm dressing up.

Chloe runs out wearing a similar getup—her sweatpants and sweatshirt under a frilly summer party dress.

You have to use your imagination when in Siberia.

"You look fabulous," Chase says, leaning over to kiss me. He doesn't look too bad himself, in a pair of wool dress pants and another red sweater my mother sent him for Christmas. He's a regular elf.

Justin is crawling on the floor, zooming a car out of the bedroom. He's wearing a pair of blue corduroys and a sweater, looking every inch a miniature replica of his father.

He's going to break hearts from one end of the globe to the other too.

"Let's go," Chase says, scooping up the kiddos. We don't bother to bundle them for the quick dash to Olya's house.

I check for Lydia as we climb through the fence. She is penned up in the back and strains at her leash, barking frantically as we approach the back door. Good dog, good dog.

Olya opens in a moment. She is decked out in a black sweater and a gray skirt, *valenki* on her feet. She's swept her raven-black hair back into a clip and has even put on makeup.

Chase gives her a kiss on the cheek. Olya hugs me.

Their house is an exact replica of ours but without the fresh coat of paint. Same fraying brown furniture, same black-and-white fuzzy television set (finally, I get to catch up with *Santa Barbara*!), same gargantuan coal furnace in the middle of the room.

The one difference is the festive atmosphere of the kitchen. The table has been pushed out from the wall and set with beautiful, albeit chipped, china and bowls of Russian delights—winter salad, pickles, cutlets, brown bread, and even, yes, a cake.

I've seen many a Russian cake. This one looks like it's grown warts. Giant, brown warts.

Uh-oh. I recognize that cake.

I love cake. But I hate Russian cake. Especially gourmet Russian prune cake.

Because Russian prunes taste like they've been soaked in kerosene. And Russians love them. They love them in vodka and cognac. They love them in cookies and pies. And they love them in their cake.

I should have known that Olya would have a kerosene prune cake on her table. And this one looks like it's garnished with extra prunes.

I just won't look at it.

Vasilley is sitting at the table. He rises, and I notice he's clean-shaven for this event, wearing a brown sweater, black pants. He only looks slightly scary. He takes Chase's hand and glances at me with a nod.

"*S dnem rozhdeniya*," I say to Olya, giving her birthday greetings and handing her the gifts we purchased for her—a spray of silk flowers and a can of lilac air freshener.

Before you judge, let me say that wouldn't you like a blast of spring during the dark days of winter? That's what I thought.

Besides, I learned long ago in Moscow, during the days when my neighbor gifted me with all manner of personal hygiene products, that anything goes for gift-giving in Russia. Even pantyhose. I kid you not.

As all Russians are wont to do, Olya sets the gift aside to open it later, outside the view of guests. To their way of thinking, it's not polite to pay attention to a gift when you have guests. They might actually have something there.

"*Nu, Pogodi!*" Justin says and wiggles out of Chase's grip to land on the sofa. Chloe, however, climbs onto a chair, puts her little paws on the table.

To my shock, Vasilley looks over at her and smiles.

Olya gestures to me and Chase to sit, and I realize we're the only guests.

The only guests.

I'm not sure what to say, think, feel . . . especially when Vasilley fills a tiny shot glass in front of my plate with vodka.

And not just any vodka. A prune-enhanced home brew. It's roughly the color of motor oil.

Oh no.

Even Chase eyes it with some fear.

Before we sit, Vasilley raises his glass and looks at his wife. Is that a shine I see in his eyes?

Or just the vodka?

Oh, I'm so judgmental. I lift my glass, smile, and nod as Vasilley toasts his wife. It's something sweet, with lots of loving words. And then he clicks my glass and downs his drink.

Shoot! I glance at Chase, who is looking a little green, but he closes his eyes and downs his own.

As does Olya.

I put the vodka to my lips, intending to only pretend, when Chloe launches herself at me. "Mom! Me some juice!"

The vodka spills down my lips, into my mouth. Turns it to fire.

"Josey, are you okay?" Chase says as I cough, sputter. I'm wondering if I still have lips or if they've been burned off.

Vasilley looks at me with a smile.

I knew I shouldn't trust him.

Olya comes to the rescue with two glasses of prune juice, called *sok*, and hands them to Chase and me. At least it isn't spiked. Chase takes a long drink.

"How are the trap lines?" Chase asks Vasilley. I know he still longs to go out into the bush to get one-on-one with these men, burrow deep into their souls and discover ways to encourage, to bring light. On top of that is the slim hope that the hunting hasn't been destroyed by the pre-Christmas deforestation.

Vasilley gives him a long look, one I can't translate. And then says (in what I consider the tone of an Italian hit man), "Why don't you come out and see?"

Gulp.

"I'd like to do that," Chase says, just as Olya arrives with a plate of steaming boiled potatoes from her stove.

"*Na zdorov'yu!*" Vasilley raises his glass to us, looking at Chase. It means "to your health," although I have serious concerns about said health at the moment. Chase considers for a moment, then lifts his glass, taps it to Vasilley's, and finishes it off.

I eye him and he doesn't meet my glance. I've never seen Chase drink, thanks to the legacy of alcoholism bequeathed to him by his father. Chase chases the vodka with a sip of prune *sok*, probably in an attempt to feel the inside of his mouth again.

I dish up a plate for Chloe, call the kitty and then Justin. He barely looks up from his cartoon.

Chase is piling his plate high with potatoes, cutlets, and salad. Olya is smiling, and it turns into a full-wattage beam when he starts to make noises. Chase is an interactive eater—when he loves something, he *hmms* and *ahhs*. It's a joy to experience.

Almost makes a girl want to cook something. Almost.

"To Olya's potatoes!" Vasilley says, grabbing the bottle of Nectar of Kerosene and pouring it into Chase's glass, then mine, topping off Olya's as well. He scoops up his glass and raises it high.

Oh boy.

Chase taps glasses, winks at me, and downs it.

I give a weak smile and put my glass back down.

Olya finally sits, and I listen to Chase and Vasilley talk about politics and people in the village and America. Olya keeps glancing at Chloe and smiling.

"Olya tells me that Josey wants to sell her boxes," Vasilley says, filling up Chase's glass for what might be the eighth time. Chase must hold his liquor well, because although he seems to be keeping up with Vasilley, he doesn't have even a hint of Vasilley's shiny eyes or slurred speech. "To Josey!"

To Josey, indeed. Olya has long stopped keeping up and now just gives me a sad smile. Out of my peripheral vision, I see Chase down the drink.

I think I'm going to be ill. Not from Olya's delicious food (aside from the prune cake), but from the change I see in Chase before my very eyes. Has he forgotten the nights he snuck out of the house, having narrowly escaped his father's drunken rampages? Or worse, the days when he didn't escape and showed up on my doorstep a little broken?

Chase always swore to me he'd never touch alcohol. And I counted on that, especially during my own high-school rampages.

Now I need that promise even more. He reaches over and takes my prune *sok*, takes a drink, moves my glass over to his plate. I don't why—he has plenty left. But I didn't want mine anyway.

"Justin, Chloe, I think it's time to go home." I touch Olya's hand. "Thank you for the meal. Happy birthday."

"I think I'll stay," Chase says, touching my hand. He pulls me down and kisses me on the cheek. "Don't worry," he whispers. But I'm past worry and on my way to an all-out panic attack.

Chloe and Justin are tucked into their beds, the house is warm and quiet, and I'm in my jammies and wool socks, under the covers, trying to read, when Chase steals in. I hear him load the coal stove, stoke it for the night. Then he pumps water and fills up the overhead water storage above the sink.

Finally, he locks the door, and I see his form appear in the doorway to the bedroom. Against the darkness of the rest of the house, the light of the bedroom illuminates him, shows the lines on his face I haven't seen before. I do recognize the five-o'clock shadow, the tousle of his hair. I expect his eyes to be bloodshot, but they're remarkably clear. He crosses his arms, leans against the door.

"Do you trust me?"

I put my hand over the page in my book. I'm not even sure what it's about, having read the same line for roughly the last hour. My heartbeat repeats his question. Do I trust him?

I trust him to love me and the kids to the best of his ability. I trust him to take care of us to the level he believes we need to live. I trust him to play with his children and do the best to parent him. I trust him to want to help.

But I don't trust the Chase I saw tonight.

I don't answer. Look back at my book.

"Vasilley asked me to go hunting with him," he says finally, pulling off his clothes, then climbing in beside me. "He says that he wants to show me how they hunt. I think they're not as angry with me about the pine trees as I thought."

Or maybe it's just that in his current woozy perspective, everybody's a friend. Please, God, don't let Chase get hurt.

He puts his back to me as I lie there in the bath of lamplight.

a little bit of sunshine

. . .

"Maybe we can fix up the playground?"

"Or the fountain in the center of the square?"

The conversation is lively and not unlike that of a potluck dinner I might find at the Gull Lake church. The women bring in their supplies, lay them out, and go to work. We are in what I'm dubbing the community center, located next door to the *detskiy sad*. Old wooden and metal chairs are shoved up against painted propaganda signs and faded pictures of long-gone leaders. A red curtain, worn and ripped, hangs from the ceiling above a small stage.

The wind rattles the windows, and a layer of snow and ice slides in under the door, around the cracks in the windowsill. Everyone still wears their winter coats, although mittens have been discarded for work purposes. I no longer think it odd to see women wearing mink coats with homemade knitted mittens. I tried wearing my leather gloves once and lost all feeling in my pinkies instantly.

I'm still holding out on the Cossack boots, however. Remember, I made a vow long ago in Moscow, and a girl can only sacrifice so much before she loses herself. I found cute, wide-heel boots lined with fur that lace up the front like something out of the sixties. I can mostly feel my toes.

I now wear two layers of everything. Turtleneck and sweater, plus jacket. Wool tights and jeans. Knitted gloves, plus the mittens Olya gave me.

Olya has decided we are friends. Especially after the birthday party dinner, she's a regular on my doorstep, armed with a hot pot of corn kasha, or better yet, *shchi*, a cabbage stew made from sauerkraut.

She even showed me a picture of Albena in Moscow. Everything inside me hurt, especially when Chloe came running up and launched herself at Olya.

The day we met Olya and Lydia flashed back at me, and for a moment, I had a full and vivid understanding of how painful it must have been for her to see my kids.

I probably would have winced also.

To Olya's credit, she picked up Chloe and even gave her a little pet when my daughter purred and made kitty paws. Hey, it's more than I would do. Good thing cats have nine lives.

I'm hoping Chase has nine, or even two lives. I can't even think about his upcoming trip with Vasilley. What if it's a ploy to get Chase into the woods alone, where there are no witnesses, and enact revenge for seventy years of Cold War? Or for two months of cold, fruitless trapping? Or what if Vasilley gets sopping drunk and shoots Chase?

What if they freeze to death?

Do you trust me? The question dogs me like the wolves I occasionally hear in the woods outside Bursk. Howling, haunting.

Driving fear into my soul.

I used to trust Chase enough to follow him to the ends of the earth (read: Siberia). Can a girl submit when the one she is "obeying" betrays her?

I'm not ready to answer that.

Instead, I've focused the past three weeks on setting up our eBay account, taking inventory of gifts, and snapping digital pictures, creating descriptions. I've even decided to send Justin and Chloe to preschool for a full day two days a week.

I'm not a bad mom. I'm not a bad mom.

The payoff is that I've learned more about the village and women of Bursk than Chase could ever put in a report.

Like, for example, the women often feel alone and forgotten.

Or, if they had it their way, they might even return to the life they had years ago—a close-knit subsistence society. With their television sets, of course.

And fur coats.

Boy, do I want a fur coat. I admit it, I'm jealous. Not that I'd give up my washing machine, mind you, but imagine, all that fur, all that warmth.

And fur coats don't make noise when you walk. Seriously. Have you ever listened to a person in a puffy parka? They can't go anywhere without making it clear that they are on the way. And that they are fat. I don't care if you're a size two—in a parka, you are never thin.

Just once I'd like to glide into a room in a fancy mink coat.

I don't think, by the way, that the women of Bursk would really like to return to cooking dinner over open fires and sleeping in a yurt. But I do think they'd like to feel as if they are contributing.

Hence, the full house at the community center, the excitement, the tentative smiles arrowed my direction. See, I knew God sent me here for a reason. Clearly, Siberian women and Minnesota girls aren't so different.

Just as I predicted, we already have orders. With Olya's help, we commandeered cardboard from the vendors at the market and have fashioned small boxes. We also have homemade wrapping paper printed with a design one of the ladies whittled into a chunk of wood.

They are a creative bunch, these Siberians.

I'm getting ready to send out our first batch of orders when I feel a change in the room. The conversation slows, a few look up, past me.

I turn, expecting to see Chase. Instead, it's Nathan standing at the door, thumping his boots, clapping his hands together. His cheeks are red, and he hasn't shaved for a day at least. Frost clings to his eyelashes. He smiles wide. "Hey, Jose. I just came by to see how you're doing."

I hold up a package. "We already have at least ten orders! They're going out today." I motion him over to the table full of packing supplies. "Help me package these."

Nathan pulls off his gloves and shoves them into his jacket pocket. He, too, wears a parka now, a black one that makes him look like a puffy mobster, especially with his knitted black stocking cap. He unzips the jacket, and I notice the red scarf wrapped around his neck that Chase and I gave him for Christmas.

"Ten orders already? That's amazing."

"It's fantastic," I say, glancing at the women. "I can hardly believe I'm getting this much participation. I expected maybe two or three women. But the entire town?"

He picks up a wooden box, begins wrapping it in paper. "They're looking beyond their lives, seeing potential. Frankly, I think it's one of the greatest gifts Westerners, and especially Americans, have given to the Russians . . . a vision of what could be."

I smile at that. Josey Anderson, purveyor of hope. "There's even been talk of redoing the central square. Updating the playground."

"If anyone can do it, you can." He looks up and grins at me. "I told you that you'd make a terrific pastor's wife."

Except, a pastor's wife has to be married to a pastor.

And last time I checked, pastors didn't drink vodka.

"Nathan, can I ask you a favor?" The request has been tumbling through my mind for three weeks and is the only logical answer to my current Chase dilemma. I spot my open door.

I never thought in my wildest imaginings (and I've had many—after all, Chase has always lived with one foot in adventure, one foot in reality) that I'd have to worry about him turning into his father.

I wrap a birchbark box tight in paper, folding the edges down to wedge it into the cardboard container. I can't look at Nathan. "Chase and Vasilley are going hunting next week. Will you . . . " I look up at him, swallow, aware that my voice has thinned. "Will you finagle a way to go with them?"

He is watching me, and now something enters his eyes, something that makes me want to cry. Mistrust of my sweet Chase. "Why?"

"I just . . . I don't trust . . . Vasilley." And that's true. "He drinks. And I'm worried about Chase."

Nathan puts down the box, lowers his voice. "Is Chase drinking?"

"I don't . . . we went to a birthday party. There was vodka." I lift a shoulder, but I can't look at Nathan. I feel as though I've just plunged a knife between my husband's shoulder blades. "It's not like he even got . . . " I can't say the word *drunk*, but it's there, hanging, ugly.

Raw. "It's just not like Chase at all. He's a good man. I don't want anything to happen to him." I close the cardboard box, but my hand trembles.

Nathan's hand covers mine. It's cold, but when he squeezes it, the kindness sends warmth to my heart. "I'll take care of it, Josey. Don't worry."

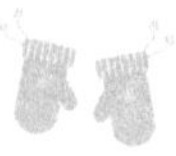

The Secrets of Siberia in your home!

> That's right! Straight from Siberia, the land of ice and cold, come handcrafted gifts for the nature lover! Birchbark vases, jewelry boxes, and kitchen containers are great for keeping herbs, grain, and even milk fresh longer! The Nanai people are among the few Siberian craftsmen who have preserved the art of carving and pressing birchbark into intricate shapes, designs, and unique items for the home. Each piece is handcrafted. Find the perfect gift and take a piece of Siberia home today!

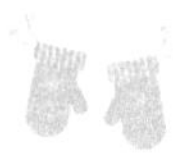

I'm going to have to start paying rent at the government office. And get a pillow for my backside. Outside, I see the hour is late, and I'm going to be late picking up Justin and Chloe if this picture doesn't finish loading.

We've completely sold out of our initial stock, and I have the ladies working every day at the community center, stockpiling bread boxes and jewelry containers and making place mats, coffee cups, napkin rings, hairclips, and even necklaces.

I wake in the middle of the night with designs in my head.

I am the queen of my empire.

Or, at least, I'm frantically trying to keep up. At least all this business keeps me from thinking about Chase, who left yesterday for parts unknown in the middle of Siberia with Vasilley. And, thank the Lord, Nathan.

C'mon, load. I spy Anton leaning against the door frame. He's frowning. He hasn't asked about my health for a while now. I'm not sure why.

Everything's going to be fine, really. Chase dug out a backpack and sleeping bag and packed it full of warm clothes, socks, and even a first-aid kit.

I sat on the bed, petting Chloe, and tried to hold my tongue.

But it wasn't until Nathan showed up with his own stuffed backpack, not until he gave me a smile and the smallest of winks, that I began to breathe.

I hate that I enlisted backup for the man I most believe in. Or at least, want most to believe in.

Oh, God, please help me to trust Chase! He does deserve my trust, doesn't he? Doesn't he?

The pictures finish loading, and I disconnect, shut down the computer. Five more orders today. The post office is sending them out as fast as we can package them, but it's not like they offer delivery confirmation. At least H is sending them on to the right locations.

All I can do is pray.

Which I seem to be doing a lot, especially since Chase's jaunt into the nether hills. The good news is that Nathan brought along our company's first paycheck, wired to a Khabarovsk bank from our online account. I sell on consignment, taking only enough to cover the eBay and mailing expenses. The rest I pay out to the ladies.

I have to admit, I've never seen a woman cry when she got paid. But as I sat there in Olya's kitchen, as she counted her rubles, she put her head into her hands and began to sob.

I'm thinking that was a good cry.

I decided that it might be good if I cried too. See, this is why I could be a pastor's wife, if, say, Chase was a pastor. Because I can empathize. This is why also, last week, I had a packed house for my study of the first chapter of John.

It just takes time to win hearts and minds.

I pass Anton in the hall as I leave. I'm sure he recognizes me, even though I'm dressed in three thousand layers, with only my eyes showing between my knit cap and scarf. Still, although I lift my hand in greeting, he ignores it.

Okay, so not *all* the hearts and minds of Bursk.

The wind picks up trash it has culled from corner dumpsters, and an empty bottle rolls across my path. The late-January winds have pushed snow into drifts against swaying fences, lining footpaths to homes. The street is ice-packed, scarred now and again by hoof prints or sledge furrows. Every house I pass has a trickle of gray smoke curling into the sky, evidence of life in the otherwise darkened houses, now shuttered closed for winter. We elected to put plastic over our windows, and every day a hazy sun shines in.

The *detskiy sad* yard is well-used, even in winter. The teachers bundle up the children for the ice age and spend the requisite hour outside, playing. To my surprise, Justin and Chloe haven't been ill once this winter.

We might all need to play outside for an hour a day. Learn to get along with the other kids while wading through the snow (while remembering to stay away from the icy pipes). I think there are some metaphors for life there.

Justin and Chloe are the only ones swinging on the swing set when I arrive. Maya is in the yard, wrapped in a wool coat, looking her French model best. She gives me a small shake of her head as I retrieve my children.

"*Izvinite,*" I say. "Thank you for watching them. I appreciate your time."

She gives me one of those eerie Maya looks and adds a shrug.

I swing by the corner market, peruse the items on my way

home. Olya isn't there today—I'm hoping thanks to her recent payday—but I spot a vender with what looks like chocolate chips. I stare closer, pulling Chloe to a stop. My daughter is thrilled and begins our daily tug-of-war.

Sure enough, Nestlé's Toll House chocolate chips! I can't believe it. My supply ran out weeks ago, and the ladies have been begging for another batch.

I reach into my pocket for rubles when I see, down the street, standing beside an abandoned bread kiosk, what looks like Ulia. I recognize her by her *shapka*, a sort of swirled whipped-cream shape made of leather and mink.

And with her, leaning close, is a man I don't recognize.

In fact, he leans down and whispers into her ear. She laughs.

She doesn't see me, despite the fuss Chloe is making, and I quickly turn away, feeling as if I've just seen an episode of *Santa Barbara Goes to Siberia*.

Oh.

"Mommy, me seeds!" Justin is pointing to a woman selling sunflower seeds in a little bag.

"No, Justin. You don't know how to eat them." I'm pulling him away as fast as I can. Chloe's decided that she is a turtle and wants to try sliding along the icy path on her back.

"Get up, Chloe," I hiss through my teeth. Please, don't let Ulia see me. I feel dirty suddenly. I haul Chloe up by the back of her fur coat. "Please walk with Mommy."

"*Nyet! Nyet!*"

Okay, that's about enough Russian culture for one day. I hike Chloe up by the belt and carry her down the street like a suitcase.

Justin is sliding beside me. "Mommy, where's Daddy?"

He's in the bush, where's it's safe. Where people don't see things they ought not to and are forced to look the other direction. My stomach burns as we arrive at our house. I let the kids free. Justin runs through the yard, pretending to shoot imaginary wildebeests.

Nu, Pogodi! indeed.

The house is cold. Chase has carried in enough coal to last his trip away from home. I put on my gloves, load a couple coal chunks into the still-burning furnace. Push it around with the poker.

It's a skill I'll bet my mother never learned. But more than likely, one I share with my grandmother.

"Soup!" Justin says, climbing onto his chair. His cheeks are still rosy from the walk home, and his blond curly hair sticks straight up. Those blue eyes look at me, sparkling with hope, and I'd give him the world.

"Coming right up."

Nathan, bless him, has left his room-and-board pot of borscht in the fridge, and I heat it up slowly on the stove, serve it up with *smetana* and bread.

We read a book, I give the kids a warm bath in a large metal basin, and then I send them to bed.

The house is quiet and dark as I stare out at the stars. Chase is out there, under them. I imagine him in his sleeping bag, wool hat on, laughing with Nathan. My Chase spent much of his high-school years sleeping out under the stars.

I don't need to worry.

I don't need to worry.

Once upon a time, back in Gull Lake, I was the one who caused the worry. I was the one who might forget her boundaries. I'll never forget the night I went joyriding with Lew and the gang, shortly after we took home the state football title. I'm horrified to admit that I don't remember how, exactly, I got home.

Except to say that it had to do with Chase and his attention to details—like the fact that I wasn't in the parking lot waiting for him after the team bus arrived home and all the other football players had showered and moved on to victory events.

Chase spent half the night looking for me, and found me, apparently, on Lew's porch furniture.

I woke up on the beach of Berglund Acres, wrapped in a stadium blanket. Chase was sitting beside me.

He said nothing.

I said nothing.

And he covered for me when my father found us. Said we'd come out to watch the sunrise.

I can trust Chase.

I wrap my arms around my waist, turn off the light, climb into our cold bed, and shiver.

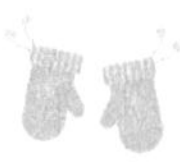

Don't you think there should be some warning, especially from God, when you are going to have to pull out your spiritual arsenal? I know that the Bible says, "Be ready in all seasons," but really, just like a race or a boxing match, there should be a designated warm-up period.

Yes, yes, I know, it's called daily quiet time, but I have twins.

And it's two o'clock in the morning. I know, because I've been asleep for at least four hours—long enough to have bad breath and matted hair. And it's greasy hair to boot because Chase has been away for three days, and there's no one to pour water over my head and wash out the suds.

I realize too late that I'm still half asleep—a girl with all her faculties doesn't open the door to crazed pounding in the middle of the night.

I don't recognize the snowy person that stumbles into my foyer, bringing in the frigid night air. I gasp, now fully awake as the air climbs up my nightgown despite the coat I've wrapped around me.

"Hello?"

I know those eyes, but it takes a moment for me to place them. And then I'm speechless. Frozen in place.

Why would Maya be at my door in the middle of the night, bleeding from the mouth?

"Can I stay here?" she gasps, and I see that her mascara has run down her face, her face blotched from the chill. I close the door behind her, nodding.

"Are you okay?"

She is trying to nod, but it's not working, and she puts a hand over her face, probably to hide the fact that she's crying, but I'm pretty savvy. Even in the wee hours. Okay, maybe not right away . . . maybe I'm a slow savvy, but I can spot sobbing with the best of them. I ease off her jacket, hang it on a hook. She's still not looking at me. I hang mine up and open the inner door, grab her elbow to move her inside where we can feel our toes.

The coal furnace needs stoking, so I open it and push around some blocks. Chase's supply of coal is dwindling, but he'll be back tomorrow, in plenty of time to dig coal from the pile outside. I motion to a chair. "Would you like some tea?"

She moves, somewhat stiffly, into the chair and nods, taking out a handkerchief and pressing it to her eyes, her mouth. She checks out the blood.

"Are you okay?" I ask again. "Do you need some ice?"

She shakes her head, but her hand is trembling. I put the teapot on the stove and sit down opposite her, taking her hand. It's also ice cold. "What happened?"

She glances up at me, and now I see, truly see, what is behind all those flashes of honesty.

Pain. Brokenness.

"What is it, Maya?" I ask softly.

She sighs. "Can I stay here tonight?"

Why not? The couch is empty. "Of course. Are you afraid to go home?" I occurs to me that I don't even know where Maya lives. Which is odd, because now I know where nearly everyone in town lives. Three hundred and twenty-seven people suddenly feels very large.

She looks down at the blood on her napkin. Nods.

"Who hurt you, Maya?"

She closes her eyes and takes a long breath. Another. Finally, "I was born in this village. My father was an elder."

The teapot's lid starts to jiggle against the steam, but I ignore it.

"He committed suicide when I was thirteen." She stares at her fingernails. They're polished, a deep red. "My mother couldn't take care of me, and she didn't have money to send me back to boarding school, so . . . "—she lifts a shoulder, and the way she does it spears pain through me—"she gave me to a man in the village to marry."

Oh.

She sighs again, and it's easier this time. Glancing up at me, she gives a flicker of a sad smile. "He might have loved me. But mostly he drank, and I kept his house." She shakes her head. "He wasn't always mean."

I imagine her, a young girl, afraid, trying to keep everything in order. No wonder she runs a tight ship down at the kindergarten.

The pot of water begins to boil, and I get up, turn off the heat, bring the pot to the table. I'm reaching for the cups when she puts her hand on my arm. "He would have killed us both that night."

I sit back down.

"I know it. He was drunk, but he barricaded my door before he fell asleep on the sofa. I smelled the smoke, knew he'd fallen asleep with his cigarette. And I tried to get into the room,

I tried to save him, but by the time I got out the window, the house was engulfed." She moves her head as if to shake free from the memory. "The council said it was an accident. They gave me a room at the community center, in the back, behind the stage."

So that's where she lives. Right next door to the *detskiy sad*. No wonder she's always there.

I retrieve the cups, set them in front of her. "You're safe here, Maya. Whatever happened tonight, you're safe here. And when Chase gets back, he'll find out—"

"*Nyet!*" Her eyes widen. "No, it's not . . . I can't . . . "

"Calm down. I just want to help—"

"He will kill me if anyone finds out."

The clock on the wall ticks behind me, thunderous seconds, as I let her words sink in. Who will kill her? If anyone finds out what?

I take her hand. "You're safe here, Maya. I promise. And we don't have to know anything. Except, if my children are in danger . . . " I raise an eyebrow, and she shakes her head.

"He wouldn't come here."

Hmm. I get up and bolt the inside door just the same.

Maya fixes herself a cup of tea. Her hand shakes just a little as she sips it.

"Thank you," she says softly.

I nod, but I'm not drinking tea. I'm leaning forward. "Maya, why did you come to me?"

She takes another sip, measures me with her eyes. "Because I've been watching you, and I think I want to believe you."

Believe me? Is anyone else lost?

"Because He loves me, you said. And I want to believe that. But I'm not sure how I can."

Oh. He. As in God, He.

"Why not?"

She shakes her head, looks away. And I recognize a look I've seen way too many times on my own face. Guilt. Shame. The morning-after dread on the shores of Gull Lake.

Thankfully, I also have an answer for that look. "I long ago learned that God doesn't keep score. It's all one big lump of sin to Him. And His one big remedy is forgiveness. Just like that. He doesn't promise to make all our problems go away. But He does promise to forgive us, and to walk with us here on earth, give us wisdom and hope, and to give us life after we die. One of my favorite verses says that God knows the plans He has for us, and they're good plans. But we need to seek Him to find those plans."

Her dark eyes are in mine, as if testing my words, my resolve. And then, just like that, as if the sunshine has found Siberia, she smiles. It's small. But enough. "I think, maybe, I can do that."

the hot and cold

• • •

I THINK MY MARROW HAS FROZEN. FOR SURE, EVERY CELL IN MY body has slowed and is turning to ice. I move like a ninety-six-year-old woman, and it hurts. I think I've lost all feeling in my fingers, and I've taken to holding my hands over the steam of potato soup, hoping to thaw them.

Outside, the wind has turned into a snarl, and a blizzard whiteouts the yard, the street. My coal supply is buried under a blanket of frosting—I keep praying over the furnace, but if Chase doesn't get home soon, I'm going to have to dig.

Good thing we gave away the cow, because she and her milk would be ice cream in the backyard.

And all I can think is . . . Chase is out there. A day late already.

Maya left early yesterday morning, before the kids woke up, and I cleaned the house and waited for Chase, nearly bursting with the memory of my conversation with Maya.

Waited, and waited . . . and . . .

I'm not going to worry. I'm not. Going. To. Worry.

I stand at the window, staring at a swirl of snow, and everything inside me is tight.

"This is not what I signed up for, Lord." My voice sounds thin against the wind, the rattle of windowpanes. Chloe and Justin are still asleep, bundled up in layers of comforters and wool blankets. I pull my sleeves down over my fists, tuck them under my arms. "I'm not ready to be a single mom."

I go over to the coal bucket, stare into its emptiness as if God might suddenly fill it. But it stays empty.

It only takes a second for me to succumb to the tempting pull of the Cossack boots. I pull them on, add my jacket, a hat, and Chase's works gloves, and grab the bucket.

The wind nearly takes me down. My nose immediately hurts, and water runs into my eyes. The blizzard isn't a peaceful drift of thick snowflakes but a torrent of ice crystals hitting my cheeks, the fury of Siberia unleashed.

I bend my head and trudge over to the pile, pick up a shovel, and work out a few rocks. I'm not sure what coal in America looks like, but in Russia, it can be huge, dirty black boulders. One tumbles down from the pile, lands at my feet. I pick it up and drop it into the bucket.

Coal is also heavy. I fill the bucket half full and trudge inside. No, this is not what I signed up for at all.

Humble. Gentle. Patient. Peaceful.

Be worthy of the calling.

I was worthy yesterday. Today, please, just leave me alone.

I go inside and dump the bucket into the fire. A blaze of heat begins to fill the house.

I stand back, pry off my layers. Warm my hands. Hmm. Wow, I did that. All by myself.

We might survive living in Siberia. Perhaps even help people solve the problems that have plagued this village for years. And help Olya reunite her family. And show Maya the way to hope. And even help Nathan start a church. Maybe, Siberia isn't as difficult as I thought.

I start a pot of hot water for cocoa and again stare out the window. It's getting darker, even though it's supposed to be early morning.

We are in for a doozy of a storm.

Please, God, keep Chase safe.

I go and climb back into bed, warmed by the bodies of my two little Chase replicas.

"Josey, Josey, wake up."

I am warm, so warm. I take a deep breath.

And smell smoke. I sit up and whack something, hard.

"Ow!"

A Chase-ish form pulls back, his hand on his forehead.

"Chase!" I reach up to put my hands around him, but I can barely see him through the fog of gray smoke that layers the ceiling.

"Grab Chloe!" He scoops up Justin, along with a blanket. Panic ignites me as I throw off the covers and drag my daughter off the bed. I follow Chase through the house, putting my hand over my mouth, cradling my daughter into my chest. "Are we on fire?"

Chase grabs a jacket and throws it over me, and I slip on my boots as I dash out into the snow. "What's happening?"

Justin is awake now, blinking at his dad. Chloe is just starting to move. The snow hits my face with a bite.

"What did you do?" Chase rounds on me now that we're outside. The blizzard roars in my ears, and he looks a little wild-eyed with all that snow caked on his *shapka*, his four-day beard growth.

"We're all clear." Nathan comes out of the house now, behind me, holding the plastic sheeting that used to cover our windows. "It was just the coal furnace smoldering."

Chase's eyes are red-rimmed, and he closes them as he turns away from me. I see him pull Justin tight against him, lean his face into his neck.

"What happened?" I ask.

Nathan pulls off his jacket, puts it around Chloe. "Your coal fire was smothered. The entire house is filled with smoke."

I stand there a long moment as realization sinks in. Cuts off my breathing. "We could have died."

Nathan looks at me, then turns to Chase. "Buddy, you okay?"

Chase glances at me, and for a second, I think I see his eyes glisten. He nods. "Yup." But it's a short assent that makes me believe the opposite.

He was scared. I haven't scared Chase in years, or at least since the jellyfish, perhaps. "I'm sorry," I say, my voice barely functioning. Chase reaches out and wraps his arm around my neck, pulls me to his cold, puffy jacket. I feel him tremble as he holds me.

"I'm sorry," he says. "So, so sorry."

I'm not sure what he's apologizing for, but I've learned never to turn down an apology from a man. I hold on.

We're a little family package of gratefulness as Nathan walks around the house, opening windows to shoo out the smoke.

"How did it happen?" Chase asks.

"I dumped the bucket of coal in, stoked the fire . . . ?" I prop Chloe on my hip, pull the coat over her even as she fusses with it.

"You dumped the bucket?"

"Yeesss . . . "

"You can't dump coal dust on a fire—it'll only smother it. Just put the pieces in, by hand."

Oh, I'll be sure and file that away in my Coal Furnace Maintenance Manual. I sigh.

"I'm just thankful we got here in time."

I'm not able to answer that.

"*Zhozey! Zhozey!*" Olya is running across the yard, through the fence, Lydia behind her, yapping. "*Dym idet!*"

Yeah, I know about the smoke. But I'm heartened to see Olya in her housedress, her *valenki*, her *shapka*, and a ragged coat wrapped around her, running next door to save our lives.

She wraps me in a hug. "*Vy v spokoynyy?*"

"Yes, we're safe," I answer in Russian.

I notice Vasilley has also climbed through the fence. He looks like Chase and Nathan—icy eyebrows and beard, his fur hat covered in snow. "Was there a fire?"

Chase shakes his head, briefs him.

I don't look at Vasilley, because I know I'm getting one of those "stupid American woman" looks.

Let's be nice to the foreign girl who didn't grow up with a coal stove.

"Why didn't you wait for me?" Chase asks me in English, dialing his voice low.

"Because I didn't know when you were coming back." Or *if* he was coming back. Or what condition he'd be in when he came back. "And it was getting cold in the house."

He wears another stricken look. "I should have never brought you here. This is all my fault. I should have never left you alone."

I'm not sure why, but everything inside me tightens. Begins to burn.

"*Poydem,*" Olya says, taking Justin from Chase's arms.

I'm not sure where I'm supposed to follow her to, but

anywhere is better than here. "Welcome home," I snap as I follow Olya back through the fence.

Coal smoke is black. I know this because it now embeds my curtains, my bed sheets, my walls, my carpet, and my pores. And because it's about negative two hundred outside, I can't wash anything.

Including myself. Because even my pots are covered in coal smoke, and I can't get the water hot enough to wash it off without also taking off my skin.

Yeah, it's been a cold, silent, and sooty week.

Nathan has brought new plastic sheeting from Khabarovsk, and Chase is out trying to locate nails with Vasilley.

Now, raise your hand if you would have known *not* to put coal dust in the stove. Yeah, thought so. Which means I don't deserve to be treated like a two-year-old. However, I do take back that comment about surviving Siberia. It is harder than I thought.

I thump the pot of hot water down on the center of the table.

"He blames himself, you know." Nathan picks up the teapot. Pours water into a cup already armed with a teabag. "Not only for being late, but also for bringing you here in the first place."

I really have nothing to say to that. Because, in a way, he's right. But more than that, those words rake against me. I'm not exactly helpless.

Really, I'm not.

"But in truth, it's my fault."

I raise an eyebrow at Nathan. Why, did he bring us here? If we're going to blame someone, maybe we should blame God.

Although Nathan has his angelic moments, I'm pretty sure he's not God.

"How's that?" I pour water into my cup, sit down. Chloe and Justin are at *detskiy sad*, a fact I now welcome, knowing they'll be warm and fed.

"Vasilley wanted to know why I was here, which led to a discussion about spiritual beliefs. We talked late into the night and overslept a bit the next morning, and the storm was closing in. We had to wait until it passed before we could pack up. Chase drove us crazy—he made us leave at the first sign of daylight."

Oh.

"Did Chase mention that Vasilley gave his life to Jesus? He became a Christian out there on our hunting trip."

Nathan is smiling, giving me a look that I've never seen before. "He's the first man in Bursk to get saved." He touches my forearm. "And that, Josey, I blame on you."

His words make me feel warm, right to the center of my cold soul. Because I'm feeling pretty unworthy, unhumble, ungentle, impatient, and the furthest thing from peace-making these days. "Why?" I ask, needing more.

I'm such a glutton for words of affirmation.

"Because if you hadn't said yes to Chase, he would never have come here. And it's because he came, and told Anton to sell the trees—"

"He didn't tell—"

"—and then humbly drank vodka with Vasilley, and was willing to shoulder that blame for the trees, that he got invited hunting. And then it's because you were afraid of Chase getting hurt that you made me invite myself. And . . . " He shrugs. "See, your fault."

My fault. There are certain things I'm willing to take the blame for. Vasilley's redemption is definitely in that category.

Not forgetting, of course, that it is God who draws man (and woman!) to Him. But I got to be a part of it. I'm on the team.

"By the way, you might want to ask Chase about that night at Vasilley's. He wasn't drinking."

I eye Nathan. "I saw the vodka go down. Shot glass after shot glass."

"Not to disgust you or anything, but did you also see him spit it back out, into his juice?"

Okay, a little disgusted. But as I rewind those events in my memory, I see Chase taking a drink of prune *sok* after every shot.

Ew. But, yay Chase!

"How do you know that?"

Nathan takes a sip of his tea. "I had to level with him to get him to invite me on the trip."

Oh. No. "Nathan, then he knows that I—"

"Didn't trust me?" Chase stands at the door. He's carrying a hammer and a handful of nails. I look up, meet his eyes. Swallow.

"Chase—"

"Save it." He comes inside, grabs the plastic. Nathan squeezes my arm and gets up to help him.

I watch them struggle to pin up the plastic as they pound in the nails, creating a barrier between us and the cold.

Or perhaps, locking in the cold that's seeped into our lives.

"I'm going next door," I say, hoping for a reaction.

Nathan nods. Chase the Ice Cube says nothing.

I garb up, slip through the opening in the fence, wave to Lydia, who is tied up to the outhouse and instantly hysterical, and knock on Olya's back door. The smell of something delicious baking filters through, pulls me inside.

"Yum," I say, and that's a word that translates easily. "What are you making?"

"*Pirog*," she says. Pie.

Actually, it's more of a bread with stuffing inside, like eggs or salmon. "*Kakiye?*" I ask. What kind?

"Potato pie—Vasilley's favorite."

Olya looks good today—her hair back in a high bun, wearing a sweater and pants instead of her usual housecoat. And is that a touch of makeup?

"Where's Vasilley?"

"At the post office. Sending a letter." She doesn't mention who it's to, but I can guess. To Moscow.

To her daughter.

Blame me, blame me! I shed my coat, my boots. I don't care that Chase is hurt. Okay, a little, but how was I supposed to know about his little ploy?

If anyone says something like "a lifetime of knowing Chase," then someone is getting hurt.

Shoot. I didn't mean to hurt him.

But what about him trusting *me*? Why didn't he tell me that he wasn't getting snockered with Vasilley, that he had a plan? He could have even told me at the table—it's not like our hosts would have understood his English all of a sudden. Then again, Chase is ultra-aware how rude it is to speak English in front of non-English speakers. Personally, I think we need all the help we can get.

Olya pulls the pie from the oven and sets it on the table, covers it with a towel. Then she comes over and touches my hair.

That is my personal space there, Olya. Russians really aren't into personal space—not in Siberia or Moscow or anywhere else.

"*Poydem k banya*," she says.

It's not until she grabs a couple towels and a bag of shampoo that I get it. She's noticed the buildup of grease and coal dust that's got my hair glued to my head.

"Oh, no, Olya, I can't—"

But she's got me in a Russian armlock.

What am I going to do—go home?

I'm not a girl who usually likes to get naked in front of other people. Yes, okay, there was that skinny-dipping incident as a senior, but that was a dare.

And you all know what happens when I'm dared to do something.

Which is probably how Olya gets me into a steam room, naked, with twelve other women.

I did put up a fight, however. I had a flashback to when I was twelve and forced to change clothes in front of the girls on the swim team. I excelled in dressing underneath my towel.

I should have recognized the public bathhouse by the word *banya* (as in "bath") written across the door, but of course, I was looking for something like a Japanese spa, not a log cabin. The building looked like the town hall. A main entry door led to a long hall of doors. But once inside, we veered appropriately into the *zhenshchiny*, or women's, section. Inside, a locker room made of cement and lined with rough benches managed to capture every gulag nightmare and trap the Siberian deep freeze.

"You don't seriously expect me to take my clothes off," I said, hoping to add levity to the moment. Apparently, Olya didn't share my humor. She proceeded to strip.

I wanted to yell "Stop, stop, my eyes aren't ready!" But of course, before I could get the words out, she'd turned me around and started shucking off my clothes.

Again . . . uh, personal space?

"You have to get naked if you want to get clean."

Okay, Dalai Lama, I got it.

I took over and utilized my dormant towel abilities, showing only the barest of skin before I wrapped a towel around me.

Alas, it would be a short-lived covering. Nevertheless, I clung to hope as I hung my belongings on a hook, then followed Olya.

There is a *banya* procedure, not unlike that of washing clothes. First is the steam room, where a gal sweats off the grime of the day (or last five months). Then, the cold plunge, and finally, the showers.

Couldn't I just skip straight to the showers?

I entered the steam room to find . . . well, naked women. I was so, *so* not ready for this. Where to look? Horror rose inside me when Olya reached over and yanked off my towel.

Ah. I was again twelve as I frantically tried to cover places.

And then I realized . . . I've had babies.

In Russia.

Probably this is a billion times less humiliating.

Besides, the sauna room is dark and . . . hot. Really hot. I stood there, the heat seeping into my pores, finding those frozen bones. I found a spot on a bench and sat down, keeping my head down.

Now, ten minutes later, I know I just might be in heaven. Heat—precious, delicious heat. I'm just starting to listen to the chatter of the women around me.

Someone greets Olya.

And then me. I raise my hand. Close my eyes. Focus on the heat.

"Can you believe that Sophia was going to betray Ken with that guy C.C.?"

Ah, the update on *Santa Barbara*. I sigh, breathing in the hot air, nearly crying with the warmth of it.

"Ken deserves it. He is terrible to her—ignores her, and now he's left, and I'll bet he cheats on her again. Too bad she felt too guilty to go through with it."

"I wouldn't. I'd leave him."

I glance up, surprised at the venom in the voice. My eyes have adjusted, and through the haze and the curtain of my hair, I see . . . Ulia.

Oh no.

"Sophia loves Ken, even if he is bad to her," another voice says. "She should stay with him. They have history."

"Sophia could be happy with C.C. C.C. listens to her. Especially after everything she's been through. He wants her to be happy." There is some heat in Ulia's voice.

Uh-oh. Methinks we're not talking about Ken and Sophia anymore.

"Maybe Ken just needs to appreciate her. Maybe Ken needs to notice that he's losing her."

A woman gets up, walks out. A whoosh of cold air rushes in. But Ulia's words sink in. Yeah. Maybe Ken just needs to appreciate her and all she does. Maybe Ken is a big lout.

"I think Sophia should leave him and be happy with C.C.," Ulia says, getting up. "She needs to think about what's best for her." Ulia exits also, and I climb up to the highest bench, sit in the back. Sweat pours down my face, drips off my chin. It's hard to breathe, so I head toward the door.

Olya meets me there. "Time for the cold plunge," she says. I am instantly afraid. (C'mon, wouldn't you be too? Cold? Plunge?)

The cold plunge takes my breath away, because it's exactly as it's advertised—a pool of freezing water. Olya jumps in and then grabs my hand and pulls me in too.

My breath is gone, and a thousand icicles pierce my skin. "Yow!" I scream, and Olya laughs as she climbs out. "Now the shower."

Ah, the shower. I lather my hair, three times. Use conditioner. I feel like singing. *I love the banya. I love the banya.*

Why didn't I do this sooner?

"Ready for round two?" Olya asks.

If it includes more heat, I'm all over it.

We do four rounds, and by the time we're finished, I'm a noodle. A clean, happy, holding-lots-of-Bursk-secrets noodle.

I've just discovered the Russian version of bunco night.

And I think Ulia is going to leave Anton.

happy valewomen’s day

. . .

When I first moved to Russia, the desserts enthralled me. Beautiful creations drizzled with chocolate or frosted with glaze, delicate confectionaries that tantalized from kiosk windows. I remember, with not a little sadness, the day I succumbed to the call of these desserts, purchasing a sugar cookie with a floral design, almost too pretty to eat. The sky was high and blue, fragrant with autumn, the wind swirling leaves at my feet. I bit into the cookie . . .

. . . and it was tasteless, like sand. It morphed into glue as I chewed. Then it sucked every bit of moisture from my salivary glands, and my mouth turned into the Sahara. Apparently, the city sugar-cookie factory had run out of sugar and made the cookies anyway. I coughed and stumbled to a nearby beverage kiosk and purchased the first liquid I found, which turned out to be a glass of Kvas, a nonalcoholic beer-tasting drink made from fermented black bread.

Yes, I said fermented black bread.

I’m still in recovery. Thus, when Olya appears at my door with a metal mold and a can of sweetened condensed milk, announcing that we're going to make Russian cookies, I'm leery.

Olya's been in spirits unseen before, and I'm wanting to get to the bottom of all this. So I let her in.

Roll up my sleeves.

She takes down a pot from the shelf and fills it with water. Puts it on the stove. Peels the label off the sweetened condensed milk and puts the can in the pot. The water covers the top.

"What are you doing?"

She gives me a cryptic smile. Turns the burner on high.

"That's going to . . . " I search for the word *explode* and come up blank. "Boom!" I accentuate with the appropriate accompanying hand gestures.

She laughs and shakes her head.

O-kay.

We make a dough that resembles a tea cake—butter, flour, walnuts, honey (where I might have used vanilla). She forms it into balls and smashes them into the mold. I check the can. It's boiling nicely, although its texture still seems hard.

One needs to have a sense of humor in Russia. Especially when you're cooking potentially explosive materials.

She turns on a burner and holds the mold over the flame like she's roasting marshmallows. Clearly, I'm the only one afraid of burning the house down.

"What are we making?"

"*Oreshki.*"

Nuts. I take a pot out, fill it, and put on water for tea. Check the can. Still boiling.

I take down two cups and place them on the table. I notice that the bucket under the sink needs emptying. At least the cold doesn't take my breath away when I go outside. Instead, it just seeps into my pores, finds the nooks and crannies where I'm not quite warm, and bites. I'm starting to wonder if I'll ever see spring again.

Maybe I'm just overreacting to the cold chill from Chase's side of the bed.

I did, after all, apologize. And I saw the old Chase in the way his eyes softened, the way he reached out and caressed my cheek. "There's nothing to forgive," he said. "You were trying to help."

I *was* trying to help. We all know that, right?

Olya has taken the mold off the burner and lays it aside to cool. The teapot whistles, and I pour water into our mugs, hand her a sugar cube. She surprises me by filling her saucer and drenching the cube with tea. Apparently, she knows that trick too.

I'm saturating my own cube when she says, "What did Chase do to Vasilley?" She puts down her cup, and I know she means this in a good way, because she's smiling.

Hmm. "What do you mean?"

"He's better. Calmer. Doesn't drink as much." She leans back, and I notice she is looking better these days. With a smile that touches her eyes. I didn't expect their problems to change overnight with the news of Vasilley's salvation, but maybe my expectations were too low.

"What did he tell you?"

Olya grows a little red at this, looks down at her cup. Oh, Olya, we've come so far. Don't retreat now. I wait for it.

"He said he realized what a terrible man he'd been. And that he found forgiveness."

I cover my hand with hers. She looks up at me, and her eyes glisten. "He is a better man, every day. Nathan gave him a Bible. And visits us. He is teaching Vasilley about Jesus."

I didn't know that, but warmth swells inside me at Nathan and his depth. And for Chase, that he persevered and even tasted vodka so he could earn Vasilley's trust. I should have trusted Chase. I know that now.

"Is this why Vasilley is different?"

It's why I should be different too. "Yes. Imagine you are Vasilley. He knows he's hurt you, and others. If God were to judge Vasilley based on his past, do you think he'd let Vasilley into heaven?"

She makes a face, shakes her head.

"But Vasilley's been forgiven by God. He's been given a second chance to live this life on earth, and because of God's forgiveness, he'll live forever in eternity. I suppose that's what is making the difference in his life."

The can starts to bang against the pot. I get up to turn down the heat, but she stops me. "Let it boil. It needs to boil to become a sweet filling."

She takes a towel, lays it out on the table, then takes the hot pads and dumps the shells from the mold. Golden brown, they look like hollow walnut halves.

"I want to be a better wife too," Olya says as she sits down, and this time she meets my eyes. "Can you tell me how?"

I'm not sure . . . because while there are days that I've thought I had that job nailed, I'm not so sure now.

"I know that being a wife is more than just following your husband across Russia," I say, more to myself than Olya. "It's about forgiving and being patient and gentle and learning how to make peace. But I know that I can't do that without help. God's help."

She's looking at me hard, and I'm trying to find the right words. "I know life hasn't been kind to you, Olya. And I know this is going to sound too easy, but God loves you. You know how you feel about being apart from Albena? That's how God feels about being apart from you. But you can have a second chance too, just like Vasilley."

She says nothing, and we watch as steam rises from the boiling pot, gathers on the ceiling, dissipates. The room is warm, almost too hot.

Finally she gets up, and using tongs, takes the can from the pot. She sets it on the counter to cool.

"Vasilley and I have been married ten years," she says, her back to me. She takes a can opener and gets the lid off the can. "I think it's time for a second chance."

The milk has thickened into a light brown caramel and smells sweet, like boiled sugar. She takes a walnut half and, using a spoon, fills the hollow with caramel. She fills another half and then puts the two halves together.

"Boiled sweetened condensed milk makes caramel?" I hand her a plate, and she puts the cookie on it before handing me the spoon.

I take it and fill my own nut cookies, delighted with the sweetness inside the hard cookie crust.

"Do you want me to take these to the post office?" Olya has a box full of orders, packaged up. The ladies are barely keeping up with demand, but the happy group has full coffers and is trying to decide what to do with their cash.

Most importantly, Olya nearly has enough for her tickets to and from Moscow.

"Yes, thank you," I say. Olya is smiling as she leaves the community center, her arms full of goodies.

I leave right behind her, going back to the house before I return to the *detskiy sad*. The smell of chicken soup cooling on the stove is evidence that Nathan has been here, and it's confirmed by his duffel in the entryway. He must be here for his weekly Bible study with Vasilley. After my chat with Olya, even I've noticed the change in her husband. For example, the way he helps her milk the cow. I know, but still, nothing says "I love you" like holding old Bessie while your wife milks her, and then carrying the milk inside.

As for me, I am looking forward to Nathan's visits more and more.

At least he talks to me.

Chase drinks his tea and listens to us.

I've always loved Chase's ability to fit in, to listen before he talks, to analyze his role in a new society, to blend. Too many people think Chase is Russian.

What plagues me is exactly this blend-in ability, however. I know that Chase managed to do an end run around Vasilley and his birthday imbibing, but that trick can only work so many times. And worse, what if Chase adopts the male mindset of Bursk?

It certainly feels like he's turned into Ken. Not Barbie Ken, but Santa Barbie Ken, the One Who Ignores His Woman.

By the way, Sophia was right. Ken *was* cheating on her, and she should have left him, because she can be happy with C.C., who adores her. But no, she has to pack her bags and fly off to surprise Ken. And she's going to be bitterly disappointed because he doesn't love her. Maybe he never did! He doesn't see how she felt betrayed, how he's losing her—

So I'm getting my weekly updates from the Banya Girls. At least Ulia hasn't left Anton yet, and although I've never been so clean in my life, I feel like a dirty little spy. A naked, double-crossing secret agent. Because all this information I hold would be invaluable to Chase and his study, not to mention his friendships. I think a guy would like to know if his wife were about to leave, so he could fix things, don't you?

Or maybe that's meddling . . .

I get so confused about these things.

By the way, Chase sailed right by Valentine's Day without a nod.

Okay! Yes, I forgot it too. It's not like they celebrate it here in

Russia, or at least in Bursk. Everyone's just trying to keep warm. (Although, one would think it would be a mandatory holiday for exactly that reason.)

So I'll cut Chase some slack.

Especially as I enter the house and notice the bouquet of flowers sitting on the table. Roses of all colors, wrapped in baby's breath. Oh, Chase! He remembered the International Day for Women!

Not sure where Chase tracked those down, but then again, this is the man who brought home a washing machine for Christmas.

I breathe in the smell, let it fill my cold, nearly iced-over senses. I touch one of the flowers. It's smooth and soft, and silly tears prick my eyes. Of course Chase and I are going to be just fine. I don't know why I worried. Even though I jumped to conclusions, he knows I'm on his side.

After all, I *am* here in Siberia.

And right now, Siberia seems to be in the clutches of a deep freeze. Here I thought the ice would break at the beginning of March.

Instead, I got a blizzard. What is the saying—in like a lion, out like a lamb? What about in like a wildebeest?

Thankfully, life doesn't stop in Siberia when the mercury freezes over. The people trudge on and find celebration in any moment. Hence, the all-village attendance of our *detskiy sad*'s annual Women's Day celebration. I bundle up again, smell the flowers one last time, and head out to the community center.

The place is humming with conversation. Olya and I spent most of the morning packing away our supplies, labeling boxes, and hauling chairs for the afternoon program by the kindergarten and grade school. I find a seat.

"Oh, look at that Chloe." Nathan sits down next to me. I'm wearing my parka and, yes, finally, the Cossack boots. I can't believe I've been cold-pressed into wearing the furry boots out in public. On Women's Day, no less.

I'm an embarrassment to fashionable females around the globe.

On the bright side, under all this padding, no one would really know that I'm a woman. More of a thing. A blue, puffy thing in fuzzy footwear.

I guess that thought should depress me.

"I know, isn't she adorable?" I wave to my daughter, who is wearing the traditional brightly colored dress of a Nanai native. Under her costume, she's also wearing three layers of snow clothes, boots, and mittens, but the costumes are designed to be large.

And her hair has grown enough to sprout tiny high pigtails above her headband.

She waves at me as the teachers line the students up to do a little dance. Maya sees her wave and follows with a wave of her own. She seems different lately. She smiles when I greet her in the yard.

Justin is also in line, fiddling with his shirt—a silver and blue pullover that goes over his own snow attire. He isn't smiling.

He told me yesterday that boys aren't supposed to dance. Thank you for that, Chase.

"Where's Chase?" Nathan asks.

Yeah, that's a good question. I scan the room. I don't see Olya or Vasilley, of course, but there's Ulia sitting in the front row, and a few other ladies from Bible study. I can't look at Ulia without feeling like I'm an accomplice in her crime.

"Chase?" He's probably out skinning fish with his teeth. Or something.

Uh-oh, I think I might have said all that out loud, with the way Nathan is looking at me. "He'll be here," I add.

The music starts, and my little Nanai children skip in a circle, clapping and singing with their classmates.

"What are they saying?" I ask Nathan.

"I don't know. It's traditional Nanai. But probably something about Mom and spring and fertility."

Perfect.

Justin isn't smiling, and he keeps kicking the boy in front of him. Apparently, Chase and Justin are correct about the nondancing thing.

Chloe, however, is twirling, watching her skirt fly out. Oops, there she falls. Oy, there goes the entire circle . . .

Just when should a mother get involved? Pull her child out of a mass of bodies?

"You want me to get them?" Nathan asks as other mothers rise.

I sit there in silence, grimacing. See, this is part of motherhood—dealing with your child's foibles.

"By the way, I stopped by the house," Nathan says. "I went ahead and put your flowers in water."

I glance at him. He's giving me the strangest look. Like, almost . . . embarrassed. And pleased.

Like how a man might look if he gave a girl flowers.

Oh. No.

"Did you . . . are the roses from . . . "

"They were on sale in Khabarovsk. I thought you needed something friendly to put a dent in these gray days. I had to wrap them inside my coat to keep them from freezing on the snowmobile ride north. I wanted to thank you for letting me sleep on your sofa and invade your kitchen."

I dredge up a smile.

But inside, everything turns just a little colder.

"What's the matter, Josey?" Nathan's smile is gone, and he's frowning.

"Nothing." But by the catch in my voice, it doesn't sound like nothing. I try and turn the wattage on my smile brighter.

I probably look like a hyena.

Nathan isn't buying it.

I've got to come up with something. So I lower my voice and keep my eyes away and blurt out the first thing that comes to my mind.

"I think Ulia is going to leave Anton."

See, I'd make a horrible spy. One hint of bright lights and I'd spill all.

Nathan lowers his voice. (He'd make a better spy than me.) "What?"

"I'm not sure, but the way she's been talking . . . "

Now I feel sick, like the time I ratted out H for breaking the window at the high school during our girl scout meeting.

"Maybe I'm wrong."

Nathan scoots his arm around me, turns toward me, his face tight with concern. "What makes you think this?"

Umm . . . okay, the way she agrees with Sophia and C.C., and, oh boy, never mind.

"I'm probably jumping to conclusions. *Banya* does make a girl a little thickheaded."

Nathan isn't appeased, though. "The last thing this village needs is the mayor's wife leaving him. Who knows what that kind of behavior will start?"

Oh.

"You'll tell me if you hear anything. I could talk to Ulia or Anton—"

"No, are you kidding?" The effect of my shrill voice laced with panic is betrayed on his face. I quiet it to a stage whisper. "That's the last thing he needs to hear. He's already mad at me. Won't talk to me. Wait until I know for sure, and then we'll tell him." Hey, not only is *banya* at stake, but let's remember that I'm dependent on Anton's benevolence to keep our little village business running. No need to rush things or make a mountain out of a molehill.

Besides, see, Sophia is staying with Ken, for now. Maybe things will turn out all right.

On stage, Chloe has untangled herself, and the teachers are helping the children down from the stage. Justin, however, is still wrestling with one of the boys.

Chloe is streaking toward us. I hold out my arms.

"Daddy!" She yells and barrels past me.

I turn.

Chase is sitting behind us. He doesn't look at me as he scoops up Chloe. But as he pulls her tight, he closes his eyes.

As if he might be in pain.

I love this Siberian village at night.

Did I actually say that? Use the word *love?* Okay, I did. I've fallen for Bursk the way one might fall for a mangy puppy with sad eyes, or a worn-out teddy bear. Bursk does have its charm. Take, for example, the sight of the stars blinking against a velvet black sky, undiminished by city lights. Or the pastoral elegance of snow piled up along a faded blue fence, trampled only by booted feet. A dog, face marked by the black mask of a husky, trots out from a yard, looks at me, and heads down the street. Snow drifts lazily from the sky and, like frosting, blankets the roofs, the yards, the expanse beyond the centrifuge of houses.

The village is quiet at this time of day, right before dinner, when light pushes through the cracks in the shutters and the smell of coal smoke hints at stoked furnaces. A cow lows, waiting for relief. I relish the walk home from the community center, alive with the excitement of our flourishing business. We have stayed overtime three nights in a row now to complete orders for Mother's Day, which is still nearly six weeks away. My early eBay reminders are paying off.

My feet squeak on the fresh snow, and I stick my mittened hands in my pockets, digging my nose into my wool scarf. I'm warm, despite the winds, because I now dress like I'm an arctic explorer.

Light is also on at our house, fuzzy yellow as it pushes against the plastic.

I open the door and am greeted with the smell of soup—perhaps chicken—simmering on the stove. Hanging my coat on the hook and unlacing my boots, I slip into wool slippers and enter the house.

I'm not surprised to see Nathan sitting at the table with Chase.

I am, however, taken aback at what they're up to. They have a bowl of dough before them, and flour covers the table. Chase has a small rolling pin and is rolling out little circles the size of a biscuit. Nathan is filling them with meat, pinching them along the edge, then curling them to touch corners.

It's a work of art.

"What are you doing, and please tell me those are edible."

"Making *pelmeni*, for the soup," Nathan says, as if that should have been obvious. He looks up and smiles though. "It's something I just learned in Khabarovsk, from my Russian landlord. Like a meat-filled dumpling. It's delicious in chicken soup."

Chase's reception isn't as warm. "You're late. I was getting worried."

I'm going to translate that to "I missed you and didn't want anything bad to happen to you. Which makes me sort of irritable and is a disguise for how much I love you."

I think every marriage could use some creative translation now and again, don't you?

"Can I help?" I ask as Chloe runs to me and hugs my leg. Justin rolls off the sofa, where he's watching a Russian cartoon, and jumps at me.

"Sure. You can roll out dough," Chase says as he scoots over. "I'll help Nathan make the *pelmeni*."

I can do that, probably. My first few are misshapen disks, but after a few, I start to get the hang of it.

I'm mesmerized watching Chase. He takes the dough, plops in the meat, closes it with the other hand, and deftly twists it into a ball. I always knew he was magic in the kitchen.

Only, it's not his artform I'm marveling at.

It's his speed.

And the fact that Nathan has picked up his game and is matching it.

Chase is now moving nearly as fast as I am rolling out the dough. Nathan grabs one from my hand, and Chase gives him a dark look.

"That was mine."

"She handed it to me."

"No, she didn't. You leaped over me to get it. It's not yours."

"Why would I do that?"

Chase says nothing, but I see his jaw grinding.

"I'll go faster," I say. "I can keep up with both of you."

"No!" they both bark.

O-kay . . .

"Maybe I'll just add this to the soup," Chase says, picking up the tray of dumplings.

"It's not ready yet. It has to be boiling. Don't rush it."

"It's ready. Don't worry, it'll be fine."

"You're going to turn them to mush, wreck the entire supper."

Chase dumps the *pelmeni* into the pot. “It's my soup. Make your own.”

He chucks the board into the sink and walks away.

Oh.

Nathan looks at me, something on his face I can't read. Then he puts down the piece of dough he's been folding. “I'm going to go out,” he says, and gives me a tight smile.

I'm left alone in the kitchen with flour, half a bowl of dough, and raw, ground chicken.

Perfect.

My *pelmeni* don't exactly look like Chase's or Nathan's, but I finish a half hour later and put the board of little dumplings out in the entryway (aka freezer).

I ladle out soup for the kids. Nathan was right—the dumplings are mushy.

Chase is sitting on the bed in the dark, peeling flour and dough off his hands when I enter.

“Hey,” I say, sitting down on the bed. “Good soup.” (Liar, liar, but I'm using the adjective *good* in the sense that he made it for us and is taking care of us, which is good. And translates, thus, to good soup. So I'm not lying, if you take a step back and work with me here.)

He leans his head back against the wall. Sighs. In the darkness, I see the fatigue on his face. “I think I'm beginning to understand why Siberian men feel overwhelmed.”

Pelmeni did that? In his voice I also hear disappointment. Frustration.

“I totally forgot Women's Day,” he says, his eyes now cutting to mine. “I'm sorry.”

My smile comes easily. “I forgive you.”

“You shouldn't. You should be really angry. You should probably not talk to me, for at least a month or two.”

Uh . . . okay. I reach out to take his hand, but he pulls it away.

"What are we doing here anyway, G.I.?"

I'm sitting in the dark, brushing dough off my sheets.

Oh, perhaps he meant something bigger. "Helping?"

"Yeah, but how?" He leans forward, takes my hand. "How?"

I open my mouth to speak, but I have no words, because I have no answer. I have all sorts of cosmic platitudes, but none of them seem right. Because we're helping their economic base? We're teaching them how to use eBay? We're putting a dent in their collective social depression?

"Nathan has had more of an impact than I ever hope to." Chase is looking at me now, something strange in his eyes. "Maybe he's right. Maybe you *would* make a good pastor's wife."

Except, Chase, you're not a pastor. I'm frowning at his words when he smiles. I see it's forced, and it makes my stomach hurt.

"I have to go to Moscow next week for a six-month recap to Voices International."

Bagels. I get bagels! I get to see Maggie! Okay, maybe my priorities need a little adjusting. But I get bagels! I flip on the light.

Chase is wearing a look I've seen before. It's more of a grimace than a smile, and last time he wore it, I confronted him about his ambush with Marc that got me to Siberia.

Yeah, *that* look. Everything inside me tightens.

"What?"

"They only sent one ticket."

Of course they did. "That's okay."

Chase, however, leans forward, takes my hand again. His is sticky. "No, it's not." He stares at me then, and suddenly gets up, pulling me off the bed with him.

"Is Nathan still here?"

I shake my head.

"I'll be right back."

He pulls off his apron, wads it into a ball, and chucks it into the kitchen on his way outside. In a moment, he's back with Olya, who's grinning.

What's going on?

Chase kisses me, grabs my hands, and pulls me through the house. "Come with me. I want to show you something."

I glance at the kids, but Olya is already sitting with them, singing them a little song. Practicing for when Albena returns, I hope.

We bundle up and head outside. Night has fallen. Chase turns toward the river side of the village.

"Where are we going?"

He takes my hand, or rather, my lump, because it's hard to hold hands in mittens. But we shuffle and slide together down the street. It is getting warmer out, the days almost above freezing. Spring could be fighting for purchase.

I hear a sound in the distance, something like wind chimes, I suppose. Overhead, the sky is perfect and clear, a million stars winking at us. There is little wind, and in the distance, I hear a village dog howl.

The tinkling sound continues, a crackling, almost. I glance at Chase, and he's wearing a tiny grin but refuses to look at me.

"What is that?"

"Don't rush it," he says, but he pulls me faster.

We reach the dip in the land the village calls the harbor. The snow is caked along the shore, and the moon glints off a thousand pieces of ice that move with the rhythm of the awakening water. The noise now takes up space, and I have to raise my voice to be heard above it. "What is that?"

"Close your eyes." Chase turns to me. "Close them, G.I."

I do, and his arms go around my waist, his hands in the pockets of my coat, pulling me to him. His breath is in my ear. "What do you hear?"

"I don't know—"

"Shh. Think. What does that sound like?"

I lean my head against his chest. Let the sound envelop me, slide through me. Raindrops on glass. Or maybe glasses at a party, clinking.

"How about the railroad? Cars going past, click, click, click."

I listen, and yes, I hear it now. The railroad tracks, like the ones near his house in Gull Lake. I nod and open my eyes. "Yes."

"It's the ice, flowing over itself." Chase finds my eyes. "The first time I heard it, you know what I thought of?"

It's a question I haven't a clue how to answer.

"That time we walked home from school. Remember? I wanted to walk home on the railroad tracks, and you were scared, but I talked you into it."

I start to smile. Yes, I would have done anything for Chase in fourth grade. And fifth. And sixth . . .

"And then the train started to come, and I got scared." He is holding my scarf now, his face close to mine. "You grabbed my hand and pulled me off the tracks, and we hid on the side until it passed."

"I didn't know you were scared."

"I was terrified. But I couldn't tell you that." He grins. "But I knew, that day, that I couldn't ever let you go. I held on to your hand and knew I loved you."

The wind catches my eyes, and they water a little. "It only took you fifteen years to tell me."

He shakes his head. "I've been trying to tell you ever since."

Oh. Well.

He thumbs away a tear that escapes down my cheek. "But I'm not doing a very good job lately."

"Chase—"

"No, listen. I'm so sorry I missed Women's Day. And Valentine's Day. And that I scared you with Vasilley and my hunting trip. I'm sorry that I put you in the middle of nowhere, without plumbing."

"I really don't care about the plumbing anymore." I smile up at him.

He doesn't smile back. "I do. And I know you miss Gull Lake." He looks out at the river.

I lean my head against his chest, and his arms go around me. "It really does sound like the tracks. Like home."

We stand there a long while, watching the moon and stars turn the dark swath of river into a tray of gems.

"I did something. I hope it's okay."

I lean back and see a sparkle light in his eyes. I'm almost afraid to ask.

"I asked H to come and visit you. You said she wanted to, so I emailed her. She's going to keep you company while I'm in Moscow. I can't bring you to Gull Lake. But maybe I can bring Gull Lake to you."

He's grinning now, and it's shy and cute and perfect. "Happy ValeWomen's Day."

Oh, Chase. I stand on my toes and kiss him. Really kiss him.

He's smiling when I pull away. "I did a good thing?"

"You did." I pat his chest, right over his thumping heart. "You did real good."

h

. . .

H AND I BECAME FRIENDS IN SIXTH GRADE WHEN HER FATHER took over as head coach of the Gull Lake Gulls. She was determined to not ever date a football player.

I lived for the whole enchilada.

Okay, I admit it, I was a football player groupie. I sat on the sidelines and watched practice. Memorized numbers (as in jerseys, not plays).

Mostly, however, I watched Chase. He started at halfback, moved to fullback, and when he began catching the ball on a regular basis, became an all-state wide receiver.

H, on the other hand, was an artist. She spent her time after school in band practice, and I'm not talking marching band. She put together her first garage band at the age of ten, by thirteen was writing her own songs, and by fifteen had gone on the road twice for summer gigs at local fairs.

H lives to play music. And not just the punk music she loves (and I don't understand), but nearly anything. Case in point—she accompanied our classical choir on the piano, punk hairstyle and all.

So I understand as she sits at my kitchen table, whining

about Rex and his decree that she should hang up her guitar and start "acting like a married woman."

"Jon Bon Jovi is married. Does he have to give up his life?"

I still can't wrap my mind around the fact that my friend is here, in the middle of Siberia. Chase left two days ago, and Nathan met H yesterday in Khabarovsk and ferried her up to Bursk on the now running boats.

She looks good, too. I can't believe I haven't seen her for three years. Last time, she had purple hair—or was it orange? —and was walking down the aisle with said oppressing husband. I had just given birth to the twins and was hoping my pregnancy weight would mysteriously vanish.

Things haven't changed much, apparently, because she still has purple hair (although now the ends are tinged with a fetching midnight black, and she's gotten another piercing, right above her eye), and let's not talk about that pregnancy weight, shall we?

"He can't expect me to just surrender everything I am for him, can he?"

I'm probably not the best person to answer that, given that I'm pumping water to add to my above-the-sink holding chamber. "Does he want you to stop playing altogether?"

"No. But he has a job teaching band at the high school and wants us to limit our gigs to the weekends—in town."

I expected Chloe and Justin, having never seen anyone with purple hair, to shrink behind me when they met H. But that thing they say about children seeing past outside appearances to the heart must be true, because Chloe went right up to her with kitty paws and purred.

Justin waved and said, "*Nu, Pogodi!*"

I translated that very loosely to "He's really glad to meet you." Nathan rolled his eyes, which I returned in kind.

"So, I moved out," H finishes, pouring herself more tea. She's tired, her droopy eyelids evidence of serious jet lag.

"Don't fall asleep," I say, sliding the sugar cubes toward her. "Let me teach you a Siberian trick Nathan showed me." I show her the cube-in-the-saucer treat, and the sugar rush revives her.

"I can't believe you came all the way to Siberia to see me." This is an understatement. It's like when Jasmine came to Moscow (only this is better because I was in labor when Jasmine arrived and couldn't take time to show her how well I surfed the subway or bartered for food at the market). Finally, I get to show someone from back home that I really do have this Russia thing well in hand. Sorta.

"I can't believe you really have an outhouse and a water pump." H leans back just in time for Chloe to crawl over, purr, and climb into her lap. She twirls one of Chloe's pigtails around her finger. "Tell me about this guy who picked me up."

"Nathan? He's a friend of Chase's. He's from South Dakota and is planting a church here in town. I hold the weekly women's Bible study at my house."

"Still doing that Bible thing, huh?"

"Still doing it." I get up, pour water into the bucket above the sink. I splash water onto myself as I pour, and it's so cold it takes away my breath. "The truth is, H, I'd never make it here without God's help."

"He'd better help. He got you into this mess."

Ah, yes, H, my loveable agnostic.

"There's a verse in James that says that when we go through trials, our faith is refined. Like, all the waste and everything fake is burned off. I've heard that Siberia brings out the best and the worst in people." I am remembering, suddenly, the sweetened condensed milk. "I'd like to hope it's made me a better person. And if that's the case, then yes, I'll be happy to blame God for that."

H is staring at me, an expression I've never seen on her face.

"I don't get you, Josey. Your husband drags you all the way to the end of the world, and you're happy about it?"

Happy? Let's define that for a moment. Happy is . . . what? Seeing Olya and Vasilley walk hand in hand down the street? Smelling soup on the stove when I tromp in from a blizzard? Listening to the crunch of snow as I walk through the village on a crisp, sparkly night?

Hearing Justin and Chloe laugh as they slide down the street on their sled. Snuggling in close to Chase's warm body as the frigid wind buffets our windows.

"Yeah, maybe I'm happy."

"Unca Nate!" Justin springs across the room as I see the door open. He jumps into Nathan's embrace. Nathan grabs him up, puts him on his hip.

"Hope I'm not too late to help with dinner." He holds up a bag of frozen chicken thighs and leg quarters.

Oh yeah, right. Still, I appreciate his implication that I have anything to do with food preparation in the house. "No, you're right on time. In fact, why don't you take it for tonight?"

He winks and moves past me as I sit down at the table.

"Bush legs," he says as he pulls them out of the bag. "Named after President Bush One, when he started sending humanitarian aid to Russia."

I'm assuming the trivia is for H, who is watching him with some interest. He pours water into a pot, sets it on the stove to boil. Adds a bouillon cube.

Now, just for the record, I have started to do more cooking. All this watching Chase and Nathan over the past few months has taught me much in the way of culinary skills. I'm now a whiz at peeling potatoes. And opening a can of tomato sauce? I'm a master.

Nathan disappears into the entryway, and I hear him rustle around the potato bin. When we arrived and Chase informed me we had *two* fifty-kilogram bags of potatoes, I thought, what, are we feeding the Vikings' defensive line?

Yeah, we're on our third bag. Ask me how to prepare

potatoes and I have flashbacks of Bubba Gump Shrimp—baked, boiled, fried, mashed . . . I'll be happy if I never see another potato.

Nathan returns, a pile of potatoes cradled in his arms. He dumps them on the table. "Start peeling, soldier."

I giggle and grab a bowl, a potato peeler.

If Russia holds the market on anything, it's potato peelers. It molds into my hand, and I have developed the hand strength of a sixty-year-old babushka. If I *was* planning to eat potatoes again once I got stateside, I would bring this back to America with me.

Nathan sits down opposite me and grabs his own potato. Soon we're racing, and I've piled up naked potatoes on the table.

"When I was a kid, my mother would make potato pancakes on Sundays. I would peel all Saturday afternoon. I think she did it on purpose, to make my hands sore for Sunday, so they'd stay folded." He laughs. I love Nathan's laugh. It's warm and deep.

H is watching me, holding her teacup. "I remember Josey hiding out on Saturdays, when Jasmine and her mom rolled out three billion pecan buns." She quirks an eyebrow.

"I would have rather mowed the lawn than bake." I finish the potatoes and dump them back into the pot for Nathan to wash. "I was never a chef."

"Although you make a mean chocolate chip cookie," Nathan says, picking up the pot. He releases water from the upper chamber and lets it run into the sink. "And you're pretty good at everything else."

His compliment turns my face warm. He's so sweet.

Justin drapes himself over my lap. "I need to go out."

Right. I slide him into a jacket, and we tromp out to the outhouse. The sun is low, but the smell of spring hangs in the air. No longer do my ears hurt or my sinuses sting when I leave the house. The streets are turning muddy. And I smell a freshness, a new life, in the breeze.

Out like a lamb.

H is outside when we finish, leaning against the house, smoking a cigarette. I prod Justin inside and wait for her.

She is wrapped in an army jacket, a purple scarf, and black boots that lace up to her knees—hey, I have a pair of those . . .

"Nathan come here a lot?" she asks, watching the sky.

"About once a week," I say. "He's a great cook."

"Mm-hmm," she says. She takes another draw on her smoke. The wind curls in, lifts my hair, whistles in my ears. Maybe I was wrong about that spring thing.

"I'm not sure I should be taking marriage advice from you," she says, blowing out smoke through her nose.

Now, wait, I never said . . . but her words hurt.

She drops her cigarette, smashing it with her boot. "I think I understand, now, exactly why you're happy in the middle of Siberia."

I'm not sure what I did to make H angry, but she's treating me like the time I asked her if Jeff and she were still going out, and if not, would she mind if I took a shot at him. Offended.

Okay, yes, I broke the universal girlfriend code with that smooth move, but it's not like she had dibs on Chase, so I haven't a clue why she's acting like I've sold her out for a song.

More than that, I've done everything I can to show her a good time. Nathan and I taught her to make *pelmeni*, and we showed her around the village, stopping in at Olya's for some of her delicious plum *pirog*. Yes, I opted out of *banya* (c'mon—it's one thing to get naked with a bunch of Russians, but I'm definitely not going there with my own kind!), but I did spend the afternoon making birchbark boxes with her and *introducing* her to the Banya Girls. Nathan had a delicious pot of tomato borscht waiting when we got home. And one night, we invited Maya over for dinner, Nathan made potato soup, and we spent the night laughing over the foibles of Justin and Chloe and the other munchkins at the preschool. I know we don't live the high life here in Siberia, but we're trying to keep her warm and fed.

So there's no need for the pout fest as we sit outside *detskiy sad*, waiting for the twins to be done with school for the morning.

"How's Lew?"

My party friend, turned football coach, used to be one of H's best pals too.

"He left his wife for the secretary at the school."

Oh.

"And Jasmine? Do you talk to her much?"

"Not since she moved to Minneapolis. She left your parents to run Berglund Acres. There's talk of them selling out."

This news has me around the neck, and I'm trying to breathe.

Apparently H has the heart of an executioner, because she says nothing to soften that blow.

H throws her cigarette down, smashes it into the mud. Spring has arrived in the breath of five short days, and I can even see the smallest of buds tracking down the trees. Birds occasionally sing.

I've gone back to my lace-up Italian boots.

"Sell Berglund Acres?" My voice is barely above a whisper.

H crosses her arms over her chest, watching the kids, her face hard. "Yep. I guess you can't count on anything to last anymore."

I frown at her, but at that moment, Chloe runs up.

"Mommy!" She hugs my legs, and I swoop her up and give her a kiss.

Set her on my lap.

Oh . . . Chloe. "Honey, what happened?" She's wearing her leggings and a pair of winter snow pants, but she's soaked through.

"I go *ah ah!*" She covers her mouth with her hands, her eyes wide, the little drama queen. But this is not good.

"What is *'ah ah'*?" H asks, eying my expression.

"It's Russian for she wet her pants." I put her down, take her hand, and walk over to Maya. Sometimes we chat long enough for me to walk her home, to the community center.

Or occasionally she comes over for tea. She's even hinted that she might be seeing someone, and by the blush, I know it's not the man who left her bleeding and hiding three months ago.

"Chloe had an accident," I say in Russian.

Maya nods. "She doesn't have a change of clothes here."

Of course not, because my daughter hasn't wet her pants in months. "Okay, time to go home." I turn and see H coming toward me.

She, by the way, hasn't let Siberia stand in the way of fashion. She's wearing her high-top boots, a leather jacket that looks like it might be from some 1960s vintage rack, and has painted her lips black.

Yes, we got quite a few looks the first day out on the town.

"Can you hold on to Chloe while I get Justin?" I hand over Chloe.

H smiles down at her. "Did you make naughty in your pants?"

"H! We don't call it naughty. We don't want her to get a complex. She made a mistake, an error, a misjudgment."

"Right." H's smile dims. "Sorry." But I can tell by her tone she doesn't mean it. "Did you error in your pants, sweetie?"

I roll my eyes, turn, and scan the yard. "Do you see Justin anywhere?"

"Mm-hmm."

I glance at H. "Where?"

"Oh, he's the one making a . . . misjudgment with his middle finger at the teacher." She nods toward a group of kids.

Sure enough, in the center is my darling three-year-old.

Giving one of the elderly teachers the bird.

Lovely.

"Now." H turns to me, a sweet smile on her face. "Would we call *that* making naughty?"

"Justin!"

My voice scares every kid on the playground. Maya stares at me, wide-eyed, as I stalk over and grab Justin's hand.

He looks up, terrified.

Perfect. I have a wet daughter, a hoodlum son, and now I'm the Hulk of the play yard.

I walk past H, who regards me with a raised eyebrow.

It's a long, quiet journey home through the mud. The streets are swamps, and the sidewalks, if you can call them that, are trails of mud through patches of matted grass. Every previously hidden empty vodka bottle and newspaper wrapper is now exposed by the receding black snow.

Chloe falls and plasters herself. I haul her up by the arm and drag my two delinquents home.

Where I find Chase in the yard, just getting in from the ferry. He looks refreshed, clean-shaven, his hair soft and conditioned as if he's just spent a week in . . . civilization. Without crabby children and a grumpy what's-her-problem houseguest.

He has a life.

I have a village.

Still, despite the gurgling sense of unfair, I want to cry with relief. I trudge toward him and lay my head on his chest. He throws one arm around me, still holding his satchel.

"Hey, G.I." He kisses the top of my head. I still have a firm grip on the hooligans, who are jumping up and down. "Miss me?"

Desperately. I didn't realize exactly how much until this moment.

"Hey, H. How are we doing?"

H trudges by, shoots me a look. "Naughty. We're all very naughty."

Dear Jasmine,

Hello from Siberia! I hope you're liking your new home in Minneapolis. H was here for a week, and she caught me up on the Gull Lake happenings. Sounds like you and Milton are making quite a go at this *kringle* business.

I never thought I'd be the one to say this . . . but I'm glad H is gone. I can't believe she spent the week angry at me—and I don't even know what I did!

Chase had a great week at Voices International. Apparently, they're thinking of renewing our term.

Please, God, save me from Siberia.

It's not that I don't like it. Really, there are times when I know, without a doubt, that I am supposed to be here. Like yesterday, when Olya came over with a plate of raspberry blini. (By the way, you'd love blini—little flat pancakes, rolled up and filled with jelly, not unlike crepes, but yummier.) She sat down at the table, her brown eyes glowing. And then, she fished out of her pocket . . . airplane tickets. Three of them, to Moscow and back.

She's going to get Albena. And I, Jas, helped. Really helped. Maybe this was the exact reason I was sent to Russia. I don't know. But as we sat in the kitchen and cried, something went through me: a deep whoosh of joy. I wanted to capture that feeling, hold on tight.

I love seeing lives changed.

Nathan—I know I've mentioned him—said that I'd be a great pastor's wife. I can't get the words out of my head.

Sometimes I think I'd like to be a pastor's wife. Except for the fact that Chase . . . isn't a pastor.

But I am hoping that at least I am exhibiting pastor's wife qualities—humility, gentleness, patience, peace.

Even, perhaps, submission.

Chase has been different since returning from Moscow. For one, he's been keeping a journal. I think he must have started it before Moscow, because he's already halfway through it, but still, every night I see him scribbling in it, his brow furrowed. Reminds me of when we shared study hall, and he'd scratch out his English papers. I would normally go through and fix all his spelling errors, but he won't let me near the journal. Okay, yes! I tried. It was lying on the bed, and I was just going to move it, but Chase came up behind me and snatched it out of my hand.

"Not quite ready yet," he said. As if perhaps someday he would be?

Chloe is back to wetting her pants every day. I'm not sure why. Did Amelia ever have a relapse? I'm not even going to tell you what Justin did last week in the play yard. Let me just say that obscene sign language translates in every language.

Only three more months. Three.

Tell Mom and Dad not to sell Berglund Acres. I'm coming home.

I just hope Chase is with me.

Love, Josey

matchmaker

• • •

Oh, Sophia, you're so stupid! Don't you see that Ken doesn't really love you? And that woman who just hired you—that's his mistress! Run, run as fast as you can, back to C.C.!

I'm squinting through the static, trying to translate the Russian, and barely notice the knock at my door through the noise of the washing machine churning.

Run, Sophia! Follow your heart!

The knock comes again.

Shoot, not now!

Okay, yes, I might be a little addicted to the goings-on of *Santa Barbara*, but it's not my fault.

The *Banya* Girls started it.

And a gal has to keep up her side of the conversation. Especially to get her mind off the nakedness.

I am relieved to report, also, that Ulia seems to have dropped her complaints against Anton. So I might have been overreacting. Like I said, I blame the steam.

It's not like my to-do list is overflowing out here in Mudsville. H isn't responding to my email, and we have a full stock of birchbark crafts, now catalogued and stored at the community center. Olya is gone to Moscow, and Chase has commandeered my computer to write his analysis on the Nanai for Voices International.

Justin and Chloe are still attending *detskiy sad*, but I've taken to sending extra clothes with Chloe.

"Zhozey?" Olya says, now inside and standing at my door.

"Olya!" Except . . . oh, no, Sophia, don't go in there if you don't want your heart broken—Ken is there, with—

Olya clears her throat.

I look over.

And standing behind my friend's legs, peeking out with giant, luminous brown eyes, is a little girl. She has short brown hair and is wearing a white handknit sweater and a black skirt over a pair of tights. All dressed up to meet the neighbor.

"Albena?"

Olya grins and turns to sweep up her five-year-old. "Say hello, *lapochka*."

The little girl turns and hides her face in her mother's shoulder. I'm consumed with emotion, words completely gone as I look at Olya's face.

She looks transformed. Gone, without a trace, is the woman I met six months ago, broken, afraid, despairing. This woman is full of life, full of hope.

I can do nothing but come close and hug her. "Your daughter is beautiful," I am finally able to say.

"I know," Olya says, pride in her eyes. "We just got back."

I turn off the television and put on a pot of water for tea.

Tea, by the way, has become one of my specialties. I'm very, very good at unwrapping a box and dunking in a little baggie.

We sit at the table, and my eyes are on Albena, this formerly missing chunk of Olya's heart, as Olya tells me about her trip.

She's never been to Moscow, but as she talks, old memories churn up, and how I miss it—the Gray Pony, a karaoke place where I sang "Stand By Your Man" to my frustrated Chase. And the subway, where I got my traveling legs. The bagel shop, where God continually reminded me that He cares about the little things, and my friends Sveta and Thug, who took care of me, even if I said I didn't need it.

The tea water whistles, and I can't believe that I've made a new life here, in Siberia.

And that, despite my desperate moments, it's starting to feel like home.

I pour the water into cups, and Olya and I sip together. I laugh as Olya gives Albena a sugar cube dipped in tea.

"Did Chase have a good meeting in Moscow?" Olya asks.

"I think so." I'm not sure since he's been pretty quiet since his return, writing in his notebook, which calls to me to read it. But I'm not going to . . . Not. Going. To. Even if it should, say, accidentally fall into my hands, open, while I was, perhaps, dusting. Under the bed. "He's trying to figure out a way for the men in the village to create an economic future."

Olya kisses the top of Albena's head. "Maybe it's not from the outside that change will happen." Her eyes are shining. "But from the inside. Vasilley hunts for me, not for money. And now, Albena."

She presses her hand against mine. "You gave us our future, Zhozey."

Probably, those kinds of words are not good for my ego. But they warm me all the same. "I'm really going to miss you when I leave."

She withdraws her hand. Her expression turns hollow. "You're leaving?"

Uh. Well . . . "Our project ends at the end of May. I think we're going back to America."

She swallows. Panic lines her expression.

Albena spills tea down her sweater and starts to cry. Olya grabs a napkin. Tries to dab it. But it's too late; there's already a growing stain on the shirt.

Olya gets up, tears in her eyes. "I should have expected that."

I am not sure if she's referring to Albena and the tea . . . or me.

Suddenly, my eyes are filling too. "I don't want to leave," I hear myself saying.

Before I can qualify those words, however, I hear the outside door thump, heavy feet tracking inside.

I get up just as Chase opens the door and stands in the threshold. His expression is dark, and for a second, I'm even a little scared.

"What?"

He glances at Olya and opts to speak English. "Ulia left Anton." He advances into the room, boots and all. Casting a look at Olya, he lowers his voice and says, "And Anton is saying that it's all your fault."

Does anyone think that's fair? Huh? Huh? Just because a woman leaves her neglectful, sullen husband, I don't think it's right to blame it on the first forward-thinking foreigner that happens by.

Even if said foreigner did somehow manage, inadvertently, to arm the woman with her own supply of cash with which to leave.

But that's not Chase's biggest issue at the moment. No, as he ushers Olya from the room and closes the door behind her, I see something darker in his eyes.

"Ulia said, and I quote Anton, 'If Josey can leave her husband for someone else, I can too.'"

There's more than anger in his eyes. There's hurt.

As if he believes her?

"What on earth are you talking about?"

Chase shucks off his jacket, hangs it on the chair at the table. Runs a hand through his blond hair. His jaw is tight, as are his shoulders as he turns his back to me.

"Please tell me it's not true."

What's not true? I'm on my feet and I touch his back, but he flinches and stalks away from me.

"I don't know what you're talking about."

He rounds on me. "You and Nathan. Apparently he spent most of his time here when I was in Moscow."

"H was here—"

His stricken look, as if he's seen into another realm and is horrified by his vision, cuts off my words.

"Naughty. That's what she meant—"

"She was talking about the fact that our son flipped off the teacher at *detskiy sad*!"

"Really, Josey? And why would he do that? Maybe he's stressed out? Maybe he's thinking that his mother and father are going to split up?"

"He's three, Chase! He doesn't have those thoughts." But his words have hit me broadside. Split up?

I press my hand to my stomach, reach out for a chair. "There is nothing going on between Nathan and me."

"I heard you talking at Women's Day—I thought, no, it can't be me. They aren't talking about me—"

"What are you talking about?" I'm thinking back to the event, trying to figure out—uh-oh. I remember my panicked stage whisper to Nathan. *That's the last thing he needs to hear. He's already mad at me. Won't talk to me. Wait until I know for sure, and then we'll tell him.*

"I was talking about Ulia. And Anton."

But Chase isn't listening. He's got his hands over his face, shaking his head. "I'm so blind. I'm so stupid."

"Stop it, Chase. Nathan and I are just friends."

But he's beyond listening. In fact, I'm not even a part of this conversation anymore. "I let it happen. I invited him into my house, I saw the way he talked to her, listened to her. Paid attention to her . . . "

You know, I *am* in the room. As his monologue continues, however, I'm starting to see his point.

Nathan did pay attention to me. Like bringing a turkey at New Year's. And flowers on Women's Day.

Soup on a regular basis.

The increasingly frequent visits.

You'd make the perfect pastor's wife.

My mouth feels as if a hedgehog has climbed inside. Muddy, thick.

"Chase, I . . . "

He turns, his eyes red-rimmed. "I can't trust you, can I?"

What? "Hey, that's not fair."

"Apparently, I've done exactly what the elders warned me against. Here I was, fighting for your business, telling the elders to let the women have their hobby—"

Hobby? I'd say that the several thousand dollars we've brought into this community is more than a hobby.

"But Anton is right. It's more than that. Maybe you are exactly what he says—a bad influence on this society. And thanks a lot for just confirming to everyone what an idiot I am. So much for them ever listening to my ideas to help them."

I'm speechless, every thought wiped clean from my mind as I see him grab his jacket, throw it on. He breathes hard, and I'm still trying to conjure up one coherent thought in response to his tirade when he rounds, one last time, on me.

"I'll tell you one thing, Josey. Your little home business stops. Today."

He's gone, out the door before I finally find the words I want to say.

Not on your life, pal.

I live in *Santa Barbara*.

So maybe we don't have swimming pools and breathtaking vistas of the Pacific Ocean, but the river is free flowing, the lilac trees are budding, and the Banya Girls know how to blow off steam.

Or at least create it.

It's a hotbed of gossip and chaos in Burrrrsk, and apparently, I'm exactly what Chase accuses me of . . . the ringleader.

Just because a girl sits naked in a sauna and occasionally nods at the conversation around her—mostly to keep her head from filling with fog—doesn't mean she endorses the torrid affairs of others.

Apparently, that's exactly what Ulia was having. One version of the story is with a tall, handsome ferryboat captain from Khabarovsk who whisked her away at the first sign of spring. Another story says she's upriver, sailing to the mouth of the Amur with a salmon fisherman.

The only thing we know for sure is that no one has seen her. And that she took with her all the cash she'd earned from the sale of her birchbark crafts.

I'm sitting in the steam room, listening to the women assail their husbands, pretty sure I shouldn't say a word.

"Misha says I can't go to the community center anymore," says tall, thin Anya.

"So does my husband," says another woman. "And I was planning on remodeling our kitchen."

I wonder what that looks like without plumbing . . .

"My Igor took all my money and hid it."

I purse my lips at the words.

"What should we do, Zhozey?"

Me? You're asking me? I shake my head. I'm the last person who has answers, given my own crumbling marriage. Chase has practically moved in with Anton, although he slinks in every night like a jackal. I haven't seen Nathan in two weeks, and I'm dearly hoping that he didn't rap on the door looking for shelter and get a coal shovel to the head.

No, Chase wouldn't do that. Would he?

"I don't know," I finally mumble, because everyone has fallen silent.

"Are you going to leave Chase?" a voice pipes up from the back.

"Of course not!" My tone is stronger than the question deserves, but I wouldn't think of leaving Chase.

Or running home to Berglund Acres, where I'm loved.

Accepted.

Where there are flushing toilets.

"I'm not leaving Chase," I repeat, quietly. But I wish the words didn't feel so far away, so outside my body.

"But you love Nathan, don't you?"

These words, from Olya, shock me. "Of course . . . not . . . " I mean, I love him like a brother. A friend. I breathe in the thick air, turning over my memories. It's true that Nathan makes me laugh. And he listens to me. And compliments me. And he's smart and full of wisdom and knowledge. Of *course* I like him.

"We saw the way he looked at you at the Women's Day celebration. He had his arm around you," Anya says.

"We were talking about . . . " Uh, oops . . . "We were just talking."

"He picks up the kids at *detskiy sad*."

"And he's here more than he's ever been since you showed up."

"I think he's cute."

Oh, that's helping. But as I listen, I see their point.

From all outward appearances, it does seem as if Nathan and I have had a little . . . something. I close my eyes, and the truth rushes in. Maybe I did enjoy his visits more than I should have. Maybe I enjoyed his attention, appreciated that he saw me, saw my hurts, enjoyed my children. I let him open a door that should have stayed locked.

Oh, Chase.

I wince, remembering the hurt in his eyes.

"I think you need to be like Sophia and follow your heart," Anya says.

Sophia is an idiot.

And so, apparently, am I.

"I'm not leaving Chase," I say again, and this time the words find a resting place inside.

"What about the business? They can't just take that away from us, can they? It's our future." Olya's voice holds panic.

I glance at her through the curtain of my wet hair. I feel like I'm in grade school. Boys against girls.

Except somehow, we all have to win.

I get up, step out, and jump into the cold plunge before I lose my nerve, then hit the showers.

Lord, please help me fix this.

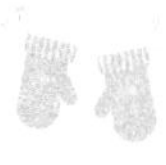

God must be on Chase's side. (Okay, let's be honest. After careful examination, I wouldn't blame Him. After all, I do look guilty. But He knows my heart, right? Even if I did like Nathan, I meant my vows. Really meant them. I just had a little issue with boundaries.) It's so utterly unfair that I find Nathan on my doorstep when I get home.

He's got his duffel slung over his shoulder.

"What are you doing here?" I hiss, looking over my shoulder. Suddenly I feel like I'm naked and running down the center of the street screaming, "Adulterer, Adulterer." I feel dirty. And sneaky. "Chase is going to be here any minute!"

Josey, that is making it worse. Please, mouth, stop.

"So?" Nathan smiles at me. So, perhaps I imagined his feelings for me.

Or maybe he's just a giant faker. I narrow my eyes at him. "You don't care that Chase is about to come home . . . and . . . " What, interrupt us? *There is nothing to interrupt!* But I leave my sentence dangling and raise one eyebrow.

He matches it. "Is this a game? Is it Chase's birthday? Did I forget a surprise party?"

Oh, good grief. "Where have you been for the last two weeks? I thought you'd been buried in a potato field."

"Huh?" Nathan slings the duffel down from his shoulder. "Are you okay?" He peers at me like he can look deep inside my soul and identify the alien that has taken possession of my body. Josey, are you in there?

"Stop it. Don't pretend like you have no idea what is going on."

He raises his hands, as if in surrender. "Okay, you got me. I'll stop pretending and say it right out. I have no idea what you're talking about." He puts down his hands and shrugs.

Now it's my turn to peer deep inside.

"What?"

I shake my head in disgust. "You haven't a clue that the entire town thinks we had an affair and that Ulia left Anton because of it?"

He actually turns a little white.

Clearly not.

"What?" he repeats, and there's something wrong with his voice. He actually takes a step back from me, like I'm emanating some toxic germ.

"Oh, stop. Like you haven't been super nice to me, complimenting me, and bringing me flowers, and a turkey, and making me dinner—"

"I'm staying on your sofa, for crying out loud. What's a guy supposed to do to show his thanks?" But his color hasn't returned.

"And what's with the 'you'd make a great pastor's wife' line? I'm not married to a pastor!"

"But you should be!"

His tone stops me, and the frustration that crosses his face steals my words.

I close my mouth. *I should be?*

My expression must betray my horror, because he shakes his head, dialing his voice back to normal, looking past me as if to assess who else, besides all of Siberia, might have heard him.

"I mean Chase. *Chase* should be a pastor. He has it in him—the desire to help, to change lives, and I think all this frustration over the past year is telling him exactly that."

I blink at him.

"And it's not every man that has a woman like you who would be willing to sacrifice and minister to people who live way out in places like Siberia."

Oh. And see, it's statements like these that get us in trouble. I don't know whether to strangle him or thank him.

"And I should know," he says, now looking away from me. "My fiancée broke it off with me when she found out God had called me to be a missionary in Siberia." His voice is tight, and for a second, I'm not sure he's even spoken. But then he looks over at me, pain in his eyes. "Chase has no idea how lucky he is, and I would be the last guy to mess that up for him."

Oh.

"In fact, the reason I've been up here so much is . . . well, I've been seeing someone."

He's turning red now, and I can't help an instant flare of annoyance. I live to matchmake, and here he found someone, right under my nose? Without my help? "Who?"

"It doesn't matter. What *does* matter is that I'm sorry I . . . damaged our friendship. And put you and Chase on the skids. And made you feel uncomfortable. And made the whole town believe a lie. I was just trying to encourage." He picks up his duffel, slings it back over his shoulder.

Oh, Nathan.

But I don't stop him as he walks past me, down the sidewalk.

I stand there in the mud long after he's walked through the gate and latched it behind him.

a blank slate

. . .

The house is quiet when I enter. Chase has agreed to pick up the kids from *detskiy sad*, and I only hope he hasn't forgotten.

The hum of the furnace backdrops the signs of life in our little bungalow. Chloe's kitties are taking a nap on the sofa. Justin has left a toy car on the television set. I go into my little bedroom, pull up a pillow, and lie on the bed, staring at the ceiling.

Now what, Lord?

Humble, gentle, patience, peace.

Yeah, I'm real pastor's wife material. Brought real peace to this little community. I'm just a stellar example of tranquility and homemaking.

I put the pillow over my mouth to stifle the scream I feel building.

But what were my choices, exactly? Throw myself over the doorjamb and demand we return to Gull Lake? Or follow my vagabond hero to the far reaches of the world for yet another adventure?

Can you fix this, Lord?

I roll over, and there it is. Evidence that I have it all together. My Bible, with the little bookmark in Ephesians where it's been for, oh, say, four months?

I sit up, open it to where I left off.

My eyes fall to Ephesians 5. You know what I'm talking about. The submission chapter.

Perfect. Submission is what got me into this mess. Remember, it was Chase's idea to invite Nathan into our lives.

Chase's idea to let him cook.

Chase's idea for me to help with the women's Bible study.

So I was a willing accomplice. Another perspective might say I was submitting.

I'm starting to think that perhaps I've misunderstood all this submission stuff, don't you? Maybe it's not about going along with everything that enters my beloved husband's head.

I track back to the *humble* verse, and read Ephesians 5:1-2. *Be imitators of God, therefore, as dearly loved children and live a life of love, just as Christ loved us and gave himself up for us as a fragrant offering and sacrifice to God.*

I stare at the verse for a moment, and suddenly I see. *Live a life of love, just as Christ loved us.*

The win-win.

Because maybe this isn't a contest about who will surrender and who will dominate, but rather finishing the race together, side by side.

I must be on to something, because in a very pastor's-wife-material move, I flip back to the submission verse and discover that the amplified words say, "Adapt yourself to your husbands, as a service to the Lord."

As a service to the Lord.

Don't know why I missed that earlier.

But I see it now, and suddenly I realize what I have to do.

I slip off the bed and onto the floor, kneeling beside the bed.

It's not often I find myself here, and perhaps that's part of the problem.

"Lord, I've made a mess of things here, but You know I didn't mean to. However, I want to serve You. And if that means serving Chase, then I'll do it."

I take a breath. "Help me to see Chase and love him the way You do."

I hear the door opening, someone calling my name.

I meet Olya at my bedroom door. She's sweaty—of course, because she's just come from *banya*—but no, she's breathing hard.

She clutches her knees. "Zhozey, come . . . quickly." She stands up, grabs my hand. "The community center is on fire!"

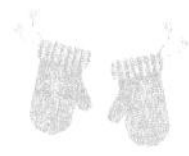

Have you ever seen a fire, up close and scorching? It makes noise, almost a growl, as it licks up the sides of a building, rolls over the top. Sparks spit from the flames, fly over the heads of the onlookers as I run up. The gray dusk of the night is lit like noon as flames pour out of windows and twine into the sky.

"Where are my kids?" I glance over to the *detskiy sad* yard, but it's empty. I see others—Misha and Anya and their two children huddled in fear around their legs. Where's Maya?

What if she was inside?

"Have you seen Maya, or Chase?" I direct my question to Vasilley, who is standing outside the boundary of the flames.

He looks at me with incomprehension, but I see relief wash over him when Olya runs up behind me.

Anton is standing away from the crowd, in the street, his hands in his pockets. Watching.

I turn back to the fire, a sick feeling in my gut. All our hard work in cinders. All the hopes and dreams of the women, of the village, turned to ash.

I stalk over to him, fire in my belly. "How did this happen?"

He lifts a shoulder, and with everything inside me, I want to send my fist into his face.

This is no time for humble. Or gentle. "Anton, I swear, if you know anything—"

"Josey!"

I turn and see a blackened-faced Chase running toward me. Tears, probably from the smoke in his eyes, run down his face. His jacket is smoky black, and he's covered in mud. "I can't find Chloe!"

I stare at him for what seems like a long, syrupy moment. It's thick and I can't seem to untangle myself from his question. "You . . . where did you last see her?"

He is wild-eyed. "We came out of the community center, and I told her and Justin to stay by the fence—"

"You didn't stay with her? She's three!" I take off, running toward the blaze, but it's so hot it pushes me back.

Chase catches me around the waist. "Maya was with her! But she ran away from her—"

I hit his shoulder and run away from him too. "Maya!"

I find her mesmerized by the flames, holding Justin by the hand, tears running down her face. "Maya! Where's Chloe?"

Maya stares at me, but her eyes are vacant. And I'm remembering that this isn't the first fire she's had in her life.

Oh, God, help us all.

"Chloe!" I scoop up Justin and fling him on my hip as I run toward the *detskiy sad*.

Please, God, just keep her safe, wherever she is.

The blaze is reflecting off the lights of the building, and I hurdle the fence. I hear breath behind me and see Chase pass me. "Chloe!"

Where would she go when she's afraid? My mind reaches . . .

Lord?

She loves the playhouse. I am angling for it when I see Chase already there. He's hit his hands and knees, crawls inside.

I hear the voice and it turns my knees weak. "Daddy!"

Chloe.

Chase pulls her out, and her arms are tight around his neck, her legs around his waist. He's holding her too, his head buried in her soft blonde curls.

I've reached them now, just as Chase looks up, grabs me, and crushes me to himself, hard.

"I'm so sorry," Chase says. His voice is in my ear. "So sorry."

He puts me away from him, his eyes scanning Chloe, assessing for damage. "Are you okay?"

She nods. I also do the once-over—first Chloe, then Chase.

He's the one who looks like he's walked through Hades. "What happened to you?"

He shakes his head, wraps one arm around me, and holds me tight. He's still shaking a little. "I'm really sorry, G.I."

I nod but can't find any more words. He takes my hand in a death grip, and we walk back to the blazing community center. The fire takes down the front wall with an explosion of flame and sparks. "Why isn't anyone putting it out?"

"They don't have a fire department."

I stare up at him. "So if something catches fire, it just burns down?"

"You found her!" Maya runs up, takes Chloe from Chase, hugs her tight.

Chase gives me a grim look. "I tried to rescue some of your crafts."

I blink at him, trying to wrap my mind around his words. He must see my confusion.

"After I got the kids out, I went in, tried to save a few boxes." I see now the sweat along his brow and realize he wasn't crying so much as sweating. "I'm so sorry. All your hard work, destroyed." He looks at Chloe. "And our daughter, lost."

I'm seeing, suddenly, not my hard work . . . but Chase's heart. Through all that black soot and the smell of smoke and the sweat pouring down his face, his one thought was to salvage my—the village's—livelihood. Maybe, in fact, the man does have the heart of a pastor.

And when he thought Chloe was gone, he had the heart of a father.

Just like that, I see it—the long hours spent listening to the elders talk about their lives. The disgusting prune vodka he consumed (or not) so Vasilley would invite him hunting. The days upon days he picked up the kids at *detskiy sad* and made me soup. Even my beautiful, sweet-smelling outhouse. All Chase, trying to love me, to love others.

"It's okay about the crafts, Chase," I say quietly. "I was going to close the business anyway."

He looks down at me, something like pain on his face. "Because of me?"

"No . . . I mean . . . maybe . . . "

I'm interrupted by Anton. "There she is! Arrest her!"

For a second, the voice yanks me back to a place in my past and I stiffen. Me? I didn't do it.

No, he strides past me and grabs Maya's arm. "She set the fire!"

Behind him are the locally appointed militia officers, who look at each other, not sure what to do.

Maya yanks her arm from him, rage and fear in her voice. "What? I didn't do this!"

"Where were you this afternoon, when the fire started? I checked with your preschool—they said you left early." Anton's voice is low, and it contains enough hatred to prickle my skin. What does he have against Maya?

The memory of the night she showed up at my house, bloodied and afraid, rushes at me, and I stare at Anton, horror slicking through me.

Who, really, was having the affair—Ulia, or Anton?

That's not fair to Maya . . . so maybe it wasn't an affair. Something dark grips my stomach, twists it.

I'm not ready to make accusations, but I do know who is innocent here. "Maya didn't do this." I glance at her, stepping closer. She meets my eyes with surprise.

"Maya wouldn't do this." That much I know.

"What do you know about this—" And he uses a bad word, one that even I know, in Russian. I feel slapped. "She probably killed her husband too."

I hear myself gasp, and all retorts are yanked from my open mouth. Maya goes pale and is shaking her head.

"She didn't do it, Anton." The voice comes from behind Maya, and it's a voice I know, that I've come to recognize without looking.

Ulia shoves her hands into the pockets of a green army coat. I barely recognize her in a scarf and jeans. "You know she didn't set this."

Anton's face hardens. "How would you know?"

"Because she was at Sasha's house, bringing her food."

Sasha, Sasha . . . I'm scanning my brain—oh, Sasha, their widowed daughter with two little children . . . I glance at Maya and see the truth on her face. Maya's been bringing food to someone in need. Reaching out beyond herself, her pain. A surge of pride and affection whooshes through me, and I can barely stop myself from throwing my arms around her.

"She does it nearly every day. I see it because I'm staying next door, at Leonid's house."

From behind her, a man who looks vaguely like the Other Man puts his hand on Ulia's shoulder. Oh, that's bold.

Except that Anton looks up at him and nods, as if to say, "Hey, it's okay you stole my wife. Let's all be friends."

I'm so confused.

"I thought you left me," he says quietly.

Uh, me too! Me too!

Ulia's voice softens. "I wanted to. I was tired of us. Tired of wishing for something better. I love you, and I don't want to leave you." She glances at Maya. "I know about your mistakes, Anton. But I . . . miss you, and it only took a couple weeks of staying with my brother to figure that out."

Oh, brother. Oh. *Brother*.

I feel like I'm in the middle of a *Santa Barbara* episode, because Anton's eyes actually get glassy. And he takes a step toward his wife. "I'm so sorry. I didn't mean to cause all this. I thought you'd left me because . . . " His gaze cuts to Maya.

May shrinks back a bit, and I get it.

He thought Maya told Ulia about their affair, or whatever. Okay, see, that was a leap, but when you're in the middle of a soap opera, those kinds of leaps are easy. Expected, even. In fact, here's another easy one—Anton burned down the community center (which is also the house of his former mistress) to destroy his wife's livelihood and keep said mistress from outing him, killing her in the process. How am I doing? I probably could write an episode of *Santa*—

"You did this?"

Obviously I'm not the only one doing the math here, because Chase, in a total Soap Opera response, lets go of me and launches himself at Anton.

He grabs him up by the shirt. "You set this fire?"

Anton has his hands at Chase's wrists.

They go down in the mud. Chase is talking half Russian,

half English, and it's not pretty. Much of it sounds like its coming from a place inside Chase, a place I don't know.

"Is this how you treat everyone who's worked hard for Bursk, to build new lives? Don't you care about anyone but yourself? No wonder Ulia left you!"

Chase dodges a punch, and I scream, push Justin's face into my jacket.

And then Nathan appears, grabs Chase, yanks him away.

But Anton isn't finished as he finds his feet and takes another swipe at Chase. Vasilley nabs him by the arm. A lot more power in Mr. Skin and Bones than I thought.

Chase rounds on Nathan, and for a second I think he's going to take a swing, but he shakes himself free.

Nathan steps back, hands up. "It's not worth it, Chase."

Chase gives him a long look. Then turns, and everything written on his face makes me want to weep.

Despair. Brokenness.

My man is down for the count.

Without a word, Chase walks away.

Now the militia guys finally pick sides. They manhandle Anton away from the crowd. I notice that Ulia follows.

Behind me, the rest of the building caves in with a thunderous roar.

"Mommy!" I turn to see Chloe tugging at Maya's hand. She's wide-eyed and afraid.

I scoop her up to my other hip, hold both my children tight. Chloe wraps her legs around me. Justin is shaking.

"Shh," I say, watching the fire begin to smolder. It's going to burn long into the night, however. "Everything's going to be okay."

Nathan stands at a distance, and I glance at him.

But he's not looking at me. He's headed toward . . . Maya. Who turns and takes his hand. He pulls her to himself, wraps an arm around her.

Oh.

She looks at me, and I see tears cutting down her cheeks. *Spa-si-bo*, she mouths.

Now I have tears too.

Slowly, I turn and walk home, my children clinging to me.

The house is dark when I enter, and Chase's jacket, a puddle of soot on the floor, confirms that he made it home. His boots, too, caked with mud, lie on their sides, as if he toed them off and flung them.

I put the kids down, de-layer them, and dump their clothes in a pile. Washday will be fun tomorrow.

Inside, the fire is dying. I open the furnace, throw in a chunk of coal, stoke it. I set Chloe and Justin on the sofa, pile toys around them, and turn on a cartoon.

Then I look for Chase.

He's sitting on the bed, his head in his hands. His shoulders are shaking.

I get afraid when I see Chase's shoulders shake. "Chase?"

"I meant to do this right."

His words still me. Meant to do what right? I hold my breath.

He looks up at me. His eyes are red. "I'm sorry about that, back there. I—probably Anton did set the fire, but I don't know. And it doesn't matter. If anyone is to blame for you losing everything, it's me."

He shakes his head. "I shouldn't have followed my ambition out to Siberia. I should have . . . taken you home."

I blink at him, and the verse I read—was it only an hour ago?—flashes through my mind. *Live a life of love, just as Christ loved us*. And love speaks the truth.

"Babe, listen. I *do* feel as though I've been running around Siberia a little bit naked, unprotected. I could have used you noticing me more. I needed to know that you're still the guy that will ride in on the motorcycle in the dead of night to rescue me. However, I'm *not* sorry we came to Siberia. I'm not so thrilled about having an outhouse, or letting Nathan so far into our lives that you thought we were having an affair—and don't look at me like that, because we're not, and didn't, and that's all I'm going to say about that—but I'm not sorry about the rest. I'm not sorry for giving these women a sense of accomplishment, about helping Olya get back her daughter, and even for holding down the fort while you went tromping about with the neighbor so he could find Jesus. And I'm especially not sorry about being stretched so far I thought I might break, and discovering I had more in me than I realized. So you don't get to take the blame for all the bad or the good stuff. God gets that."

I sit down, lean against him. "And He's bigger than you. He can take it."

Chase doesn't smile, but he puts his arm around me, closes his eyes. "Oh, G.I., I just wanted to do more here." He swallows, and I feel it reverberate through my body. "Would you read something?"

Would I read something? Like the Secret Journal of Chase Anderson? Oh, I suppose, if you insist. I school my voice. "Um, sure."

He pulls his journal from under the bed and hands it to me.

I feel like I'm being given access to his heart. The Chase I don't know. Yet.

He leans back on the bed as I open the book. "Where do I start?"

"Anywhere. But don't finish until you get to the part where I know that you and Nathan didn't have an affair, but where I wouldn't blame you if you did. And be sure not to skip over the section where I realize that everything I've done over the past four years is a failure."

What?

I close the journal without reading it. "I'm not going to read that, because it's not true."

His eyes are closed, as if he doesn't believe me, doesn't want to hear it. And now I'm angry.

"Hey, we have two adorable, incredible kids out there, who love their daddy. And unless I'm mistaken, we have one of the nicest outhouses in all of Siberia. So don't tell me that you're a failure."

I get a little smile.

But it quickly vanishes.

I put the journal down on his chest. "Could it be, though, that you were supposed to fail, in order to see that God has something bigger for you?"

He opens an eye.

I nod. "Could it be that God brought you out to Siberia, not so we could change the economic future of the people of Bursk but their spiritual future? Maybe Nathan is right—I *would* make a fabulous pastor's wife, because *you* were meant to be a pastor."

"Nathan said that?"

"Yes. And he feels sick that he put us in this position. He wasn't after me, Chase. But he knows he can't be our friend anymore. At least, the kind that sleeps on our sofa."

Chase looks at me. Shakes his head. "He told me that you'd make a fabulous pastor's wife too."

I shrug, as if, of course.

"He also told me that maybe God was doing more in my life than I was willing to see."

Oh. Well, that could apply to all of us, couldn't it?

"The thing is, G.I., I . . . uh . . . " Chase clenches his jaw, as if the words need to be wrestled out. "I came here because I was selfish. I saw my life spiraling down to nothing in Gull Lake, and I panicked. And then you were so supportive and enduring, it just made me feel worse and worse, and I couldn't talk to you, and then Nathan could, and I got jealous." He attempts a pitiful smile. "You wanted the guy who would show up on his motorcycle. I wanted to know that you'd still jump on the back and ride with me anywhere."

Oh, is there any doubt? I lean over and kiss him, and his arms go around me.

"Forgive me, babe?" he whispers.

I love forgiveness. Especially when it includes Chase holding me, his lips on mine, making me remember just why I went to those high school football practices and braved the Minnesota cold. I suppose it was just a warm-up for the real thing. He tastes salty, though, like tears. This is a new Chase.

He finally sighs, leans back. "Nathan asked me how long I was willing to wait to become the man God plans for me to be."

I touch Chase's hair, smile into his eyes. "And?"

"Not a day longer." Chase sits up and takes my hand. "Maybe I could be more." Something gathers in his eyes—something that fills my heart—and I see the Chase I knew years ago, when he first dreamed of following God into the hinterlands. "Maybe I want to start over," he says softly. "Be a blank slate for God to write on."

A blank slate. I love that. A do-over, except with everything we know now.

"Except . . . I'm not sure how to get there, Jose."

I take his hand, run my fingers over the calluses. "Olya told me not long ago that you have to get naked to get clean. Seems like a good place to start, huh?"

So, for the second time in the day—I find myself on my knees. And it's okay, because beside me is the man I'd follow anywhere.

already home

. . .

Dear H,

I owe you an apology. Because I get it. Really get it.

Nathan and I weren't having an affair. But I let him inside my heart, and you saw that. It wasn't on purpose, and it happened one day at a time, without my knowledge, but definitely with my consent. I suppose if I had let myself, it could have been something more, but, well . . . because of you, and God, and even my beloved *Banya* Girls, it wasn't.

In fact, what I didn't know is that Nathan has been seeing Maya—you remember her, the pretty woman who came to dinner?

Did I tell you that the community center burned down? Yes. Anton, the mayor, set it on fire. He blamed Maya, but I knew she couldn't do that—not after the way her husband died. And when Anton's wife showed up, apologizing for leaving him, and then confronted him, he admitted what he'd done. Apparently, not long after her husband's death, Maya and Anton had a brief affair—something she cut off but he kept pushing for. Eventually he hated her for not giving in. Maya felt so guilty she started taking meals to Anton and

Ulia's widowed daughter, Sasha, and her children. But I think that was more about redemption and restitution. Ulia got that part, thankfully. But Anton was afraid of losing his wife, and he thought maybe the business gave her too much freedom, so in desperation, he burned our business down, hoping to scare Maya with the fire too. He claims he wasn't trying to kill her, and maybe that's the truth. He's in the town jail, awaiting trial.

I know. I'm telling you, there's more drama in frozen Bursk than on a Saturday night in Gull Lake!

Forgiveness is contagious, and the entire village is going through a sort of revival. Nathan has started a church, and even the men are attending.

Anyway, I wanted to tell you that there ARE things you can count on. Like, it doesn't matter where you live, just who you live with. And submission doesn't mean that you have to surrender your brain, just your heart. I think the best relationships are the ones where everybody wins. Marriage is a partnership, not a division of labor. A life of carrying burdens, and joys, together. Helping each other. At least, that's what I've learned living in Siberia.

I believe you and Rex are going to make it, H. Even in Gull Lake. Don't be afraid to give up what you think is most important . . . because God has a way of making your surrender feel like a reward.

Forgive me, please, for letting you down?

Rock on,

Josey

I KNOW I SHOULDN'T BE SURPRISED THAT THE NEWS OF THE FIRE made it all the way to Moscow. After all, it's not every day that a man burns down the biggest building in town over a jealous fit.

And, of course, Chase had to give his analysis of it to Voices International.

I am surprised, nonetheless, when Dalton and Maggie Calhoun appear at my gate nearly two weeks later. "I like what you've done with the place," Maggie says as she opens my gate.

Maggie is walking elegance, even in a Siberian village. She's wearing a jacket lined with rabbit fur, and I notice the boots—supple brown leather, and obviously imported.

"I especially love the outhouse," she says with a smile.

I've decorated it for spring with a spray of lilacs, and it's hard not to enter without coming out woozy from the smell. The fragrant floral smell, I mean.

I drop my shovel where I've been digging up rows for a garden. I'm not sure why—we leave in just a few weeks, but I figure that Misha and Anya will appreciate having their potato seeds in the ground.

The sun is high, and we've set our clocks forward, but I can already sense the days lengthening.

I embrace Maggie, and then little Steven, who runs into the house, looking for Justin and Chloe. Dalton wraps me in a one-arm hug. "I hear you have a decent sofa." He smiles, and I'm trying to figure out how, even in its unfolded state, it will hold two.

Not that I'm complaining.

"What are you doing here?"

"Chase told us about your little village home, and I just had to see for myself," Maggie says. Her brown eyes are twinkling.

I should insert here that it was Maggie and her state department connections that really got Chase's peanut butter cottage industry off the ground. And I have a feeling she's not just here to share a cup of tea.

I find out the reason for their visit at dinner—we've graduated from soup to mashed potatoes and cutlets.

"Chase told us about your business, Josey. And we want to help." Dalton reaches over, forks another cutlet onto his plate. "In fact, we'd like to start similar businesses in native villages all over Russia."

I stare at Chase, and he looks as surprised as I feel. But he can't be, because behind my surprise is the shock that he was even talking about me, or my village business, in Moscow.

Chase smiles at me. "Want more potatoes, Chloe?"

"No tatoes!" Chloe says and pushes herself away from the table. As she gets down, she paws the ground, bends her wrists, and lets out a neigh.

Oh, we're moving onto larger animals. My little pony.

Maggie doesn't notice the equine in the family room. "And the best part is—we want you and Chase to move back to Moscow and run the business. You will have offices in WorldMar, and we'll fund your first year, just to get you off the ground."

"Are you saying it'll become an NGO project?" Chase directs his question at Dalton.

"No, no. It'll be a business. But one that we'll both have equal stakes in."

"We can have investors lined up in no time," Maggie says, as Steven pushes off her lap and gallops in a circle with Chloe. Maggie is pregnant again and has the smallest, cutest bulge. I wonder what it's like to have them one at a time.

"Listen, with Maggie's State Department connections, we can figure out how to fast-track shipments out of the country. It'll streamline everything, and we could even set up a warehouse in New York City. Think of it—you and Chase can travel to the villages, help them create and develop their own designs. With Chase's experience working with the elders, I'm sure he can bring them to agreement, especially when he shows how the proceeds can benefit the village with medicines and vaccinations. Chloe and Justin can attend the best schools in Moscow"—Maggie leans forward, gives me a sly smile—"and Josey can have indoor plumbing!"

I'm starting to like my outhouse, aren't I?

Okay, not that much.

"What do you think?" Dalton says, wiping his mouth with his napkin. "Can we lure you back to Moscow?"

It's late by the time we clean up, get the kids in bed, pull out the sofa, and finally climb into our own bed. We keep our voices low, because Maggie and Dalton are in the next room. I'm not sure why that's creepy when it never was when Nathan slept on the sofa.

Chase's hand finds mine in the darkness. "So, G.I., what do you want to do? Move to Moscow? Or . . . " He rolls over, and I feel his whiskers brush my cheek. "Should we go home?"

Oh boy. What do they say about history repeating itself?

"Me, cake!" Justin is sitting at the table, his grubby little fingers just itching to take a swipe out of the chocolate frosting I'm layering on his and Chloe's birthday cake. I can't believe they're four.

Or that I made a cake from scratch. It's not unlike cookies.

Most of all, I can't believe that four years ago today, I learned that God loves me in ways I never imagined. And it seems He hasn't slacked off, either.

The plastic is off our windows and they're open, allowing in a slight breeze that smells of jasmine and lilac, of overturned garden dirt and the fresh start that spring brings. Chloe is dressed all in pink, in short sleeves, her hair in high curly pigtails. She's trotting around the yard, snorting, and I think I miss the kitty.

"Olya sent over a salmon pie," Chase says, walking into the house with a plate covered by a towel. He's looking cute and American in a pair of faded jeans and a pullover long-sleeve shirt that makes his blue eyes shine. Yeah, I'm still crazy about the man who stole my heart. "She said she'll send Vasilley over in a bit with prune *sok*."

Perfect. But I *am* glad for the help with Chloe and Justin's birthday party. Besides the cake, I've done my part by baking eight dozen peanut butter cookies (thanks to Maggie and Dalton's re-supply gift).

Chase sets down the pie. "I invited Nathan." He looks at me, gauging my response.

I give him a nod. "I hope he brings Maya." I'm proud of my Chase, seeking out Nathan, apologizing without coming to blows. The fact is, Nathan asked the right questions, made Chase spot his potential losses as well as his hidden gifts, and every guy needs a friend like that.

Even if the friend needs to work on his boundaries. Like not giving flowers to other people's wives.

I finish the cake, put it in the center of the table, and go outside where Chase has set up a long picnic table and benches with boards. I cover the table with a sheet and decorate it with orange flowers I find growing along my fence.

Already, green buds of potatoes are sprouting through the dirt we furrowed. It'll be a good start for Anya and Misha when they move back in. Not to mention Chase's award-winning outhouse.

Chase comes up beside me, puts his hand around my waist. Kisses me. "Just think of the garden you'll have in Gull Lake."

I touch his hand, then turn and twine my arms around his neck, lay my head on his chest. We've decided to turn down Maggie's offer. The last thing my twins need is more time away from Mom. I've taught Olya the ins and outs of the Internet, and she's taken over most of the eBay responsibilities for the crafts business. Chloe and Justin are back to all half days at the *detskiy sad*, and both of them are "error"-free and keeping their sign language to themselves these days.

Even Vasilley and some of the elders have joined in on the new business, making breadboxes and cutting boards. I'm amazed at their skill. And their partnership.

As for Maya, although she lost everything in the fire, the town has banded together and not only furnished for her a room at the *detskiy sad* but also given her clothing. I'm not sure she likes the style, but I know she loves the grace she's been given.

I'm also able to spot the grace I've been given. I like the village life—the crow of the rooster in the morning, the low of miserable cows, the smell of coal smoke. I love the fact that I only have to step through the fence to visit my neighbor, and that when I go to the post office, I can't get out without seeing someone I know.

In fact, perhaps Bursk isn't so different from Gull Lake.

"Hey there, lovebirds, none of that in front of the young'uns." Nathan's voice makes me smile, and I give Chase a quick kiss before I greet him. Nathan is holding Maya's hand, and I recognize a smile on her face that I know comes from healing.

"Want a cookie?" I loop my arm through hers as she laughs.

Before we can go into the house, more people come through the gate—Ulia and her brother, Misha and Anya, the Banya Girls, who I now have begun to recognize fully dressed. Olya and Vasilley and little Albena, who breaks away and runs to find Justin and Chloe.

All the commotion attracts Lydia's attention, and she shoves her head through the fence, barking her hellos. I grab a cookie and toss it to her as I turn and greet our guests.

Everyone's brought goodies—sauerkraut, pickles, *salo*, salad. Bread.

"Congratulations!" Olya says as she gives me a kiss on the cheek.

"Why congratulations?" I receive a kiss from Vasilley.

"We also congratulate the mother on the birthday of her children," Olya says. She's still shining, as if Albena just arrived home yesterday. Or maybe it's because in about six months *she'll* be accepting congratulations.

I hear a shriek, followed by pounding feet, and Justin flies out of the house, followed by Albena.

"Mommy! Chloe ate the cake!"

Of course she did. But Justin's far from innocent, because he's wearing a beard of chocolate frosting.

I roll my eyes and turn, but Chase stops me. "I'll handle it." He gives me a wink. Hmm.

"So, have you guys decided what you're going to do?" Nathan asks as Olya and Maya lay out the treats on the table.

I frown at him, and he makes a face. "Apparently Chase hasn't mentioned it to you."

Uh-oh, here we go again. "Hasn't mentioned what?"

"I'm headed stateside, to finish seminary." He lowers his voice. "I'm going to put it off just a bit longer . . . " His gaze flashes to Maya, and I see tenderness cross his face. "But I need someone to take up the reins of this ministry. Someone with a heart and understanding for the Small Peoples of Siberia." He pauses, looking for something in my response, and finally sighs. "I guess Chase didn't mention that I asked him to consider it."

My throat is tight. And not because Chase has kept this question from me . . . but I suddenly realize how much he loves me. It's way more than he loves himself.

Chase knows how much I love Gull Lake. And he wants to give me my home.

I'm wondering, though, if I'd miss Bursk more. Because maybe it's not about where I live but how. And with whom.

And *I* want Chase to be everything God intends for him.

In fact . . . "You told me once, Nathan, that I'd make a good pastor's wife. But the fact is, all I've wanted to be is a good wife. One who loves her husband. And if God wants to do this amazing work in and through Chase, I'm going to help . . . by not standing in the way."

Before Nathan can say anything, Chase appears. He's clutching Justin under one arm, Chloe under the other. They're both covered in chocolate and giggling.

Especially since Chase is also smeared with chocolate. He comes near, trying to give me a kiss, and I laugh and dodge him.

But he'll catch me. He always does.

And as I watch him race the other kids around the yard, little weapons of chocolate destruction under his arms, I realize it doesn't really matter where we live.

Because together, we're already home.

epilogue: ready, set...go!

. . .

"ARE YOU READY?" I'M SITTING CRAMMED IN A RADIO FLYER wagon, perched atop Bloomquist Mountain. Below, Gull Lake sparkles under a perfect summer sky.

"Josey, really, this is crazy. I'm going to win, and you're going to get hurt." Chase is sitting in a matching wagon, all grins. He looks just as cute as he did twenty-some years ago, in his cut off T-shirt, his faded jeans. And here I am again, poised to race him down a gravel hill. I might turn over into the ditch. I might even get hurt.

But I know I'm going to win.

"I can't believe it's our last day here." I'm stalling for time as I eye the hill.

Chase has his legs over the side and is rocking his wagon back and forth. A golden tan has browned his face and arms from working at Berglund Acres over the past year, getting it ready for the new ownership, namely my brother Buddy, who is moving with his fiancée back to Gull Lake.

Has it already been a year since we left Bursk? I can still see them—Olya and Albena and Vasilley, waving to us from the dock, along with my clothed *Banya* Girls. And Ulia, standing with Sasha and her children. Last I heard, she's moved in with her daughter while Anton serves his sentence for arson. And then there's Maya and Nathan at the Khabarovsk airport, as we *fly* out, thank you very much, courtesy of Chase's insistence that Voices International treat us to plane tickets.

It's been a contemplative but busy year, ending with our commissioning service last week at the church.

Buddy is already manning the coals for the big Berglund Acres barbecue. Probably Myrtle and Uncle Bert have arrived, along with H, who is already starting to show, a cute lump under her hot pink maternity shirt. (It's hard to tell which is glowing more—her shirt, her hair, or her face. I knew she could do it.)

So they're all here. One family ready to send us back to the other.

"Caleb and Daphne called this morning. They'll meet us at the airport in New York. Apparently Caleb wants to show her Central Park."

"It's the last glimpse of mowed grass they're going to have for four years," I say. "But I have a feeling that Daphne is going to love Bursk."

I reach over, grip his arm. "Say it again."

"Indoor plumbing, I promise." He grins. "I've already contacted Vasilley, and he says they're working on it. And not just for us—they're contracting with the region for plumbing for the town. He makes a great mayor, if you ask me. And oh, Olya is doing fine. She and the kids send their love. You were smart to put her in charge of Secrets of Siberia. She has to fight for dial-up time with Maya, however, who spends all her free time on the Internet talking to Nathan. Apparently, she's coming stateside for Thanksgiving this year. Nathan told me last time we talked that he might pop the question."

I'm so glad Chase still has Nathan in his life. I wonder what else they talk about. Like, Chase's own Bible classes he's been taking by correspondence? Or perhaps the way he is devouring God's word? He went through Ephesians in just a week! Where's the fairness in that?

The breeze stirs the pine, the poplars, reaping the last smells of summer. I can't believe it's nearly over.

"Your parents are probably back with Justin and Chloe from the pool. I know they've loved all this grandparent time. And they're starting to get the hang of instant messaging, and I already installed the webcam. I tried it on Jasmine last night. She and Milton said they'd leave right after church."

"She'd better be bringing *kringle*."

"She mentioned that, and bagels."

I laugh. See, my true friends won't forget, regardless of how far I roam.

"We'd better get going if we hope to get any ribs."

I stare again down the hill. It's not as steep as I remember. More of an incline, really.

"Are you sure about this?" Chase says, looking down the hill. His smile dims, and I see the same uncertainty in his eyes I saw the day we received our acceptance letter from Mission to the World.

Dear Chase and Josey Anderson,

We're pleased to inform you that you have been accepted as career missionaries . . .

"I'm sure about this," I say, and hold onto the handle of the wagon. "But can you keep up?"

His smile is back, and in it I see a little bit of danger, a little bit of challenge. My stomach does a small roll of delight.

"Ready . . . set . . . "

"Go!" I yell, and push off.

Chase is behind me, laughing, yelling.

And my face is to the eastern wind.

Thank you for reading *Get Cozy, Josey*! I hope you loved the final story in my Josey Series. If you missed where Josey and Chase's love story began, be sure to get your hands on *Everything's Coming Up Josey* and *Chill Out, Josey*.

everything's coming up josey | the josey series, book one

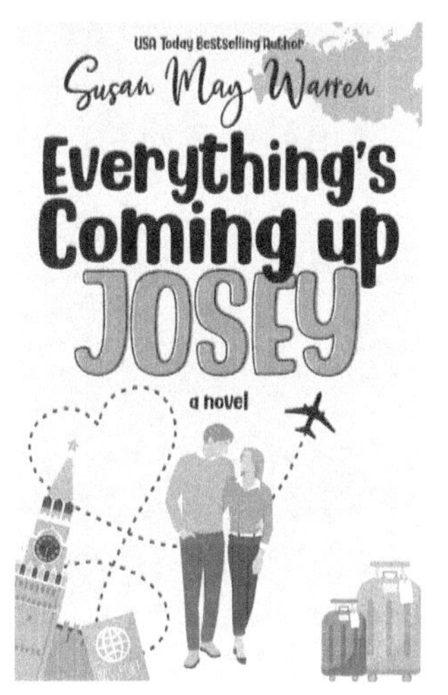

'I need you,' the tall, ridiculously good-looking missionary had declared, his words reverberating through the entire church. Wait—he wasn't talking just to Josey? Oops, because suddenly she's not in Gull Lake, Minnesota anymore. Instead, she's found herself in Moscow, Russia, as a missionary for a whole year. Oy!

Really, she just wanted to escape her chaotic hometown, where her sister ran off and married her ex, and her heart still pines for Chase, 'the one that got away.' But life has a funny way of throwing snowballs, and now she's in Russia, spreading the good word and navigating a land of vodka, fur hats, and passionate hearts.

As she immerses herself in the vibrant Russian culture, from haggling for fruit at the Moscow market to braving the icy weather, Chase's memory lingers . . . and just when she starts to think she's finally moving on, fate throws them back together. Will Josey take a chance on love and rekindle the flame with her hometown sweetheart, or will she embrace the allure of Russia, and a new love that sets her heart ablaze?

With Susan May Warren's signature blend of humor and heart, "Everything's Coming up Josey" is a vintage rom-com that will leave you laughing, swooning, and rooting for Josey's happily ever after in this hilarious and heartwarming tale.

Get your copy now!

chill out, josey | the josey series, book two

Josey Anderson had dreams of being the perfect wife, and everything seemed to fall into place during her fairytale wedding to Chase. Well, almost everything—there was that hilarious moment when the matron of honor unexpectedly went into labor! But hey, life is full of surprises, and Josey knows how to roll with the punches.

Now, Josey sets out to find her dream Cape-style house, conquer her role as a reporter at the Gull Lake, Minnesota paper, and become a baking whiz and sewing extraordinaire. Piece of cake, right? But just when she's settled into the rhythm of her new life, Chase lands a job in Moscow, turning Josey's dreams upside down. Suddenly, the city without year-round hot water, decent takeout, and even maternity clothes becomes her new reality—and it's far from the perfection she envisioned.

As Josey grapples with the challenges of her new surroundings, she discovers that being the perfect wife isn't about having a flawless life—it's about embracing the unexpected and finding joy amidst the chaos. Will Josey be able to redefine perfection and find happiness in the most unexpected places?

With Susan May Warren's trademark blend of wit and

warmth, you'll find yourself laughing, cheering, and maybe even shedding a few happy tears as you follow Josey's hilarious journey of self-discovery.

"This heartfelt and humorous novel is sure to leave you with a smile on your face and a renewed belief in the power of love, laughter, and happily ever afters." – online reviewer

Available now!

Looking for more love and laughter in beautiful Minnesota? Dive into Susie May's Deep Haven contemporary romance novels, beginning with *Happily Ever After*.

God has answered Mona Reynolds's prayers and given her the opportunity of a lifetime: she is about to open her own bookstore-coffee shop, the Footstep of Heaven. Now Mona has no time for love and no hope that a man can ever be the hero of her dreams. But when she hires mysterious drifter Joe Michaels to be her handyman, she discovers that it isn't only in fairy tales that people live "happily ever after."

Keep reading for a sneak peek into Mona and Joe's love story!

happily ever after | deep haven, book one

CHAPTER 1

Eight Months Later

Mona leaned over the steering wheel of her Chevette and gunned the hatchback up the shoreline climb. The car nearly sailed over the top of the hill overlooking Deep Haven, but Mona didn't care if she touched down right into a speed trap. Delight drove her foot into the floorboards as she spied the town spread out before her like a red carpet—the place where years of dreaming and planning would reach their vivid finale. After ten long years she'd made it back. Finally, she would find peace. *Thank You, God.*

Mona stomped her brakes as she entered the forty-mile-per-hour zone and narrowly missed a pale-haired grandmother pumping her arms on a morning power walk. The woman glared at her. Mona returned an apologetic look.

As she motored along Main Street, Mona decided Deep Haven had changed little over the years. The lighthouse on the craggy point needed a paint job, and she noticed a number of new gift shops. Essentially, however, the population seemed intact—tourists and retirees. She turned off Main, clung to the shoreline drive, and headed for World's Best Donuts. She would spend her first moments back in this slice of heaven sitting on a boulder, propping coffee between her knees, and folding a sugary elephant ear into her mouth. It was an adolescent treat, but Mona wasn't quite ready to give it up.

She parked in front of the dime store and trotted over to

World's Best. Squeezing into the packed bakery, she got in line and fifteen minutes later emerged with a crispy ear wrapped in a grease-dotted napkin.

Mona headed straight for a jagged outcropping on the shore of Lake Superior. Settling herself on a rock, she inhaled deeply, losing herself in the crisp, pine-laced lake air. Indeed, peace could be had in Deep Haven. She only had to inhale the fresh aroma of the forest and hear the scrape of waves on the beach to revive her father's memory in her heart. Finally, she could live the dream she'd waited a decade for already. Finally, nothing stood in her way.

She hoped her business instincts hadn't betrayed her. Although only a microdot on the Minnesota map, Deep Haven represented the only place to wrestle away a few days of privacy and calm from the stress of life in Minneapolis or St. Paul. When traveling the five hours north on I-35, tourists set their cars on cruise and started their holiday in the driver's seat, enjoying the jeweled countryside. Following the crisp Superior breeze, most vehicles found their own way to the tiny village nestled among the birch and maple trees, Norway pine, and balsam fir.

Very few people actually lived in Deep Haven. The town functioned like a large outside mall, where everyone met to slug down coffee and a donut, swap tales, and bemoan the horrors of life in the city. A few homes dotted the hillside, but Deep Haven had outlawed private building permits anywhere along the shore, except by approval of the local planning committee: Edith Draper.

Mona sipped her coffee—black, no sugar—and said a prayer of thanks to the good Lord for giving her mother, Verona, the sense to become Edith's friend thirty years ago. Mona checked her watch. Thirty minutes until Chuck's Real Estate opened and she picked up the keys to her future. It was all clicking together according to plan—from Edith's approval of her living quarters above the shop; to the down payment the size of her nest egg; to the agreement of her roommate, Liza Beaumont, to be her business partner.

Mona watched dawn spill across the water, turning the lake a sparkling indigo. Lake Superior's waves lapped easily a stone's toss from her feet. Oh, how her father would have loved it. He would have been beside her, swilling his own java—two creams, no sugar—and gesturing with a half-eaten chocolate cake donut at the seagulls dipping about on the waves. "Mona," he would have said, "there's a little bit of heaven to be found here. We just gotta keep our eyes out for it."

I'm looking, Pop. A gull, brave and cocky, landed near her and waddled close, its white head bobbing and its beady eyes fixed on the scrap of elephant ear. Mona tossed it to the scavenger, and the bird caught it before it hit the ground. She brushed off her sugared fingers and picked her way back toward the street.

"You all set?" Chuck sat behind his desk, a corduroy jacket over his plaid flannel shirt, appearing infinitely more at ease than he had eight months ago. Sunlight skimmed off his shiny head from the side window, and he had the gentle eyes of a man who'd spent his life serving people. The roller chair creaked as he leaned back.

"I think so." Mona smiled and held out her hand, palm up.

"Not so fast." Chuck stood and rubbed a chubby hand over his balding head. "I know you're excited, and frankly, it is a good idea, this bookstore thing. But I know how much it means to you, and I just want to make sure you know what you're in for."

Mona lowered her hand. "And what's that, Chuck?"

He met her eyes with a fatherly gaze. "The house is in

rough shape, Mona, rougher than I thought. You have a lot of work ahead of you to be ready by tourist season."

Mona flexed her arm. "I've got Norwegian blood in me!"

Chuck smirked. "That you do. Okay. If you need some help, give me a call." He yanked out the drawer of his metal desk and rustled around until he found a long silver key. He held it out to Mona.

The Footstep of Heaven Bookstore and Coffee Shop. She had known that would be the name since the day she had sat on the beach with her father. Wrapped up in a bestselling hardcover, he had glanced up at the gathering fire on the horizon and said, "This place is the footstep of heaven." Somehow that phrase wound around Mona's heart and strengthened her during his funeral and over the past ten years.

Mona stood on the wide steps of the two-story Victorian, heart pounding, and knew this place was perfect.

She could see it clearly in her mind: the wide porch would be filled with intimate round tables covered with lacy tablecloths that fluttered in a fresh lakeside breeze. Sitting at them would be a handful of contented tourists, drinking freshly brewed coffee out of Liza's handcrafted mugs, eating gourmet muffins, and diving into classics they had unearthed in Mona's bookstore. Strains of Brahms or Chopin, as gentle as a whisper, would drift from the house and float along the street, and all of Deep Haven would bless her for bringing a little bit of heaven to their shores.

Mona hummed as she bounded up the steps of the house. She leveled off in a high-pitched scream as her foot sliced through the top step and sent her sprawling. She heard a car door slam, then laughter. She winced.

"Some place, Mona!" Liza Beaumont caught Mona under

the arms and hoisted her to her feet. "Glad I made it for the grand tour."

Mona wrinkled her nose at her best friend. "Just one step, Liza. That can be fixed."

Liza propped her hands on her hips and nodded, brows arched. At least she clamped those ruby lips together.

Mona dusted herself off and stepped up to the door. The key worked, and she pushed the door open. A shaft of sunlight flooded in over their shoulders and lit a dusty hallway. Mona made a face and shivered when she spotted a wide spiderweb stretched from banister to ceiling. Liza pushed her into the house, whistling approval.

Once inside, the place looked cleaner. The hardwood floors suggested a silky amber glow if polished, and a magnificent chandelier in the dining room refracted the sun in a kaleidoscope of colors. A wide staircase ran up from the foyer. Down the hall, two leaded-glass doors opened into a fairly modernized kitchen. Or so Chuck had said. Poking her head into the room, Mona decided Chuck's description had been generous. Perhaps lime green cupboards and lemon countertops had been modern in his time . . .

"Our rooms are upstairs?" Liza asked.

Mona whirled, and the smile on her roommate's face bolstered her sagging enthusiasm. She nodded and held her breath as Liza raced up the steps two at a time. Thankfully, they didn't break.

Mona wandered to the family room on the first floor, envisioning floral arrangements on the oak mantel and a cushion on the bay window seat. Over there, in the dining nook off the family room, she would install her coffee bar, where patrons could belly up with a frothy mocha and swap quotes from their favorite literature. Mona would set up Liza's pottery in the other side of the house, in the parlor, with the two windows that seemed gateways to the sun. Liza's trademark bold colors would sparkle and draw customers like bears to honey.

A sense of gratitude filled her. So the place needed some elbow grease. It was still the only property along the shore to be offered that year, and she had been fortunate to land it. And soon, with Edith's help on the zoning papers, the lakeside home would become a legitimate business. *Her* business.

"Come up, Mona!" Liza leaned over the banister. "There's a bathroom for each of us!"

"Finally!" Mona answered with a playful laugh. She climbed the stairs, registering the squeaks for future notice, and found Liza lying spread eagle on a bright orange shag carpet in the master bedroom.

"What are you doing?" Mona leaned against the frame of the French doors and folded her arms across her chest.

"Dreaming of furniture," Liza said, sighing. Mona's roommate looked the part of a French Indian princess, with her black hair splayed out, loopy gold earrings glinting in the sunlight, and her fuchsia, fake-leather jacket akin to a brilliant royal robe. Mona shook her head teasingly and grinned.

The other room upstairs included two dormer windows that overlooked the slanting veranda roof, with a window seat built into each alcove. "This is my room," Mona declared, delighted.

Liza poked her head in. "You sure? The other room's bigger."

"Yeah, but the other room has a bathroom built onto it—perfect for cleaning all that clay off your body." Mona wrinkled her nose in disgust.

Liza's eyes narrowed in mock suspicion. "You just don't want to clean up the gigantic water stain I found under the sink."

That night, as the birch trees hurled shadows into the furnitureless bedroom, Mona and Liza huddled in their sleeping bags and counted the Victorian's casualties.

"Two broken windowpanes, a leaky kitchen sink, that big water stain on the dining-room ceiling, and the rotted floor under the fridge," listed Mona.

Liza buried her head into her folded arms and continued where Mona left off, her voice muffled from the folds of fluffy down. "A broken front step, three rotten boards on the veranda, two useless electrical outlets in the parlor, and did you notice my bathroom door won't close?"

Mona groaned in reply.

"But—" Liza popped her head up like a jack-in-the-box—"the good news is that most of the problems are cosmetic. And we can work around the rest." She flopped over onto her back. "I hope you know how to hammer because I'm doing the painting!"

Mona grinned at a cobweb on the ceiling and tried to ignore the idea that a spider winked back. Six weeks till opening day. Six weeks to remodel, paint, buy furniture, and assemble her lifelong dream.

But it would be all right. A little spit and polish was all they needed to turn the place into the Footstep of Heaven.

Two days later, Mona was ready to blame Chuck for selling her a Victorian from nowhere but south of its heavenly name. Two shutters had fallen off, another front step splintered when the movers arrived with the industrial oven, and an entire section of plaster cracked around the stain in the dining room. Liza heard it, and like Henny-Penny, she flew out of the room screaming, "The sky is falling!" A minute later the section gave way and littered the floor with chunks of rotted plaster.

If that weren't enough, Mona created a miniature Old Faithful in her kitchen when she stripped the nut on the faucet in an attempt to stop a leak. She managed to dam it up with some plumber's putty, but the plug looked iffy at best.

Then Liza walked in with the zinger. "You got a parking ticket, my unlucky friend." She tossed the offensive yellow slip at Mona. It drifted toward Mona's feet, and she stomped it to the planked floor.

That night, as the sun slid beyond a platinum lake, Mona sat on the porch and cradled her first decent cup of coffee. A half-eaten elephant ear lay soggy and cold in a donut bag crumpled beside her. It wasn't much of a supper. Liza had brought home a frozen pizza from the Red Rooster and had already wrapped up like a mummy in her bag. Perhaps tomorrow their furniture would show up, and they could sleep in their own rooms, off the pumpkin-colored carpet.

Mona sipped slowly, considering the repairs and the days remaining until opening day. Discouragement hit her like a cold Superior wave. *Lord, I wanted so much to build the perfect place. A place where people could enjoy the simple pleasures in life.* She squeezed her eyes shut and fought the lump forming in her throat. *I just want to do something right, something good and lasting.* The Footstep of Heaven seemed like such a good idea—even a God-ordained one. The goal had kept her forging ahead through a series of mindless jobs. Even the stint she had done as a Whopper flopper during college seemed worth it with Heaven in view. Now her one, God given chance was slipping through her fingers. *Please, Lord, just a little more help?*

Mona set her empty mug next to the crumpled donut bag and sank her face into her hands.

Joe Michaels ran his hand over the dented hood of the Ford pickup. The paint job was even, except for a few rust spots over the wheel wells, and the black vinyl dashboard gleamed like a piece of onyx.

"She's a good runner," commented a ponytailed salesman in an ill-fitting tweed blazer. He looked and smelled like he had spent a few lifetimes under the hood of a hot rod, smoking something foul while he did it.

Joe grimaced. "Well, she's not a beauty queen, but her engine seems clean, and she hums like a song. How much?"

"Three grand."

"For this clunker?"

The salesman backed up, a hand out as if to push away the comment. "Okay, okay. Two and a half."

Joe examined the dirt and kicked a stone with his dusty boots. Money wasn't the issue—he just liked to run 'em around a bit. He made a face. "How about two?"

The salesman reacted like he had been shot. "You're killin' me, man." He paused for effect. Joe knew the salesman hoped he would recant, but he held his ground. There were other used-car lots, and he didn't need anything in particular. Just a change of pace. "Oh, okay," the salesman finally huffed. "I guess I gotta move her. Come inside; we'll sign the papers."

Joe bit back a grin. He loved winning.

They sealed the deal inside a ramshackle trailer. Joe peeled crisp one hundreds from a worn leather wallet and slapped them on the faded desk.

The salesman handed him the keys. "Stay light on the gas; she's got an itchy accelerator."

Joe hiked out to the pickup. The sunlight glinted off her polished forest green hood, and she twinkled like a Christmas bulb. Joe flung his army duffel in the back and climbed into the cab. He liked stick shifts, especially those on the early models that groaned and wheezed as you wrestled them into gear. They seemed nostalgic, and he preferred them to the computerized SUVs of today. Simplicity had its merits. No computer to bog down this engine. Just an old-fashioned carburetor he could take apart on the side of the road and rebuild if he needed to.

Joe saluted the salesman and roared out of the lot. Where to next? North. To Deep Haven. He knew his destination as if it had been whispered into his ear. It was time to visit Gabe.

He had been shirking the responsibility for over a decade, appeasing his brother with letters, presents, and the occasional phone call. But he knew he couldn't procrastinate a day longer. After fifteen years of avoiding the backwoods smudge on the map, God was forcing him to return. Last week's visit to his mother's grassy grave site had revived her last words to him: *Take care of Gabe.* He'd tried to protest, to reason away the shame. He *had* kept his part of the deal. But the excuses tasted bitter in his throat, and guilt, a heavy-handed motivator, sealed his fate.

He owed it to his mother to visit, if not love, the son she had sacrificed so much for. After all, Joe was the only family Gabe had left. God kept pointing that out until Joe surrendered. His goal: to stop in, say hi, make sure the kid was being well taken care of, and ditch town before the dust settled beneath his feet. And, if God intervened, he might also figure out how to untangle the mess he'd woven during his past eight months of fruitless roaming. A trek along the western seaboard and through northern Canada had left him with nothing to show for his time, something his boss didn't need to know—yet. It wouldn't take much for the wrong people to find him in Deep Haven, but he was one step ahead, and he still had weeks before his promises came due.

Maybe, if he kept his eyes open, a brief stopover in a sleepy tourist town just might provide the opportunity he needed to make good on his promises. At the least he might be able to scrape up a tidbit to throw to the wolves that ran his life.

Joe cracked open his window as he drove north up I-35. A

road sign flew by. Duluth—thirty miles ahead. He would never forget his first trip north, the first time he had ever seen Lake Superior. He had been eleven, on a church camping trip heading toward the Boundary Waters Canoe Area, and when he smelled the crisp lake air for the first time, he was intoxicated by it. The smell of pine mingling with fresh water and a ripe amount of mossy undergrowth had so overwhelmed him, it had changed the course of his life forever.

Eau Claire, Wisconsin, had suddenly seemed claustrophobic. He strained at its borders. His mother must have sensed it, for on his eighteenth birthday, she let him go without a fight.

He had spent his first summer alone, hiking the Boundary Waters Border Trail, catching lake trout, eating wild berries, and letting the love of nature embrace his soul. That summer he came to know God as his best friend, his Savior, his Creator, his Lord. For fifteen years, he'd carried that summer with him all over the world.

As Joe topped the hill overlooking Duluth, caught the rich smell of pine, and beheld the vast Superior spread out like an endless blue blanket, his heart swelled and quickened in his chest. For a moment he wondered if returning to the North Shore might again change his life, pull him out of the dead-end rut he'd wallowed in for so long. Something had to change—and fast, or his days of freedom were numbered.

Joe threaded the pickup through Duluth and stopped for lunch at the harbor park. Throwing the remnant of his chili dog to the seagulls waddling over the grassy knoll in front of the museum, he watched an oceangoing iron-ore tanker skid under the massive aerial bridge, headed out into Lake Superior and beyond. He waved to an assembly of sailors working the deck. A few returned the gesture. He felt sorry for them. He knew too well the life and the loneliness of months at sea.

He was back on the road by midafternoon, his windows at

half-mast, a violent wind skimming through his short-cropped tawny brown hair. He stretched out an arm along the top of the bench seat and whistled an old tune, trying to ignore the squeeze in his chest as he ate up miles toward Deep Haven. Would Gabe even know him? Joe wouldn't blame his kid brother if he gave Joe one look and tossed him out on his ear. The yearly cards, gifts, and the occasional phone call didn't fill the gap left by their mother's death.

Gabe never gave any indication of offense, however. All his letters, carefully etched out, proclaimed a feeling of open arms, inviting Joe to his home. At least Gabe had a home to invite him to. Joe hadn't had a home since he packed his bags fifteen years ago and left his mother's two-bedroom ranch on Linner Lane.

Lost in the past, Joe nearly broadsided a dog. He glimpsed a brown blur dart into the road and, going sixty-five plus, only had time to crunch his brakes and swerve madly. Thankfully, traffic was sparse on this sunny stretch of road. Joe angled the truck into the ditch and buried his head into his forearms. His heart had rammed into his throat, and it took some seconds for him to swallow it back into place.

Then dread roiled through him. Had he hit it? He jumped out of the cab. "Hey, pooch!" he hollered.

No sign of the mutt. The road behind him curled around the far-off jagged cliffs like a black ribbon. He scanned the other stretch of highway. Again, empty. Joe put two fingers in his mouth and whistled. No blur of brown, no whining lump in the ditch. Relief crested over him. The dog must have headed home.

Joe climbed back in the cab and had just shifted into drive when something banged against his passenger door. Joe glimpsed two muddy paws smearing his not-so-clean-anyway window, and a long pink tongue dangled sideways out of a grinning canine mouth.

"Howdy, boy," Joe said to the lop-eared dog as he leaned

over and opened the door. A large, dark chocolate Labrador retriever scrambled inside and stared at him with droopy, nut brown eyes. The dog panted in heavy gusts, and drool dripped from its mouth.

"You're messing up the truck," Joe said with a mock frown. He reached out a tentative hand. The dog watched, clamped his snout shut, and sniffed. Joe obviously passed inspection, for the mutt laid his muzzle into Joe's palm. With his other hand, Joe found the soft spot behind the dog's ears and rubbed vigorously. The Lab groaned happily.

"Well, you're not a stray," Joe said. "You're somebody's pal. Whatcha doin' out here?"

The dog had hunger in those glassy, sad eyes.

"Stay put." Joe climbed out of the cab. Cupping his hands around his mouth, he yelled into the woods, "Anybody lose a dog?" The wind devoured his words; the trees hissed in reply. Joe pushed a hand through his short hair. Well, he couldn't just leave the animal in the woods. He climbed back in the truck.

"It's not much farther to Deep Haven. We'll see if anybody there knows you."

The dog settled down on the seat, laying his massive head on grimy paws. He sighed deeply.

"Feeling lost, bud?" Joe pulled out and gunned the truck to sixty-five, laying a hand on the dog's matted fur. "Aren't we all?"

Get your copy now!

thank you for reading

Thank you again for reading *Get Cozy, Josey*. I hope you enjoyed the story.

If you did enjoy it, would you be willing to do me a favor? Head over to the **product page** and leave a review. It doesn't have to be long—just a few words to help other readers know what they're getting. (But no spoilers! We don't want to wreck the fun!)

I'd love to hear from you—not only about this story, but about any characters or stories you'd like to read in the future. Write to me at: susan@susanmaywarren.com. And if you'd like to see what's ahead, stop by www.susanmaywarren.com .

And don't forget to sign up to my newsletter at www.susanmaywarren.com.

Susie May

about susan may warren

With nearly 2 million books sold, critically acclaimed novelist Susan May Warren is the Christy, RITA, and Carol award-winning author of over ninety novels with Tyndale, Barbour, Steeple Hill, and Summerside Press. Known for her compelling plots and unforgettable characters, Susan has written contemporary and historical romances, romantic-suspense, thrillers, rom-com, and Christmas novellas.

With books translated into eight languages, many of her novels have been ECPA and CBA bestsellers, were chosen as Top Picks by *Romantic Times*, and have won the RWA's Inspirational Reader's Choice contest and the American Christian Fiction Writers Book of the Year award. She's a three-time RITA finalist and an eight-time Christy finalist.

Publishers Weekly has written of her books, "Warren lays bare her characters' human frailties, including fear, grief, and resentment, as openly as she details their virtues of love, devotion, and resiliency. She has crafted an engaging tale of romance, rivalry, and the power of forgiveness." *Library Journal* adds, "Warren's characters are well-developed and she knows how to create a first rate contemporary romance..."

Susan is also a nationally acclaimed writing coach, teaching at conferences around the nation, and winner of the 2009 American Christian Fiction Writers Mentor of the Year award. She loves to help people launch their writing careers. She is the founder of www.MyBookTherapy.com and www.learnhow-towriteanovel.com, a writing website that helps authors get published and stay published. She is also the author of the popular writing method *The Story Equation.*

Find excerpts, reviews, and a printable list of her novels at www.susanmaywarren.com and connect with her on social media.

facebook.com/susanmaywarrenfiction
instagram.com/susanmaywarren
x.com/susanmaywarren
bookbub.com/authors/susan-may-warren
goodreads.com/susanmaywarren
amazon.com/Susan-May-Warren

also by susan may warren

THE JOSEY SERIES

Everything's Coming Up Josey

Chill Out, Josey

Get Cozy, Josey

THE CHRISTIANSEN FAMILY

I Really Do Miss your Smile (novella prequel)

Take a Chance on Me

It Had to Be You

When I Fall in Love

Evergreen (Christmas novella)

Always on My Mind

The Wonder of Your

You're the One that I Want

DEEP HAVEN COLLECTION

Still the One with Rachel D. Russell

Can't Buy Me Love with Andrea Christenson

Crazy for You with Michelle Sass Aleckson

Then Came You with Rachel D. Russell

Hanging' by a Moment with Andrea Christenson

Right Here Waiting with Michelle Sass Aleckson

Once Upon a Winter Wonderland

DEEP HAVEN SERIES

Happily Ever After

Tying the Knot

The Perfect Match

My Foolish Heart

The Shadow of your Smile

You Don't Know Me

NOBLE LEGACY (Montana Ranch Trilogy)

Reclaiming Nick

Taming Rafe

Finding Stefanie

A complete list of Susan's novels can be found at susanmaywarren.com/novels/bibliography/.

www.ingramcontent.com/pod-product-compliance
Lightning Source LLC
Chambersburg PA
CBHW030606310726
48979CB00003B/597

* 9 7 8 1 9 6 2 0 3 6 1 6 0 *